Unto Us a Son Is Given

Donna Leon

W F HOWES LTD

This large print edition published in 2020 by
W F Howes Ltd
Unit 5, St George's House, Rearsby Business Park,
Gaddesby Lane, Rearsby, Leicester LE7 4YH

1 3 5 7 9 10 8 6 4 2

First published in the United Kingdom in 2019
by William Heinemann

A CIP catalogue record for this book is available
from the British Library

ISBN 978 1 52888 969 8

Typeset by Palimpsest Book Production Limited,
Falkirk, Stirlingshire

Printed and bound by

For Maxim Emelyanychev

The good we wish for, often proves our bane.
I pray'd for children, and I gain'd a son,
And such a son, as all men hail'd me happy.
But who'd be now a father in my stead?
The blessing drew a scorpion's tail behind.

Handel, *Samson*, Act I, Scene 3

CHAPTER 1

'You know I don't like to meddle in things,' Conte Falier told Brunetti. 'But since, in this case, he's so close to me, I feel I don't have a choice, not really.' Brunetti, seated opposite his father-in-law in one of the overripe armchairs that filled Palazzo Falier, had been listening to the older man for some time, aware of how difficult il Conte was finding it to begin telling the story he obviously wanted Brunetti to hear.

Il Conte had called him that morning and asked if Brunetti would have time to stop by and have a drink on his way home from work because there was something he'd like to ask him about. Brunetti's first response, given that it was a warm day in early spring, had been to calculate the easiest way to walk from the Questura to the *palazzo* without becoming entrapped in the by now normal migration paths of the herds of tourists. Because of the clear sky and benevolent temperature, walking up Riva degli Schiavoni would be impossible, crossing Piazza San Marco an act of madness. The vaporetti coming from the Lido, however, were generally no more than jammed, not too crowded to board, so

1

he had accepted the invitation, tossing to the winds his usual reluctance to use public transportation when he could walk, and had taken the Number One to Ca' Rezzonico and arrived early.

'I don't like gossip,' il Conte insisted, recalling Brunetti's attention. 'Never have.'

'Then you're living in the wrong city,' Brunetti replied mildly, smiling as he said it to remove the sting. 'And probably should avoid speaking to other Venetians.'

The Count's answering smile was broad and relaxed. 'The first is not true, as you know,' he told Brunetti. Then, his smile even warmer now, he continued, 'The second might well be true, but if it is, there's nothing I can do about it: it's too late. I've known Venetians all my life.'

'Is one of them the source of this gossip about Gonzalo?' Brunetti asked, interested that his father-in-law would want to discuss gossip about his best friend and curious to know more.

'Yes. And he's a lawyer.' Perhaps thinking that Brunetti would ask him who, il Conte held up a restraining hand and said, 'It doesn't matter who told me. It's the story that's important.'

Brunetti nodded in agreement. Like most Venetians, he was accustomed to swimming in the swirling froth of information and misinformation that flowed through so much of daily life; unlike most Venetians, however, he took little pleasure in it: long and tangled experience had shown him how unreliable most of it was. Brunetti the police commissario had heard tales so scabrous they reddened his cheeks, and Brunetti the reader was familiar with Suetonius' descriptions of the pleasures of Tiberius. Brunetti the thinker, however, knew how prone Venetians were to exaggerate the deeds of those they'd never met, how careless of the consequences of what they blithely repeated, how fundamentally unreliable they were.

He was certainly interested in what people did, but he seldom believed they had actually done it until he had accumulated sufficient evidence. Thus whatever his father-in-law might have been told was, to Brunetti, a case to be proven, not a truth to be believed.

While he waited for il Conte to make up his mind about how to tell him, Brunetti's own thoughts turned to a decision the family had been avoiding and postponing for years: what to do with the family villa near Vittorio Veneto, which il Conte and la Contessa no longer used and where Brunetti's family had all but stopped going during the summer. As the family dithered, water had started to seep in under the north-facing windows, and the caretaker had announced he wanted a significant raise in salary.

As if he'd read Brunetti's thoughts, il Conte said, 'It's not the villa I want to talk about, however much Gonzalo sometimes reminds me of it.'

Brunetti, surprised by the comparison, said, 'I didn't know he had water coming in under his head.'

Il Conte ignored Brunetti's lack of seriousness and insisted on explaining his remark. 'You got to know them both at about the same time, Guido; you had a lot of happy times in their company; and now both of them are showing the effects of time.'

His parents-in-law's friend, Paola's godfather and unofficial uncle, Gonzalo Rodríguez de Tejeda had been part of the Falier family for as long as Brunetti could remember. He had come from London for Brunetti and Paola's tenth anniversary dinner, when he had given them a piece of twelfth-century Kufic pottery, desert-pale, about the size of a salad bowl, decorated with what they had always assumed was a Koranic inscription running up the inner sides. A prescient Gonzalo had had the bowl suspended inside a Plexiglas box that could be hung on the wall and thus help the bowl avoid the assaults and accidents that afflict any house with small children. It still hung on the wall of the living room, between the two windows that gave a distant view to the bell tower of San Marco.

In recent years, Brunetti and Gonzalo had occasionally met on the street, or in a shop, or a café, and they had always been happy, chatty times spent drinking *un'ombra* or a coffee. They'd met by chance some months before on the street near Campo Santi Apostoli. When he entered the *campo*, Brunetti saw Gonzalo coming towards him, a hand raised in salutation, and noticed that the older man's hair had passed from iron to snow, although

4

as he approached Brunetti, his back was as upright as a drill sergeant's, and his glance still a piercing blue, perhaps the trace left behind by some Northern invader of Spain.

They'd embraced, said how glad they were to see one another, the older man adding – speaking in an Italian entirely devoid of accent – that he was late for an appointment and couldn't stop to talk, but to say hello to Paola and the kids, and kiss them all for him.

He'd touched Brunetti's cheek with his hand in a sign of affection he often used, then said he really had to go, turned and walked away quickly towards Fondamenta Nuove and the *palazzo* where he lived. Brunetti had stood still and watched him go, happy to have seen him, as he was always happy to see Gonzalo. He had resumed walking, and then, for no particular reason, paused and turned to look for the retreating back of the man making his way through the crowds. At first, looking for someone walking quickly, Brunetti had failed to see him, but then he'd noticed a tall form, moving away, but slowly, head bowed, elbow jutting out, one hand placed on his hip, as though to quell some secret pain. Brunetti glanced away immediately, as though he'd come upon the man doing something embarrassing and wanted not to see him do it.

Pulling himself back from his reverie, Brunetti saw that il Conte was watching him carefully. The older man asked, 'When did you last see him?'

'A couple of months ago, perhaps a bit more,' Brunetti answered. 'We met in Santi Apostoli but only for long enough to say hello.'

'How did he seem to you?'

'He seemed like his old self, I'd say,' Brunetti answered, automatically defending one old man from having to hear that a friend had succumbed to the forces that were lying in wait for both of them.

Avoiding il Conte's gaze, Brunetti studied the portrait of a young gentleman hanging on the far wall and felt his gaze returned. Vibrant with youth, muscles screaming to be freed of the stillness demanded by his pose, he stood with his left hand on his hip, the other on the pommel of his sword. No doubt he was an ancestor of Paola, some distant Falier who had died in battle, or of disease, or drink, leaving behind this image of himself to show what he had been when he had been.

Brunetti saw, perhaps fancifully, some traces of Paola's face in the young man's, though hundreds of years had softened the angles in hers, leaving only – at least in times of sudden anger – the hawk's eye seeking its prey.

'You really had no time to talk?'

Brunetti shook his head.

Il Conte lowered his glance, pressed both hands on his thighs and kept his eyes on them. What a handsome man he still was, Brunetti thought. He took the opportunity provided by il Conte's obvious distraction to have a closer look at him and was surprised to realize that his father-in-law had grown smaller since the last time they'd met. No, since the last time he had paid attention to the older man's appearance. Though his shoulders were narrower, il Conte's jacket still held those thinner shoulders in a soft embrace. Perhaps he had had it altered, but then Brunetti noticed that it had that year's lapels and so was new.

Il Conte continued to study the back of his hands, as if looking for an answer there, then he glanced across at Brunetti and said, 'Your situation is always ambiguous, isn't it, Guido?'

Was that a question, Brunetti asked himself, or a statement of the Conte's opinion? Did it refer to the difference in rank between him, the son of a man from the lower classes whose life had been a series of defeats, and his wife, daughter of il Conte Falier and heiress to one of the largest fortunes in the city? Or perhaps between his professional responsibilities and the demands that friendship and love might make upon him? Or was it his situation as a commissario of police married into the family of this man before him, whose business dealings might not bear close examination?

Unwilling to ask to what part of his life il Conte was referring, Brunetti temporized by saying, 'I think many of us lead ambiguous lives. The world we live in makes that necessary.'

The older man nodded and moved his hands to the arms of his chair, where they rested easily. 'I remember, years ago, Paola came home for a visit while she was at university in England. Most of the time she was here, she was reading a book she had to write a paper about.' His face softened at the memory of his only child, home from school, doing her homework.

Brunetti waited, familiar with the Conte's narrative habits.

'It wasn't until the third day that she talked about the book and what she wanted to say in her essay.'

'What did she tell you?' Why, he wondered, are we always so interested in the past experiences of our best beloved?

'That I should read it,' the Conte revealed. 'I tried to, but not until she'd gone back to England.' He shook his head as if confessing something. 'I'm not drawn to that sort of thing – it was a religious book – and I couldn't read it.'

'What book was it?' Brunetti asked, curious about what Paola would have been reading while a student.

'*The Cloud of Unknowing*,' the Conte said and paused. 'I've always thought it would be a wonderful title for an autobiography. For anyone.' His smile widened, and Brunetti smiled in return.

Brunetti let a few moments pass and then decided that he wanted to know, no matter the consequences. 'Weren't we talking about Gonzalo?'
'Yes.'
'It sounds as though you're worried about him.'
Il Conte nodded.
The older man's hands tightened for a second

and then slowly loosened. The tension, however, migrated to his face, narrowing his eyes. 'Gonzalo's my best friend. We were at boarding school together.' He looked across at Brunetti and said, unable to restrain his surprise, 'My God, it was more than sixty years ago.'

'Where was it?'

'In Switzerland,' the Conte answered. 'My father said he wanted me to live in another country for a time.'

'For any particular reason?' Brunetti asked, curious to learn something about his father-in-law's past, to dip into the black hole that was il Conte's life.

'He said he wanted me to learn French and German. No one thought of English then,' he explained. 'But it was a ruse, I think. He wanted to remove me from the company I was spending time with.'

'Why?'

Il Conte raised both hands, palms outward, as though trying to convince an attacker of his innocence. 'I think he didn't like the political ideas of some of my friends.'

Brunetti cast his historical memory back to the years before his birth but could think of no political unrest that might have affected the nobility. The Red Brigades had been in short pants then, and the financial boom was sweeping the country towards the future.

'Did it work?'

Il Conte smiled and shifted his gaze to the window behind Brunetti. 'I learned the languages. Other things, as well.'

'You said you met Gonzalo there,' Brunetti reminded him, curious about the connection.

Il Conte's face softened in a smile. 'He taught me how to ski,' he said, and Brunetti thought that was all he was going to learn about the young Gonzalo. The smile dimmed a bit, then lit up again at some sudden memory. 'He also taught me how to cheat at poker.' Il Conte laughed with childlike delight. Before Brunetti could ask, he went on. 'He said it was so that I could recognize it if anyone ever tried to do it to me.'

'Did that ever happen?' Brunetti asked.

'Not with cards,' Conte Falier answered and offered no further explanation. 'But the signs Gonzalo taught me to look for show up in other games, as well.'

'A useful skill,' Brunetti said.

'Far more useful than knowing how to ski,' Il Conte observed, adding, 'Especially in my business.'

Whatever that might be, Brunetti thought, but let it pass through his mind, leaving no trace in his expression. He remembered asking Paola, not too long after he had met her, what it was her father did. He had not known then that she had acquired her sense of humour from an English nanny and from four years of study at Oxford, so it was with some surprise that he heard her say, 'He sits in his office on the *piano nobile* of the *palazzo* and makes phone calls.' After he realized she was joking, but not joking – telling the truth but telling it slant – Brunetti had thought of his own father, who passed his days at home, sitting and waiting for someone to come by and offer him a day's work at the docks, loading and unloading boats. Even then, at the beginning, he'd been conscious of the gulf that stood between her family and his own: her father a count, her mother the descendant of Florentine princes; Brunetti's mother a woman who had left school at twelve, his father a hopeless dreamer ruined by years as a prisoner of war.

Brunetti studied his father-in-law's face and was aware of how much of it was taken up by his nose. 'How many years were you at school together?' he asked, surprised to imagine that this man had ever been a teenager at school. Surprised, as well, to think he had once been a teenager.

The older man gave a deep sigh that was in no way melodramatic. 'Four; from the time I was fifteen until I was nineteen and went to university.' Il Conte had sunk lower in his chair as he spoke but suddenly pushed himself upright and looked at Brunetti sharply. 'I'm turning into a garrulous old fool, aren't I, Guido?' he asked, sounding amused, not embarrassed.

'Hardly, Orazio,' Brunetti answered. 'The past is always interesting.'

'The distant past, perhaps,' il Conte said and leaned forward to tap Brunetti's knee to enforce his point.

Brunetti thought of the time, it seemed like ages ago, that he had bought a new suit to wear to his first meeting with this man, who had asked to speak to the young man who wanted to marry his daughter. Brunetti had spent what he considered an immoderate amount on the suit, so much so that he failed to buy new shoes to wear with it. Not yet a *commissario di polizia*, and with a widowed mother to support, he was a poor – in every sense of the word – marriage prospect. He'd known this, could not change it, but had still agreed to go to what he knew would be the doom of all his hopes.

He remembered going to the *palazzo* for the first time. The maid had actually curtsied to him before leading him to the first floor. Stopping outside a door, she knocked, then opened the door to allow Brunetti to enter.

He'd recognized il Conte instantly, a man with whom he'd spent many hours in the same room. He saw the grey hair, the brown eyes, and the unsmiling mouth. The other man, as surprised to recognize Brunetti as to be recognized, came forward and clasped his hand warmly. 'You're the young man who's been reading about Hadrian,' he'd said, putting his other hand on the back of Brunetti's and pressing with evident warmth.

All Brunetti could do was stumble over the words, 'Yes, sir,' but then he'd had the presence of mind to ask, 'How do you know what I'm reading?'

'The librarian told me,' was the Conte's answer. 'We're old friends.'

'What else did he tell you?' Brunetti asked without thinking. About, perhaps, the way this man's daughter had sat beside the same young man one afternoon, the two of them hand in hand, laughing at the difficulty of turning pages?

Conte Falier had turned away without answering and led Brunetti to a plump chair, sitting opposite him and waving to him to sit. When both were comfortable, il Conte said, 'Nothing more than the books you've requested over the last few weeks.' Brunetti ran his mind over the titles and hoped they would pass muster: Cassius Dio, *The Augustan History*, Philostratus and Pausanius. A copy of Fronto's letters, with his ambiguous comments about Hadrian, seemed unfindable.

'He told me,' il Conte went on, 'that you expressed great interest in Hadrian.'

Brunetti's confusion deepened. He had come to talk about this man's daughter, not about a second-century Roman emperor. He noticed that his palms were damp, but he couldn't very well wipe them against the legs of his new suit. Instead, he'd said, 'Do you find that interesting, Signor Conte?'

'Of course,' the older man answered seriously. 'Could you tell me why you're interested in him?'

'Because of Paola,' Brunetti had answered before he thought. Then, realizing this made little sense, he added, 'She talked about him, and I thought she was being too enthusiastic.' He had heard how much this sounded as though Paola had been talking about someone they both knew,

13

a rival for her attentions, perhaps, and that he was reacting out of jealousy.

Hoping to amend this, he had added, 'That is, if what I've read about him is true.'

'Which is?' il Conte asked.

Brunetti wanted to ask why he was being questioned about his judgement and whether what he answered would somehow serve as proof of his unsuitability as a husband for this man's daughter. Instead, he decided simply to answer the question. 'I'm a policeman, sir, so I've developed the habit of reading accounts of people's behaviour as though they were police reports.'

'I see,' il Conte had said, smiling. 'Is this true in the case of the Emperor Hadrian, as well?' He had the grace to smile, although his interest did sound genuine.

Brunetti thought the question deserved a serious answer. 'He's known as one of the five good emperors, but it seems to me there's something dodgy about the story of his last-minute adoption by Trajan and the whole process of his succession. Then there are those senators who were eliminated just after he became emperor, all men who opposed him or were said to be his enemies.'

Il Conte had nodded slowly, as if being asked to look at a familiar story in a new light. 'Is that the only reason for your interest?' he had asked.

Brunetti had hesitated, raised one hand to push at his lips, then glanced out of the window behind the older man. 'Paola's reading a book about

14

Hadrian. A novel. An epistolary novel. And from what she's told me about it, the hero sounds like a chatterbox mixture of Marcus Aurelius and Saint Francis. He's always talking about how reluctant he is to go to war, but he's always ready to send the troopers in to hack and burn.' This was pretty much what he'd told Paola, though it had failed to lessen her enthusiasm for the book, or for Hadrian.

Il Conte had smiled and then laughed. 'When she was young, we never tried to stop Paola from reading whatever she wanted, but now that she's older, I find myself wishing she'd stick to the British novel and not waste her time with this nonsensical French drivel.'

'You've read it?' Brunetti had asked, unable to hide his surprise.

'Ages ago, but only a few pages,' il Conte had said, as though it had been the thirteenth labour of Hercules. 'It's completely ahistorical and pretentiously silly. *The Augustan History* is just as much a work of fiction, but far more entertaining and far more well written, don't you think?'

As Brunetti tried to recall the exact words he'd said in reply, he heard a voice call his name. 'Guido? Guido?' He pulled himself back from the past's consideration of the more distant past and looked across at the present. His father-in-law was leaning towards him, one hand extended.

Brunetti smiled and said, 'Sorry, Orazio: I was thinking of our first conversation.' He looked around the now-familiar room. 'It was here, wasn't it?'

15

Il Conte nodded.

'I'm glad I passed the test,' Brunetti said, having suspected all these years that it was the conversation about Hadrian, followed by coffee and idle talk he could no longer recall, that had been the first step towards his current happiness.

Il Conte smiled and opened his hands in a gesture of welcome. 'As am I, Guido,' he said. His expression suddenly changed, all softness disappeared, and he said 'I'd like you to treat Gonzalo as you did Hadrian.'

Momentarily confused, Brunetti asked, 'What does that mean?'

'Think as a policeman.'

'*Oddio*,' Brunetti exclaimed. 'What's done?'

Il Conte raised his hands again, but this time to push away the idea. 'No, it's nothing like that. He hasn't done anything.'

This answer left Brunetti confused as to why he was being asked to look at Gonzalo as a policeman and not as what he thought himself to be: something between a friend and a member of the family that had also taken Gonzalo in. 'I don't understand,' he said.

Il Conte's face hardened. 'No one who knows him could.'

'Tell me about it,' Brunetti said.

Il Conte pulled his mouth tight and raised his eyebrows in an expression Brunetti could not read. 'I don't know what or who's involved in it.' After a moment's reflection, he added, 'I can't even say for sure that anything's going on.'

Brunetti quelled the impulse to inquire why, if that were the case, they were having this conversation. Instead, he asked, 'Can you tell me what you've heard?'

17

pushed himself to his feet, saying, 'I need a drink.' He went to the credenza, e opened a bottle of whiskey without both-o ask Brunetti what he'd like and brought two short glasses, filled generously.

runetti took his, waited until his father-in-law was seated again, and raised the glass to his lips. How lucky he was that they kept nothing like this at home. How did a liquid this sharp and bitter manage to taste so wonderful?

'His sister Elena called me,' il Conte surprised Brunetti by saying. 'She's a retired doctor and lives in Madrid with her husband and son. Her other siblings and their children live there, too.'

'You know her?'

Il Conte nodded. 'We met a long time ago, the first time Gonzalo took me home with him when we were still in school. We've stayed in touch over the years.'

'And the others?' Brunetti asked, surprised to learn that Gonzalo had siblings and surprised that, in all the years they had known one another, no mention had been made of his family.

'Another sister, María Pilar, and a brother, Francisco. Gonzalo doesn't get on well with them, never has.'

'Do you know them, too?' Brunetti asked.

'I've met them a few times.'

'Tell me about them,' Brunetti said.

'There's little enough to tell. The three of them own the company together. The other two married and each had one son.' He smiled and then said, 'Berets.'

'Excuse me?'

'Well,' il Conte clarified, 'hats. But the major item has always been berets. Whenever you see anyone wearing one of those silly flat things, it was probably made by his family's company. It's one of the biggest in Spain.' He reached for his glass and rolled it between his palms, staring at the surface before replacing it on the table without drinking. 'And now their three sons work for the company and will inherit it.'

He picked up his glass and emptied it with one swallow, then sat, looking at the empty glass. 'That's what's wrong,' he finally said. 'Gonzalo wants a son.'

'What?' Brunetti asked, raising his head involuntarily and spilling a bit of whiskey down the front of his shirt. He stared at the other man, as if he'd taken leave of his senses. 'What did you say?'

'He wants to adopt a son.'

'He's mad,' said Brunetti, speaking before he heard anything more and thinking of similar cases, none of which had ended well. But he didn't know what Gonzalo's case was, did he? So he had no idea what it was similar to and should keep his mouth shut, shouldn't he?

Il Conte gave him a level look and said, 'You always were known for the moderation of your views, Guido.'

Brunetti's face grew red. 'I shouldn't have said

that.' He wiped at his shirt with his handkerchief, wondering what Paola would think when he arrived home stinking of whiskey.

'But you did say it,' il Conte responded, adding, 'And you're probably right.'

Brunetti considered what he had just been told: adopting a son. 'Who?' he asked.

Il Conte shrugged and reached for his glass. Seeing that it was empty, he went to the sideboard again and came back with the bottle. He poured them each a little and took a small swallow before setting the bottle on the table between them. Ignoring Brunetti's question, he went on. 'It was Lodo Costantini who told me about it,' he said, naming a man who was both one of his closest friends and one of his lawyers. 'He told me Gonzalo asked him a few months ago if his law firm handled adoptions. When Lodo asked him why he wanted to know, he said that it was for a friend of his who wanted to adopt an adult.' He put his fingers over his mouth and shook his head, as if in disbelief of what he was saying.

'Lodo didn't believe a word of it, said he was sure Gonzalo was asking for himself. Even though it was only a question, Lodo still thought he couldn't express his opinion, but then he heard from someone – he wouldn't tell me who it was – that Gonzalo was in the process of doing it. So he thought he could tell me because Gonzalo's my friend.' Ah, thought Brunetti, how wonderfully Jesuitical our lawyers are.

Il Conte continued. 'As you know, the law decides where most of his estate will go, regardless of his wishes.' Before Brunetti could summon to mind the relevant law, il Conte went on. 'It stays in the family, goes to his siblings, no matter how he might feel about them, no matter what sort of Philistines they might be.' So neutral was il Conte's tone that he might as well have been reading the recipe for plum cake. Then, in the same calm tone, he remarked, 'I suspect it's a law made for the convenience of the rich.'

Had this man's daughter been there to offer him support, Brunetti would have inquired, 'Aren't they all?' but her absence enjoined him to discretion and he did no more than nod.

Il Conte went on. 'If, however, by the time of his death, he has adopted someone, that person will inherit the entire estate, just as if he were a natural child.' He paused for a moment, and then added, 'Even the title might pass to him.'

Brunetti noticed that il Conte Falier, holder of one of the oldest titles in Venice, pronounced this last sentence with marked coolness. This being a problem with which Brunetti's family had never been confronted, he contented himself with observing, 'As you said, Orazio, this is a law made for the rich.'

'If you and Paola hadn't had children,' il Conte said with audible patience, 'it could eventually have been a problem for you.' He glanced at Brunetti to see how he responded to this unwelcome truth

21

before he added, 'Your brother would inherit what you and Paola have.' Brunetti was stunned by how casually his father-in-law spoke of him as joint owner of all that Paola would inherit. Il Conte gave Brunetti a chance to comment; when he did not, his father-in-law added, 'He seems like a decent person, but if he weren't, would you like it if he swooped it all up?'

Spoken by some other person, what il Conte had just said would surely have sounded irredeemably vulgar. Even as it was, Brunetti was tempted to reply that, being dead, he'd be unlikely to have an opinion on the worthiness of his brother to inherit the Falier fortune. The conversation had veered away from Gonzalo and into something close to superstition, which Brunetti had always thought was the reason people did not make wills.

'Adoption's enough?' Brunetti asked.

'Yes.'

Brunetti picked up his glass and held it to the light. He swished the remaining liquid from side to side, then around in a circle that rose towards the rim of the glass before he let it sink down again. Il Conte had said he didn't like gossip, but everything Brunetti had just heard was on that level.

He took a sip and set the glass down. 'Why are you telling me this, Orazio?'

Il Conte put his right hand to the side of his mouth and pushed the skin away and then did it twice more. The wrinkles played hide-and-seek each time, but always fell back into place. 'I want to know,' he finally said, 'if he needs help of any sort, but I don't know how to find out.' He looked away from Brunetti and then back. 'I thought you might know a way.'

'Why don't you simply ask him?' Brunetti said, not because he was unwilling to help his father-in-law, but because asking Gonzalo directly seemed the easiest way to find out.

Il Conte raised his hands in protest, as at the suggestion of the unthinkable. 'Gonzalo would be offended.'

'At the idea of needing help?'

'At the idea that I thought it.'

Brunetti was about to say that the time of luxury might be ending for Gonzalo. He was old and weak, and so there should be no loss of honour in being in need of help, but he realized in time that he was speaking to a man almost as old, though perhaps not as weak, as Gonzalo, who would certainly not like to hear any of this said.

'What did you have in mind?' Brunetti asked.

Il Conte was unable to disguise his confusion. 'In mind for what?'

'For me to find a way to help?'

Il Conte looked at him for a long time and then looked away. 'I don't know, Guido,' he answered, obviously surprised by the question. 'If I gave you the name of the young man?'

'That he wants to adopt?'

'Yes,' il Conte answered. He picked up his glass and seemed surprised to see that it was empty again. He put it back on the table and turned to Brunetti. 'Some years ago, perhaps ten, a young man lived with Gonzalo briefly.'

Brunetti pretended he was a piece of moss on a rock and sat and waited. Rain could fall, feet could walk past, animals might nibble at his edges. He would sit and wait. He did not cross his legs nor move his feet. His arms rested on those of the chair. His drink might well have been in a different room. Or on a different planet.

'It was only a few months. Not here. In Rome.'

Brunetti stared at his feet and waited.

'The young man was the son of a lawyer: good family, studied in France, seemed to have a great deal of money.' Il Conte stopped suddenly, then said, 'I know this sounds like more gossip, but it's all true.'

He returned to his subject. 'He was a wild person, this young man. He used drugs. He also sold them. To some of the people he met through Gonzalo. And then he was arrested at the airport in Bogotá with a suitcase full of cocaine.

'The police let him call his father, but he refused to talk to him. The next morning, the father called Gonzalo and told him where the boy was. But by the time Gonzalo got in touch with the police, the young man had hanged himself in his cell.' Il Conte paused here and studied Brunetti's face before adding, 'At least that was what the police said.'

Brunetti vaguely remembered the case and knew

there had been no mention of Gonzalo, either in the newspapers or in anything official he'd ever read about the case.

'How did he manage to stay out of it?' he asked.

Il Conte gave the slightest of shrugs. 'I don't know. But it's not hard to imagine, is it?'

No, not really, not for a man as well connected and wealthy as Gonzalo, Brunetti thought but did not say. One of the rules of his profession was never to reveal information to those with no official reason to know it. 'We've never had a request – not from Rome or anywhere else – to keep an eye on Gonzalo. So whoever took care of him there did a good job.'

Il Conte picked up the bottle. Brunetti shook his head and put his hand over the top of his glass. Il Conte replaced the bottle and said, 'I want to protect him from a similar mistake.' Then, before Brunetti could ask, he said, 'Yes, and I'm asking you to do it for me.'

CHAPTER 3

To stop the silence that expanded out after il Conte's last remark, Brunetti asked, 'Have any of your other friends said anything about him?'

'No, not really.'

'What does "really" mean?'

The question surprised the older man. 'No one's said anything to me about Gonzalo for some time. So far as I know, Lodo's the only one he's spoken to.'

'Would his family know anything?' Brunetti asked.

'Elena's the only one I could ask, and I'd rather not.'

'Why not the others?'

'They're a family that's grown very rich,' il Conte said. 'People like them don't like trouble.'

Brunetti restrained the impulse to say that all families didn't like trouble. 'Conservative?'

Il Conte gave a sudden snort of laughter. 'Gonzalo told me once his parents were worried I'd corrupt him.'

'I beg your pardon,' was the best Brunetti could think of to say.

'Politically,' il Conte clarified. 'They'd heard rumours that neither my grandfather nor my father had been a Fascist.'

Brunetti lacked the courage to ask if that was true.

'A few years after I was born, but before the war, my grandfather realized what was going to happen, so he had my father declared insane,' il Conte began, speaking easily, as if it were the most normal thing for a parent to do. 'He took us all to live in the villa in Vittorio Veneto,' he continued, opening up an entire volume of Falier family history about which Paola had never spoken.

'That way, with the suspicion that it might be a family trait, there was no more pressure on them to join. Nor for my father to fight. My grandfather was too old, my father was a declared lunatic, and I was still a boy.' He considered that list and then said, 'So we stayed there and were forgotten about, all three generations.'

'Your father? What happened to him?'

'He learned how much work it was to farm and take care of the land.'

'Did all of you stay there until the end of the war?'

'That was my grandfather's plan, but my father had other ideas.'

'Such as?' asked Brunetti, intrigued.

'He wanted to join the partisans,' il Conte said. 'I think he wanted to be a hero.'

'Ah,' Brunetti murmured.

Il Conte smiled. 'We surrendered to the Allies

in '43, and my grandfather asked him to wait until things became clear before he did anything.'

'Why?'

'Probably because he was older and wiser and had fought in the last war and seen how people behaved.'

'Did your father agree?'

Il Conte nodded. 'Soon after the surrender, the partisans started to come to the farm to demand the animals that hadn't been taken up into the hills. The workers had hidden most of the grain and corn and cheese, thank God, so there was something for us to eat.' He broke into a sudden smile and said, 'There was one old peasant woman – she must have been ninety – who refused to let any of them into her house. She had chickens in the attic: you could hear them from outside, but the partisans were afraid of her, so they left her alone.' Voice sobering, he added, 'The Germans came a year later. They took the chickens.'

To put an end to this talk of the past, il Conte said, 'Gonzalo's parents would not have approved of what my grandfather did.'

'Do you?' Brunetti surprised himself by asking.

'Absolutely,' il Conte said with no hesitation. 'He saw to it that his son wasn't forced to join the army and be sent off to fight in Russia or Albania or Greece or Libya. And saved his life.' After a protracted pause when he seemed to disappear into those long-gone years, he said, 'My grandfather was right: people behaved badly.'

'You were still a little boy then. How did you learn about what happened?'

'The people who run the farm now told me they grew up hearing stories from their parents and grandparents. Over the years, they've told them to me.' Before Brunetti could ask, il Conte said, 'Yes, that's one of the reasons I can't bring myself to sell the villa.' Straightening himself in his chair, he added, 'Besides, it's the first place I remember, so I suppose it's a case of imprinting: it's home to me.'

'And this isn't?' Brunetti asked, waving his hand at the wall, the beams in the ceiling, the view through the windows to the *palazzi* on the other side of the Canal Grande.

The older man's face softened; he turned his eyes to follow Brunetti's glance to the other side of the canal. 'In a different way, it is,' he said. After a long silence, he went on. 'Doesn't Saint Paul say something about having been a child and thinking like one? But now he is a man and has to put away childish things?'

Brunetti knew the lines, but had forgotten the source.

'So the villa is my childhood. But all this,' il Conte said, repeating Brunetti's inclusive gesture, 'is what came to me as a man.'

Brunetti stiffened with something approaching fear. Please don't let him start banging on about how it will all pass to Paola one day, and then to Raffi and Chiara, he thought. I don't want this to become a talk about the weight of centuries that is about to fall on our shoulders, the need to set an example to the hungry peasants and to treat them well. I don't want to be reminded that I will not be the one to assure the future of my children, but that it will be this man and their mother.

'Guido?'

Brunetti looked towards il Conte and saw real concern on his face.

He put on a smile and said, 'Sorry, Orazio. I was thinking about something else.' Then, realizing that his question would be the first step, he asked, 'Will you tell me the young man's name?'

Il Conte pulled his lips together into a grimace of resignation. He finally said, strangely serious, 'You have to promise not to laugh.'

Struck by the thought of the possibilities that request suggested, Brunetti said, 'Of course.'

'Attilio Circetti, Marchese di Torrebardo.'

His promise not to laugh had been wise because the name struck Brunetti as faintly risible, as did so many of the noble names he'd heard and read during his lifetime. Willing himself to overcome prejudice, he told himself that Attilio could easily turn out to be a modest and unassuming young man.

'You think he's the one?' he asked.

'Probably. He's been living in Venice for two years,' il Conte said.

'Do you know anything for certain about him?' Brunetti inquired mildly.

'Very little. For certain, that is.' Brunetti remained mute, forcing il Conte to continue. 'I told you I don't like gossip. But I hear a great deal of it. Because people know I'm Gonzalo's friend, they might moderate what they say about him.'

'About Gonzalo?'

'No, about this other man.'

'What little have you heard?'

'That he's often seen with Gonzalo, and that Gonzalo is very fond of him. There is often a subtext, about how very clever he is and how charming. No one seems quite sure what his profession is, or even if he has one. He's seen at dinners and parties everywhere, but no one seems to know much about him.'

Brunetti's experience suggested that this was a common type in certain circles of the city: the perfect man to invite to dinner if the number of gentlemen needed to be evened up. Discreet, affable, well-mannered, somehow familiar with almost everyone in the room, he could talk about most subjects and claim acquaintance with scores of Venetians. And yet, and yet, one never found out just what it was he did or exactly where his family lived, and he had a knack of making it seem rude to ask him.

'Have you met him?'

'I've been at two dinners where he was present, but I had no chance to speak to him,' il Conte explained.

'Is there other gossip?'

Il Conte shook his head. 'Nothing outright or clear. But there is a certain tone – more an undertone – when his name is mentioned.' That said, he looked at Brunetti, who nodded. In a closing cadence, il Conte said, 'I can't tell you more than that, Guido.'

They sat in silence for a moment, until il Conte said, 'There's one more thing.'

Brunetti showed his curiosity by raising his chin.

'I saw them on the street, about a year ago. Calle de la Mandola.' He paused but, spurred by Brunetti's silence, quickly resumed. 'They were behaving in a way I thought . . . Well, I thought it was unsuitable for Calle de la Mandola at two in the afternoon.' Then, by force of will, il Conte added, 'I said something about it the next time I saw Gonzalo.'

'You told him that?'

'Well, something like that.' Il Conte, like his daughter, had a memory that retained everything: he would remember exactly what he'd said.

'How did he respond?'

'He put his napkin beside his plate, got to his feet, and left.'

'Did he say anything?'

Il Conte looked out the window, but the *palazzo* across the way had nothing to tell him. 'No.'

'And since then, silence?'

'Yes.'

Brunetti got to his feet and walked over to the window. He had already been with his father-in-law more than an hour and was eager to leave and go home. There were many reasons he could give to refuse the request: it was improper use of police resources; he was too busy with other cases. He knew, however, that the reason was entirely other: he didn't want to be part of this, didn't want to put his nose into Gonzalo's private life.

He thought of going home and talking to Paola about it, but he didn't want her to be caught between her father and her husband, nor did he want to tell her the investigation concerned her godfather.

The boats went by; he could hear them because the *palazzo*, as part of the artistic patrimony of the city, could not have double-glazed windows, so the sounds of the motors and the horns, as well as the occasional siren, were a normal backdrop to all conversation in the front rooms. The rooms in the back were darker and quieter.

A taxi roared towards San Marco, wildly in excess of the speed limit, but there was nothing to be done about that. It occurred to Brunetti that there was nothing to be done about most things in the city.

'There's one thing I'd like you to do for me,' il Conte interrupted his musings by saying.

'What is that?'

'Lodo's giving a dinner tomorrow evening. I'd like you to go, you and Paola. I've spoken to Lodo, and you're both invited.'

Only by a hair's breadth did Brunetti restrain

himself from asking, 'To spy?' Instead, he asked, 'Will Gonzalo be there?'

'Yes.'

'With this young man?'

'Yes.'

'I'm sorry, Orazio, but I'd rather not do this.'

Il Conte sighed, then said, 'I thought that would be your reaction, but I wanted to ask you, anyway.' Then, after a moment's hesitation, he added, 'The dinner's different. I want you to see them together and then decide if it's worth trying to reason with . . .' He let his voice wander away.

Brunetti wondered if this was some sort of test of family loyalty. Would his father-in-law tell Paola how he had let the team down? Would this mark some change in his not-easily-achieved friendship with il Conte?

The older man pushed himself to his feet and paused to shake one leg of his trousers down into place. He came over to Brunetti and joined him in looking at the traffic on the canal. Finally he said, 'As more time passes, so much about this city seems stranger and stranger. Opposite us, there's a *palazzo* that was built in the fifteenth century and still has the same columns and windows. A bit farther up that side, there's a *palazzo* where Henry James wrote *The Aspern Papers* and that my daughter treats as though it were therefore the Holy Sepulchre. And I've just asked someone I love to spy on someone else I love.'

The last words battered at Brunetti's heart,

robbing him of the power of speech. He reached out his right arm and embraced the shoulders of the man beside him. The frailty of those shoulders shocked him and stopped him from trying to pull il Conte nearer to him. He bent and kissed the older man on the temple and said, 'I'll give your love to Paola and the kids.'

'Thank you, Guido,' il Conte said, his attention directed rigidly at the boats below them.

Brunetti turned away and left his father-in-law there, watching the past.

CHAPTER 4

Brunetti walked home quickly, paying almost no attention to what or whom he passed, deaf to the sound of the returning birds, the only tourists no one resented. He failed, however, to keep from thinking about what had just happened. Over the years, il Conte had treated him with, first, civility and respect and then with growing affection, and finally with the love the older man extended to his closest friends and to his family. For decades, Conte Falier had been generous with his time and, equally important, with his connections to provide Brunetti with information that made straight his professional path through complicated investigations involving politicians and those who sat in positions of power. Il Conte had access to many of them and had never hesitated to make a phone call or to introduce Brunetti to a person in possession of information that might prove useful to him. Nor had he balked at the need to apply pressure to a reluctant acquaintance to reveal to Brunetti facts concerning an event in his – or her – past that might lead to embarrassing consequences were it to become common knowledge. All this, and more, Brunetti had sought, and found, under the protective wings of this man's power.

When he reached the second floor of their building, Brunetti's heart was pounding, his breath coming in ever-shortening gasps. On the landing in front of the Lambrinis' door, he stopped, pulled out his *telefonino*, and punched in il Conte's number.

Il Conte answered after only two rings. 'Yes, Guido?' he asked.

'I'll have a look,' Brunetti said. 'And we'll go to the dinner.'

There was a long silence, and then il Conte said, 'Thank you.' The silence returned and extended, then Brunetti heard him say, in English, using a phrase he had hitherto heard him use only when addressing Raffi, his grandson, the hope of the family, the light of his eyes, 'Dear boy.'

By the time Brunetti reached their landing and put his key in the lock, his heart had returned to its normal beat, his breath to its normal rhythm. What was it Paola always said? 'Love trumps principle?' Yes. Well, perhaps.

He let himself in, hung his jacket beside the door, only then registering how much its weight and warmth irritated him. He walked over to the terrace and looked through the glass doors. The tiles had been swept and washed, and two of the chairs put back in place, though not the table. He heard the chirping of birds. Joy leaped at him: it was springtime again, the birds were back. He was at peace with his father-in-law and had saved himself from behaving like an ungrateful lout. He wished it were still daylight so that he could step outside and take off his shirt and tie and let the sun fall on his chest.

He heard footsteps coming from the kitchen and turned to see his wife approaching. In that instant, he wanted to take some sort of emotional photograph so that he could, some time in the future when things were different, pull it out of his memory and look at it and say, 'I've lived a happy life.'

'Ah, you're home early,' Paola said, her delight evident.

'Let's sit on the terrace,' he suggested, not caring that it was almost dark. He wanted to see if the day's softness still lingered.

They did just that, sat side by side, so close their thighs touched, listening to the birds across the way perhaps discussing where to build their nest this year, or perhaps bickering over a worm: it was hard for Brunetti to judge. Lights had been turned on in the windows below and beyond them, although enough light still came from the west to reflect from the rooftops and bell towers.

Slowly, he told Paola about his conversation with her father, about his first response and his second, saying nothing about why he had revised his decision and then telling her about the dinner.

'Poor Gonzalo,' Paola said when he was finished. She reached out and took his hand. 'He was so happy with Rudy, wasn't he?' she asked, naming

Gonzalo's former partner, Rudy Adler, who had left him four years before and moved to London, and since then had been heard of or seen only infrequently by people in the city. 'He hasn't been the same since he told him.'

'Who? What?' Brunetti asked.

'Since Rudy told him he'd found someone new and said he was leaving.'

Brunetti allowed a long time to pass before he said, 'I didn't know that was why.' He thought about Rudy's humour and gentleness of spirit but found only cliché: 'I'm sorry.'

Paola gave his hand a squeeze and released it to brush a strand of hair out of her eyes. 'I didn't know, either, not until I saw Rudy in London last year and he told me.'

After saying that, she pushed herself up from her chair and tried to look down into the courtyard opposite, from which loud screeches were now audible. 'What in God's name are they doing?' she demanded of no one in particular and walked to the end of the terrace, where there was a better view.

'Fighting over territory, I'd say,' Brunetti answered, then added, 'Birds do a lot of that.' Paola said nothing, still looking over the railing and down. Brunetti added, 'Humans do, too.' If he'd hoped to provoke her into speaking, he failed.

Paola turned and came back. 'Would you like asparagus tonight? I saw some in the market and couldn't resist. It's from Sicily and it looked wonderful.'

'What are you going to do with it?' he asked.

'Maybe just boil it and have it with boiled eggs.'

'How much did you get?'

'A kilo. It looked that good.'

'Would you like me to go out and get some prosciutto?'

She smiled and bent to touch his cheek fleetingly. 'I already did that.'

What better way to celebrate springtime? Brunetti thought. 'There's some champagne in the refrigerator, isn't there?' he asked, having seen it there the day before.

'Yes. It's the last of what my parents gave us for Christmas.'

Brunetti tried to remember how many cases had been delivered by Mascari: at least four, he recalled. Good grief, were they drinking it up at that rate?

'Before you start thinking about joining AA, Guido, let me remind you that more than a dozen bottles disappeared on New Year's Eve. There were at least twenty people here.'

'I'd forgotten,' Brunetti confessed.

Hearing this, Paola covered her face with her hands, turned and leaned over the railing, and, using a voice she reserved for imitating soap operas, called down into the empty *calle*, 'I spent three days preparing food for that party. Three days. And he's forgotten it.'

Brunetti ignored her and directed his attention to the *campanile* of San Marco.

From his right came the sound of choked

sobbing. He glanced at her quickly and caught her peeking at him through her fingers. 'Shall I open that last bottle, then?' he asked.

Her hands fell to her sides and she smiled. 'Oh, what a good idea.' She walked over to the still-seated Brunetti and leaned against his shoulder, then bent and kissed the top of his head. 'It was a wonderful party, wasn't it?'

'Being here with you is better,' Brunetti answered.

Silence grew between them. Church bells began to ring: the sound filled him with the same sense of completion. He got to his feet and went to get the champagne.

The next morning, Brunetti got to the Questura a half-hour early, even though there was no chance that his superior, Vice-Questore Patta, would be there before him. Indeed, it was very unlikely that the Vice-Questore would be there for some time. Brunetti went to his office and read his mail, then went downstairs in search of his superior's secretary, Signorina Elettra Zorzi, whom he found pulling daffodils from their paper wrapping and placing in a tall crystal vase. A few large sheets of the wrapping paper already lay on her desk; she was busy with the last package.

'Ah, Commissario,' she said, smiling at him as she stuck the last daffodil into the vase. She turned to the sheets of white paper and folded them neatly in half, then in fours, and then bent to put them in the appropriate receptacle to the left of her desk.

She straightened up and lifted the vase before Brunetti could move to carry it for her. She placed it on the windowsill, made two minor adjustments, and returned to her desk.

'How might I be of service this morning?' she asked, smiling again.

Brunetti had given some thought to how he should phrase this, given that it was a personal matter and had nothing to do with police work. 'There's someone I'd like you to take a look at,' he answered.

The inside lining of the collar and cuffs of her blouse were egg-yolk yellow, Brunetti noticed. Had this obliged her to bring daffodils from the market? It could just as easily have been yellow tulips, he supposed, but they did not stand up straight and scream 'SPRINGTIME' the way the daffodils did.

'And who is that, Signore?'

'His name is Gonzalo Rodríguez de Tejeda.' Then he added, 'He was born in Spain.'

'Not Poland?' she asked as she flicked on her computer.

Instead of deigning to answer immediately, Brunetti pursed his lips, glanced at the ceiling, and waited a moment. 'He became an Italian citizen about twenty years ago and gave back his Spanish passport.'

'He'll be easier to find than Franco Rossi, at any rate,' she said, bouncing her palms on either side of her keyboard as she waited for the computer to announce itself her servant.

When she began to type in the name, he added, 'There might be a title, as well, but I don't know if that got overlooked when he changed his citizenship.'

She glanced away from the screen and asked, 'Anything else, Signore?'

'He's lived here for a long time, and he owns his house, so he should be listed at the Ufficio Anagrafe. He lives over on Fondamenta Nuove. If you find the address, I'd like to know if anyone else is listed as a resident there.'

She was making a list: it pleased Brunetti to see that she still used paper and pen, however occasionally. 'And see what bank accounts or investments you can find, either here or in Spain. Or anywhere else, for that matter.' After a moment, he added, 'And if he's ever been involved in any trouble.'

She looked up at the last word. 'This might take some time. I don't know if . . .' she began, but then her voice trailed off.

Brunetti waited, but when she did not finish, he went on, 'While you're looking, could you see if he has any other property in the city? Or anywhere else.' He realized he was delaying telling her there was another person on his list.

'Spain's easy,' she said, and his memory flashed

to a burglar he'd arrested at the beginning of his career, who had told him, 'Wooden doors are easy.'

'I have friends there,' she said. Probably the head of the Central Bank.

'His family, too,' Brunetti added. 'He has a brother and two sisters. They run a factory that makes berets.'

She added something to her list.

'I'd be glad at whatever you find.'

Realizing there was nothing more to be asked about Gonzalo, Brunetti said, 'I've another name.' She nodded but did not bother to look up. 'Attilio Circetti, Marchese di Torrebardo.'

This was sufficient to cause her to look at him. Brunetti nodded. 'All I know is that he's been living here for at least two years.'

As he watched, a slow smile moved from her mouth to her eyes. 'Ah,' she said as she wrote the name. 'Then there might be something.'

He turned to leave but her voice called him back. 'Commissario?'

'Yes?' he asked, turning to face her.

'Is this . . . research, is it by any chance private?'

Brunetti remained silent, giving himself time to think, and then stalled. 'Why do you ask?'

'If he was once a Spanish citizen, and this was an official investigation, I thought you would already have contacted the Spanish authorities and would know some of this.'

She gave him a smile that mirrored the brightness

of the daffodils and said, 'Of course it doesn't matter at all. But if it's less than official, then I'll go about my research in a different manner.' She increased the temperature of her smile. 'In a more discreet way.'

'Indeed, Signorina,' Brunetti agreed, 'That would be better, I think. Discreet.'

'But,' she began, turning away from the screen; again she stopped before finishing the sentence.

'"But"?' he asked with a smile.

'But I don't know how much I'll be able to do in the time remaining.'

Confused, Brunetti asked, 'Before what or to whom?'

'To me,' she said.

Had lightning struck the building, Brunetti could have been no more stunned. Was she sick? Was she leaving? He stood and stared at her, incapable of speech. 'What,' he began, and coughed lightly while trying to formulate a way to end his panic. 'What's going to happen?' he asked, then coughed again and added, 'If I might ask.' He didn't want to know. He did not want to know.

'My vacation,' she said, looking down at her knees to brush away something but perhaps to give Brunetti time to adjust his expression. 'It's in the staff schedule for next month, Signore.'

'Of course,' Brunetti said with his recovered voice. 'Could you tell me again how long you'll be gone?' By the time he finished speaking, his voice was entirely under his control again.

'My last day is Friday. And I'll be gone for three weeks.'

Brunetti pressed his lips together and put his hands in his pockets. 'Ah, yes,' he said, stunned that he had not known this. He knew there were things he should ask her, but he couldn't think. 'I hope you have a nice time,' he said.

She smiled again and turned back to her computer.

As he walked up the stairs, Brunetti wondered how it was that no one had told him. He always knew when Vianello, Griffoni, and Pucetti would be away, so he seldom bothered to read the staffing schedule before the first day of the month; sometimes not even then. If the electricity was going to be turned off for three weeks, surely people would talk about it? He should certainly have heard. Only three days left. She would have other things to take care of before leaving, so the discreet inquiries would probably have to await her return. Well, Gonzalo wasn't going anywhere. But it would be best to inform both Vianello and Griffoni of what he had asked her to do.

Instead of going to his office, he continued on up the stairs, then down the back corridor of the building to the cubbyhole that had been given to Griffoni to use as an office. The door was open. She was at her desk, a construction a friend had made for her, its surface a single piece of wood the size of three banana boxes, to which was screwed an architect's lamp. On it stood an iPad, a mug holding pencils and, at least today, her service pistol and holster.

The corridor was so low and narrow that no one could approach her office without being heard. Without bothering to turn, she said, 'Good morning, Guido.'

'You put a computer chip in my ear?' he asked.

She turned on her chair to face him as well as to shift her knees to the side to allow him to enter, move past her, and take the other chair. She was wearing a light grey sweater, with a black jacket hanging on the back of her chair. Blondes sometimes didn't look very good in grey, but she did, perhaps because of her eyes. 'No,' she answered, 'I know your footsteps.'

He looked down at his shoes, as though to see if they had some strange defect that would give away his identity. They looked like brown leather shoes.

She smiled and shrugged. 'People sound different. I've learned to recognize everyone.'

'Even Lieutenant Scarpa?' Brunetti asked, naming her *bête noire*.

'The Lieutenant's approach is announced by the smell of sulphur that precedes him,' she explained, straight-faced. 'So I don't pay particular attention to the click of the cloven hooves.' She smiled, obviously pleased to be able to speak badly of the Lieutenant.

Brunetti nodded, wondering if there was any person whose footsteps he would recognize.

'I've asked Signorina Elettra to look for

information for someone I know,' he began. Griffoni nodded, waiting.

'She'll get to it when she comes back,' he added, proud of how calm he sounded.

'Good,' Griffoni said, then, 'What will we do without her?'

Pleased that Griffoni had said 'we', Brunetti answered, 'Pray.'

She waited a moment, and then asked, 'Who's the someone?'

'My father-in-law.'

Her expression changed, curiosity replacing amusement. 'I've never met him,' she volunteered. 'But I've passed him on the street a number of times.'

'How did you know who it was?'

She gave the smile she tried not to give when a suspect revealed something she could use to her advantage. 'As you've been telling me since I arrived here, Guido, this is Venice, and everyone recognizes everyone.'

'Does he recognize you?' Brunetti asked.

'He notices me. And we now smile and nod to one another. But we haven't spoken.'

'You could certainly introduce yourself,' Brunetti said. 'We've worked together for years, and I'm sure I've spoken of you to him.'

'Ah, Guido,' she said, 'your youth is showing.'

'I beg your pardon?'

'He's a man of a previous age. Or maybe era's a better word. Don't forget that. He grew up in a time when women did not speak to men to whom they'd never been introduced.'

Brunetti gave an involuntary snort and stared at her in disbelief. 'Claudia, for God's sake, he's not some sort of dinosaur.'

She continued to smile. 'I've seen the way he behaves when he meets people, especially women.' Before Brunetti could speak, she went on. 'He never wears a hat, but if he did, he'd probably tip it to any man he met. With women, he kisses their hands when he meets them on the street.' She paused, giving Brunetti a chance to speak, but he remained silent, trying to remember what it was like to walk on the street beside il Conte.

'It's not the way he'd kiss their hand in a drawing room. His lips don't even come close: it's a notional kiss.' Her smile broadened and she added, 'Probably because any woman whose hand he'd kiss would be wearing gloves if she were out of her home.'

Again, Brunetti was left without words.

'Men like this do not speak to strange women, nor they to him, Guido.' When Brunetti did not question this, she asked, 'Who does he want you to find information on?'

'His best friend.'

'*Oddio*,' she said, clapping her hand to her mouth. Then, slowly and with what seemed to Brunetti like regret, she said, 'Then maybe he's not.'

'Not what?'

'A gentleman,' she said in English.

49

CHAPTER 5

It took Brunetti considerable time to explain to Griffoni what il Conte had told him about his best friend and the situation in which he found himself: more than sixty years of friendship put at risk by an infatuation of which Conte Falier did not approve. Brunetti had paused at this point in his account at the realization that he had no idea at all whether his father-in-law approved or not of Gonzalo's choice, even of whether he believed he had the right to do so. Il Conte had expressed an opinion only of the undescribed behaviour of the two men in Calle de la Mandola. It had been an expression of propriety, not morality.

Brunetti continued to the end, failing to mention his original refusal to help.

'And your opinion?' Griffoni asked when he stopped. When he said nothing, she added, 'About the adoption?'

'Of course he shouldn't do it,' Brunetti said without giving it much thought.

'Because he's in his eighties and he's lost his head over a man at least two generations younger?

Why is that so bad?' Given what she was describing, Griffoni's tone sounded strangely mild.

Brunetti stared at her. 'You don't see anything odd here? More than forty years' difference in their ages?'

'If he were his real son, no one would give it a thought, Guido,' she said. 'Lots of men have children when they're fifty, sixty.'

'Their wives have babies, Claudia. They don't give birth to adult men.' He held up his hands about twenty centimetres apart. 'They have babies.'

'No need to repeat, Guido. I understood the first time.'

'I repeated so you'd understand,' Brunetti said shortly.

'I do, Guido. And I also understand that most people would assume his interest in a man so much younger would have to be sexual.'

Moderation abandoned him, and Brunetti snapped, 'Of course it's sexual.'

'Ouu, ouu, ouu,' Griffoni groaned, then put her hands up to her shoulders, palms facing him, in a sign of surrender. She was silent for a while, lowered her hands to her desk and smiled, then asked, 'And so what if it is?'

Brunetti crossed his arms. Immediately aware how defensive this must make him look, he unwrapped them and rested his hands on his thighs. He wished there were some way to stare off into the far distance. It came to him to wish he could take a longer view of the whole matter.

51

Not for a moment had he bothered to think about what Gonzalo's feelings towards this young man might be. Because Gonzalo was gay, was he capable only of lust and not of love? Would he think the same of a heterosexual man with a much younger woman? Of course he would, he realized, but he would be open to the possibility that they loved one another, would probably even wish it for them.

Griffoni stirred in her seat and crossed her legs. He wished she'd sit still: he was thinking, trying to work all this out. He studied the backs of his hands and replayed the conversation, the intensity of their voices, the emphasis both he and Griffoni had placed on single words, the tone of inquiry each had used.

'All right,' he said, still not looking at her. 'All that matters is whether this man loves him and will be good to him.' In fact, Brunetti saw, whether the young man loved Gonzalo or not was irrelevant: what mattered was whether he would be good to him. Gonzalo was eighty-five. How many years did he have left? He remembered Gonzalo the old man, obviously trying to avoid conversation, walking quickly, and then so slowly, away from him, hand on his hip as if to quiet the pain.

'Do you think Signorina Elettra's computer will be able to tell you that?' Griffoni asked in a voice as mild as a spring breeze.

He raised his head quickly and looked at her, searching for sarcasm, finding none.

It would not, Brunetti knew. But the computer might reveal the man's past, at least to a certain degree, and that might give some indication of his present and thus of Gonzalo's likely future.

Brunetti got to his feet, squeezed past Griffoni, and slipped out the door. 'I need to think about this,' he said by way of farewell. She said nothing and did not turn to him before he started down the corridor. Halfway to the stairs, he stopped and looked back, then returned and propped himself against the side of the door. She was sitting the same way, back to him, arms folded across her chest, studying the surface of her desk.

She did not acknowledge Brunetti, but her body changed, as if growing more attentive, the better to hear anything he might say. 'Thanks for saying what you did,' Brunetti said.

He saw her nod her head, but she did not turn around.

CHAPTER 6

As he started down towards his office, Brunetti thought about how taking a look at one's unconscious motives and prejudices was like walking barefoot in cloudy water: you never knew whether you were going to step on something disgusting or bang your toe into a rock. He'd always considered himself relatively free of prejudice and had even managed to temper some of his atavistic suspicion of Southerners. Well, some Southerners.

He'd also thought himself free of preconceived notions about gays, but Griffoni had shown that to be false. Was a preconceived notion the same thing as a prejudice? he wondered. Musing on this, he failed to see Lieutenant Scarpa turning into the corridor and didn't notice him until he almost walked into him.

'Good morning, Commissario,' the Lieutenant said, raising a hand to suggest a salute. Only a centimetre or two taller than Brunetti, he weighed at least fifteen kilos less and thus seemed much taller than he was. Though he stood, he seemed to loom.

54

'Good morning, Lieutenant,' Brunetti said and started to move around him. The Lieutenant leaned, but did not step, to block Brunetti. 'There was something I wanted to ask you, Commissario,' he said.

'Yes, Lieutenant?' Brunetti asked.

'It's about the visit of the Questore of Palermo.'

'Yes?' Brunetti asked, forcing a smile onto his face.

'The dinner. This evening. The Questore would like to know if you'll be attending.'

Brunetti had been trying to find an excuse for days, and now he had one: Lodo's dinner.

Before he could answer, Scarpa added, 'He said he'd very much like to see you there.'

'The Questore of Palermo?' Brunetti asked. 'I've never met him.'

'No, Commissario: the Questore of Venice,' Scarpa explained, speaking slowly as though he thought Brunetti might never have heard of, or met, his superior.

'I'm flattered,' Brunetti said, 'but I have another commitment.' For a moment, he toyed with the idea of adding that it would be helpful to have this chance to be reminded of what the Questore looked like, so infrequently was he present at the Questura, but he quelled his impulse towards sarcasm and gave the Lieutenant only a brief nod before walking away.

From behind, he heard Scarpa say, 'Dottoressa Griffoni has said she'll be there.'

Brunetti ignored the temptation to say she could take notes for him and went to his office. He refused to give Scarpa the satisfaction of seeing him close his door, went across to his desk and turned on his computer. The first thing he saw when he opened his official email was a red flag on an email from Ispettore Vianello, saying that a late-night search of the homes of three airport baggage handlers, the surveillance of whom had been handed back to the Venice Questura by the Prefetto, had revealed significant quantities of jewellery and a number of items of women's clothing still in the original wrapping and bags. Some of the objects had been reported to the airport authorities after disappearing from suit-cases in transit through the airport. All three of the men arrested had been brought in separately for questioning.

Brunetti heard a noise that only after a second did he realize was a low moaning coming from his own chest. The investigation of the baggage handlers was the Questura's very own running gag, and he had refused to have anything more to do with it. He whispered to himself, 'I will not. I will not. I will not get sucked into this again.' Disturbed by a sound from the direction of the doorway, he glanced up and saw Vianello standing there, a sheaf of papers in his hand.

'You will, you will, you will,' the Inspector said, then grinned and added, 'Unless you're very careful.'

Brunetti waved him in and pointed to the chair

on the other side of his desk. 'We've been catching them at it for I don't know how many years: we arrest them, sometimes they go to jail, more often they don't, and almost all of them go back to the same job.'

'Until we catch them at it again,' Vianello offered.

'Why don't they move to another city?' Brunetti asked. 'Or find a different kind of job?'

'Maybe they like what they do,' Vianello suggested, leaving it to Brunetti to understand the full meaning of his sentence.

'That's crazy.'

Vianello shrugged.

Calming himself, Brunetti asked, 'You said I'll get sucked into this. How?'

'I'm sure Patta's got something else he wants you to do, something he'd call a "special assignment",' Vianello began. 'I don't know what he's up to, but Lieutenant Scarpa's let drop some hints about the need to make people do what they're told to do. That sort of thing, and there's no one Scarpa would rather see being forced to do what they don't want to do. He hates you.'

This came as no surprise to Brunetti. The hatred was mutual. 'All right, Scarpa hates me. And Patta doesn't like me,' he said, as though he were about to begin reciting a litany.

'That's not true,' Vianello interrupted. 'Patta doesn't dislike you: he just doesn't trust you. That's different. And he's learned over the years that he needs you.'

'For what?' Brunetti asked.

'You never object when he takes the credit for your success or for anyone else's success,' Vianello said. 'He wants to have something to threaten you with so that, when something comes along that you don't want to do, your only other option will be to resume going out to the airport.' Vianello's smile was an unpleasant thing to see. 'He'll let you choose which one you'd prefer to work on.'

No less familiar with the Vice-Questore's behaviour than was Vianello, Brunetti was forced to see the truth of this. He pushed his chair back from the desk and got to his feet. For years, *Il Gazzettino* had praised the uncanny ability of the Vice-Questore to understand and thus outwit the criminal mind, a talent which Dottore Patta denied at every press conference he convened to show its results. Patta's success had anchored him in place in Venice: each time he was scheduled to be relocated to another province, the mayor intervened personally to keep this wizard in place, and thus the Vice-Questore's protective arms continued to spread wide over the city, not unlike those of the Madonna della Misericordia.

Brunetti walked to the window but saw nothing he liked. Personal success didn't interest him, and praise embarrassed him. He'd played soccer as a boy and had come to love the honest competition of the game; perhaps his indignation at crime was nothing more than his distaste for those who broke the rules of fair play. The important thing was that they be stopped, not who managed to stop them.

'Is there any case he wants to stick me with?' he asked, still looking out the window.

'No. Not at all. No politician's been arrested for shoplifting; no rich doctor's beaten up his wife; no bishop's been caught in the sacristy with an altar boy.'

'Nor girl, I hope,' Brunetti said in an attempt to inject the possibility of variety into the lifestyle of the clergy.

Face serious, Vianello said, 'All that's certain is that he'll be presented as the mind responsible for solving the case.'

'And welcome to it, whatever it is,' Brunetti concluded. 'I don't want to start going out to the airport every day to interview their superiors and colleagues.'

As if the idea had just occurred to him, Vianello said brightly, 'Signorina Elettra could recycle – or I could do it while she's away – some of the statements from the other investigations: there's at least ten years of them.' Then, as final evidence of the efficiency of his idea, he added, 'Many of them would be from the same suspects.' Met with stolid silence from Brunetti, he added, 'You probably interviewed them, so we'd already have tapes of the interrogations.'

This finally prised a smile from Brunetti, who raised a hand and said, 'Remember, Lorenzo, I am not going back to the airport.'

'Of course,' Vianello said. Getting to his feet, he added, 'You'll probably end up trying to cover up something for a friend of the mayor.'

'Given that choice, I'd prefer the airport,' Brunetti said instantly. His only reward was Vianello's snort of laughter as he turned to leave.

They tried to eat lunch on the terrace that day, but after five minutes, the cold won and Chiara gave up and carried her plate back to the kitchen. Brunetti gave in next, telling himself it was an act of solidarity with his daughter. Raffi joined the two of them a few minutes later and went directly to the pan containing what was left of the *tagliatelle con peperoni gialli e piselli*.

Paola came in just as Raffi was helping himself and said, making her voice as deep and rough as that of the bad guy in a Spaghetti Western, 'You take any more of that, *caro*, and it's the last meal you'll ever eat in this town.'

Raffi, Brunetti could see, was holding his half-filled plate in his left hand, a serving spoon loaded with pasta in his right. Casually, as though he'd been planning to put the spoon back in the pan anyway, he turned and set it there, then placed the lid on it and returned to his place and began to eat his diminished second helping.

Paola picked up the pan and gave Chiara and Brunetti more pasta, then set the empty pan back on the stove.

'Wasn't there enough left, Mamma?' Chiara

asked, picking up her own plate and holding it out to her mother to offer her some.

'No, thank you, Angel. I've had enough,' Paola said. 'Besides, there's *vitello tonnato*,' she continued, only to be stopped by Chiara's horrified glance. 'And *zucchine ripiene* for you,' she said to forestall Chiara's indignation.

When Brunetti saw his daughter's mouth contract, he knew she was going to ignore the house rule that no one was to criticize the food choices of anyone else at the table. Brunetti, a carnivore who had never thought it seemly to comment on his vegetarian daughter's fondness for eggs, confined himself to saying 'Chiara' in a soft voice.

'All right,' she said, setting her dish down in front of her. 'But I don't want to have to smell it. It's disgusting.'

'To some people, I'm sure it is,' Paola said in an entirely moderate voice. 'But I love it, and since I cooked it in my own home, I get to eat it here.'

'Isn't it my home, too?' Chiara asked in her adult voice.

'Yes, it is. Of course,' Paola said. 'But people who live together have to put up with one another and what they do.'

'And what they eat?' Chiara asked with the confidence of someone who expected 'no' as the only possible answer.

'And with their music,' Paola said with tie-breaking certainty.

Raffi bowed his head over his plate and put his

right hand – Chiara sat on his right – to his forehead, hiding his face and thus his smile.

Brunetti watched Chiara decide how to act, whether to be an injured victim of injustice or a person who accepts defeat with grace.

She shoved her remaining pasta around on her plate, set her fork down and took a drink of water, then used the back of her fork to wipe up the rest of the sauce.

CHAPTER 7

Brunetti went back to his office but found himself thinking about the lunchtime discussion of eating habits. Chiara had, it seemed, adopted the entire planet and now felt it her obligation to do everything she could to protect it. Thus the glass bottles of mineral water, all of them carried up five flights of stairs with the constancy and determination of ants.

Brunetti had called in decades of favours done for almost everyone in their building and had won the approval of the other residents (with the single exception of the pair of French lawyers on the second floor, who had refused him permission – a decision Brunetti chose to ignore) to leave plastic cases of glass bottles of mineral water in the crawl space beneath the main staircase. Because there was no door, the bottles were accessible to everyone in the building, although instead of stealing them – as Brunetti had thought possible – those on the upper floors carried one or two bottles each time they went upstairs and left them on their landings for the next passing Brunetti to pick up and carry the remaining distance.

In return, Chiara – and sometimes Raffi – carried down the plastic and paper garbage of three elderly couples and left it inside the front door for the *spazzini* to remove.

How different the Venice in which his children lived. He remembered his mother's stories about when she was a girl and they burned everything in '*la cucina economica*', that workhorse of a stove that heated the apartment, boiled the water both for cooking and bathing, and cooked the meals, its fuel any spare paper or wood and coal that was delivered to the house. No one had talked about pollution then, only about the fine grains of coal dust that were everywhere, the cost one paid for heat. What would she think of the current fetid air of winter and early spring, of the constant assault on every embankment from the motorized boats that passed, of the tons of plastic tossed into the garbage every day? What, in fact, would his youthful mother have known of plastic?

He hauled his mind back to the issue of meat and to Chiara's decision no longer to eat it. In the past, she had made no objection to their eating it, so long as she was given something else. But meat and fish together had been too much for her. For the first time in his life, Brunetti thought about meat, what it was, where it came from, what it did for the beings in which it . . . here, he found himself unable to find a comfortable verb. Did muscles and organs 'live' in their hosts or did they only work or function there?

He tried to recall when he and Raffi and Paola had stopped joking with Chiara about her environmental ideas and ideals. There had been no decisive action or remark, no illumination on the road to Damascus, only the dawning realization of how right she was. He was called back from this aimless musing by a noise at the door. When he looked over, he saw Signora Elettra. Perhaps because she had been at her computer much of the day, she had turned back the sleeves of her blouse, exposing the same yellow lining of the cuffs. Brunetti wondered how a detail as small as this could give such disproportionate delight.

'Yes, Signorina?' he asked.

She raised the manila folder in her hand and approached his desk. Smiling, she placed it in front of him.

'Interesting?' he asked, sliding it towards him.

'In part,' she answered, that apparently being the only introduction she was prepared to give. She gestured towards the folder. 'There are a few things I couldn't find.' Seeing his surprise, she quickly added, 'I've contacted friends who might be able to help me, but not before tomorrow.'

For a moment, Brunetti thought she might apologize for the slowness of her associates. Instead, she looked at her watch and said, 'There's nothing more I can do until they answer me, so I thought I might leave now.'

'And the Vice-Questore?' Brunetti inquired,

familiar with the fact that what little work Patta did usually got done in the late afternoon.

'He's gone home already, Dottore. Before he left, he said there was something he wanted to talk over with you but that it could wait until tomorrow.'

He gave her a steady look, but she shrugged her shoulders by way of answer, leaving it to Brunetti to fathom what Vice-Questore Patta might have in mind for him.

'Thank you for this,' he said, wished her a pleasant evening, and reached to open the folder.

Time passed. Someone poised on the roof of the building on the other side of the canal would have seen within the office across from him a robust man seated at his desk, slowly making his way through the pages that lay in front of him, just to the left of the keyboard of his computer. Occasionally, the man shifted his eyes from the document to the window, after which he folded his arms and sat for varying periods of time. His gaze was such that he would not have noticed the person on the opposite roof.

Other times, the man turned from the document to his computer, punched things into the keyboard and gazed at the screen, glanced out of the window, then back to the screen. Every so often, the man looked back at the papers on his desk; now and then he made a note on one or more of them, only to return his attention to the screen.

Once, he got up and came over to the window,

but his attention was never directed at the roof opposite. If anything, it was directed at the long open view above the roof. Occasionally, standing there, the man stuffed his hands in the pockets of his trousers and raised and lowered himself on his toes before removing his hands and returning to the desk.

Some time later, as he was gazing at the papers, the man started as at a thunderclap and smacked his hands on his breast, a gesture that would alarm any observer. But then he slipped his right hand inside his jacket, removed his phone, and put it to his ear. He listened for some time, spoke for some time, listened again, tried to speak but stopped, listened some more, said a few words, pressed the surface of the phone, and replaced it in his jacket pocket.

He appeared to say something to himself and then turned to his computer again. His attention remained on the screen for a long time, while he ran his right forefinger down the margin as he read, now and again pausing to glance away at the far wall.

He returned his attention to the printed document until he turned the last page and placed his left palm on top of it, as though he wanted to transmit some message to it, or perhaps wanted it to transmit its essence to him. After a long time, he gathered up the papers and tapped their bottoms against the desk to order them into a neat pile. He slipped them into the middle of his folded copy of *Il Fatto Quotidiano* and shoved it to the other side of the desk. He leaned closer to the screen, rubbed at his eyes and then his face and sat like that for a few moments. He covered the computer's mouse with his right hand and moved it around, then removed his hand. As he did, the light from the screen disappeared, making him invisible in the now-darkened office.

Slowly, a grey penumbra slipped into the room from the lights on the *riva* below, faintly illuminating the man and the objects in the room. The man leaned back in his chair and raised his arms above his head, grabbing one wrist with the other hand. He waved his arms from side to side a few times, freed his wrist and put his hands on the arms of his chair. He pushed himself to his feet, reached for the newspaper but pulled his hand back and did not pick it up. He moved towards the door and reached for the handle. A flash of light cut into the room as the door to the corridor opened. The man walked through the door and pulled it closed.

CHAPTER 8

Brunetti walked home the usual way, through Campo SS. Giovanni e Paolo, Santa Marina, and then over the Rialto Bridge. Without thinking, he turned at the bottom of the bridge so that he could walk along Riva del Vin and then cut through San Silvestro. Although his feet recognized the way he was going, his mind paid little attention and let them do what they chose, sure they'd bring the rest of him home.

At the bottom of the steps to their apartment, he gave no thought to mineral water and started up. It was only on the third landing, when he saw four bottles lined up beside the door of the Nicchettis' apartment, that Brunetti realized he'd walked home pretty much in a fog.

He bent and grabbed two bottles in each hand and continued up to his own apartment. Outside the door, he was still so distracted that he had to stop and consider for a moment what he had to do with the bottles before he could reach his keys. He set them down, opened the door. He picked up the bottles and backed into the apartment.

Setting the bottles on the floor, he shut the door, then picked them up again and took them into the kitchen. The counter seemed a good enough place for them.

He found an open bottle of Pinot Grigio in the refrigerator and poured himself a glass. He took it with him into the living room, leaving the uncorked bottle next to the water bottles on the counter. He sat on the sofa, pulled a cushion behind his back, stretched out his legs and placed his feet on the low table in front of him.

He had intentionally left the papers Signorina Elettra had given him in the office, wanting to force himself to remember what he'd read, thinking that the most important events would come to his memory first. As he sat there, allowing himself to relax, the information in the report lined up and started to settle into his memory.

The first fact to slip in was the most surprising: when Gonzalo was in his early twenties, his father, the owner of the hat factory, had taken out a page in the local newspaper to declare that Gonzalo was no longer to be considered his son. They did not live in Madrid, but in a medium-sized town in the North, which his family had more or less ruled for centuries. Gonzalo was first in line to succeed his father as head of the family, owner of the factory, and Viscount of . . . Brunetti could no longer remember the name of the place. The announcement, a copy of which was in the file, made it clear that something called the Deputation of Grandes of Something had drummed Gonzalo out of the club.

Because no mention was made in the document of a reason, the choice was open; Brunetti put his chips down on politics or sodomy. Spain in the late Fifties: wealthy conservative family, Francoists. It certainly wasn't because Gonzalo was trapping goldfinches.

Being disowned probably spurred Gonzalo to seek success, and fortune, on his own, and Signorina Elettra had managed to catch glimpses of him along the way. He set out for the Promised Land and found it in Argentina, where he became a farmer, then a rancher, then an exporter of beef, then a millionaire. Signorina Elettra had found no evidence that he was involved in politics in any way while he was there: he had his cows, and that seemed to be enough. Then, in the late Sixties, in what seemed an act of voluntary exile, he packed up and moved to Chile, began farming again, avoided politics, stayed through the first year of the Pinochet regime, and returned to Spain in the mid-Seventies.

His father had died some years before, but Gonzalo had apparently made no claim to the family business. Instead, he opened a gallery in Madrid, specializing in pre-Colombian art, and within a few years had other galleries in Paris, Venice, and London.

Brunetti gazed through the opening between his upraised feet. The day's light was long gone, but

71

he could see rectangles of light and, off in the distance, the bell tower: live on an upper floor, and you saw it from most parts of the city. Heard it, too.

He finished the wine and leaned forward to set the glass on the table, then went back to considering the official evidence that various bureaucracies had accumulated about Gonzalo as he made his way through the world and through the years.

The purchase of his apartment in Venice, where he apparently still lived alone, had been registered in the Ufficio Catasto, more than twenty years before and at a price that would today cause anyone searching for an apartment a convulsion of envy. Brunetti knew enough about buying a house to know that the price declared on the official documents was perhaps half the price Gonzalo had paid, but even if it had cost three times what had been declared, it was still a bargain.

The copies of the permissions for the restoration that Signorina Elettra had found in various offices suggested that the low price reflected the condition into which the apartment had fallen. The list of permissions for building work was impressive: new roof and windows, heating system, new electrical system, twenty centimetres of insulation under the roof, as well as three bathrooms and the reconstruction of three walls.

Paola had once remarked that a home was merely a hole in the ground, at the side of which the owner stood, while a deep voice from the pit called up, 'Give me Euros, dinars, francs, krone, yen, dollars, ducats, your first-born son, blood. Give me everything.' She was right, he thought.

The papers Signorina Elettra had managed to obtain spoke only of the type and extent of the renovations, not of their cost, nor of the inevitable increases in cost. The apartment was declared '*abitabile*' two years and four months after the permissions were granted, six years and three months after they were first requested. Had Oblomov worked in the office of building permits? Brunetti wondered.

In the first year of this century, Gonzalo retired from the art business: *Vanity Fair*, among other magazines, carried a story about the party he gave to celebrate his retirement; the issue contained photos of the parties at all three galleries. Brunetti, when he'd looked at copies Signorina Elettra had made of the articles, had been surprised to recognize some of the guests: a rock star and a football player in Paris, and a politician and his actress wife at the party in London. He had once arrested the lawyer, though not his wife, who appeared at the party in Venice.

Two of the articles reported that Gonzalo had sold his galleries and client list to a famous auction house for an undisclosed sum. Interviewed at the party in Venice – the one he had chosen to attend – he said he planned to spend his retirement going to museums to see the paintings and objects he had never had enough time to really study. He wished the new owners well and said that he would certainly work with them as a consultant in the next year.

And then almost nothing. Mention was never made of anything he might have done for the new owners. His photo appeared a few times in magazines like *Chi* and *Gente,* but as time passed, the photos grew fewer and smaller and moved farther towards the back of the magazines. When Brunetti thought about the photos that accompanied the articles, it seemed to him that Gonzalo had grown not only older, but paler and less vibrant.

This, Brunetti knew, was what happened to people who retired. Like photos left too long on the wall, their colours began to fade. Hair followed life and began to grow dim, the brightness of their eyes diminished. A strong jawline became harder to see; skin dried and grew more fragile. They remained the same people, but they began to disappear. Certainly, others no longer noticed them, nor what they wore nor what they said or did. They were there, hanging suspended, washed out and considered useless, trapped behind the glass of age. Dust gathered on the glass, and one day they weren't there on the wall among the other fading photos, and soon after that people began to forget what they looked like or what they had said.

'Oh, how very clever you are,' Brunetti said to himself. He got to his feet and went into the bedroom to change for Lodo's dinner.

*   *   *

Lodovico Costantini, as well as being one of Conte Orazio's lawyers, was also his friend and so, by something resembling the law of inheritance, he was Paola's friend, as well. The same law made him well disposed towards Brunetti by right of marriage. Lodo welcomed Brunetti warmly and told him that Paola was already in the *salone*: she'd come directly from the University, where the English Literature faculty had held its yearly meeting to decide who would administer the oral exams at the end of the semester.

When he entered the large and too brightly frescoed *salone*, Brunetti looked for Paola among the people in the room. He nodded to a few familiar faces, bowed to kiss the hand of Lodo's sister-in-law, and then finally saw Paola speaking to a man he did not recognize, a glass of champagne in her hand.

Because the man was at least a decade younger and not unattractive, Brunetti put his arm around Paola's shoulders as he reached them and kissed the side of her forehead. She leaned closer to him for an instant, enough to acknowledge his kiss, and said, 'Ah, Guido, I'd like you to meet Filippo Longo. He's a colleague of Lodo. He's here for a hearing tomorrow: he was just telling me about it.'

While Paola was speaking, the other man had taken a flute of sparking wine from a tray offered by a passing waiter and handed it to Brunetti, who nodded his thanks. Longo was thick: neck and chest and even his wrists, emerging from the sleeves of his jacket, seemed covered with an extra layer of muscle. His face, in contrast, was delicate and fine-boned. The effect was like seeing a Greek statue with the head of Apollo and the body of a bear.

'What sort of hearing, if I might ask?' Brunetti inquired and sipped at the wine, which was exceptionally good.

'The worst sort,' Longo said in the kind of voice a chest that size would produce: a bass baritone with a reverberation a singer would envy. 'Inheritance.' He shook his head and gave a theatrical shiver with his entire body. 'The hearings are terrible.' But then he grinned and added, 'It's my speciality, so please understand that I'm describing, not complaining.'

Brunetti asked, 'Why are they the worst?'

Longo tilted his head and looked off behind Brunetti's. 'Because things are never what they seem and often not what your client tells you they are.' He paused before continuing, as if trying to think of a way to explain exactly how terrible these cases were. He nodded. 'Yes, that's it. You think your client is being cheated by their siblings or their children or by the housekeeper of the person whose will they're fighting about, and you think they do this because they honestly believe in all good faith that they really have a right to more money or an apartment, or their mother's diamonds.'

The lawyer sipped at his wine, and Brunetti

thought how good this man would be at oral arguments: he was a man who knew how to use a pause.

'But what they're really doing is re-fighting childhood battles, getting even for old rancour, and they don't care in the least about the objects or the money, only about spiting someone who hurt their feelings half a century ago.' He took another sip and then said, voice lower and slower, and dire as a funeral cortège: 'The tragedy is that they will never realize this.'

Before the lawyer could say anything more, a different waiter came to the door and announced to the room, '*Signori, la cena è servita.*'

It was then, as the people in the room looked around for places to set their glasses, that Brunetti saw Gonzalo. At first Brunetti didn't recognize him because this Gonzalo was at least ten centimetres shorter than Gonzalo was supposed to be. And his hair, once wiry and pugnacious, pushing itself where it wanted to go, lay limply on his skull, not quite succeeding in covering the patches of pink skin beneath.

The older man moved towards the door, his head sunk forward tiredly. At a certain point he must have remembered where he was, because he pulled himself up straight. He walked to the table and moved behind the chairs, glancing at the name cards that stood in front of each place. As Brunetti watched, Gonzalo reached the end, crossed behind the single chair at the head of the table, and started slowly down the other side, looking at the cards propped against the plates.

He found his place, to the right of the host, Lodo. He placed both hands on the back of his chair, not bothering to hide the fact that he needed its help. To his right, Lodo's sister-in-law, seeing this, slipped into her chair and patted his to invite Gonzalo to sit. He lowered himself into the chair, one hand braced on the table, and turned to thank her, then responded to something she said.

Brunetti, who was sitting in the seat farthest from him, on the opposite side, had his view of Gonzalo blocked by one of two enormous bouquets of gladioli that stood in the centre of the table.

On Brunetti's right sat Lodo's daughter, Margherita, who had studied law at Ca' Foscari a few years after him and whom he considered one of his legal friends. On her other side was Paola, to whose right sat the director of a film festival in Tuscany, whom she'd met when he delivered a series of lectures at the University.

The two seats opposite Brunetti and Margherita were empty, but just as the door from the kitchen opened to admit the waiters bringing the food, a very young woman slipped into the seat opposite Brunetti and turned to Lodo's wife at the head of the table opposite her husband, saying, '*Scusa, Nonna.*' After that she sat with her head bowed until Brunetti exclaimed, 'Good heavens, you're Sandra. I haven't seen you since you were about as high as this table, and now you're a beautiful young woman.' She raised her head and smiled across at him, then looked around the table to see who else was there.

The first course, an *antipasto di mare*, was served with a particularly good Ribolla Gialla Brunetti remembered having had here a few years before. In response to his question about what she was working on, Lodo's daughter said she was currently representing the family of a worker who had died in an accident at the port of Marghera: tired after climbing up six floors of scaffolding, he had paused to lean against the wall. But it was not a wall, only a piece of white cloth draped between two upright beams, and he had fallen six floors and died on the spot.

While she was telling him this, Brunetti heard voices behind him and turned his head to see what was happening. A clean-shaven man in a dark grey suit was speaking in a low voice to one of the waiters, who listened for a few seconds, head lowered to hear him. The waiter nodded and led the man around the table to the empty seat two places to Gonzalo's right, directly opposite Margherita. He sat down quickly and muttered something that must have been an apology to the table at large. What Brunetti was beginning to think of as The Great Wall of Flowers blocked part of the man's face, but Brunetti could see enough to tell that he was dark-haired and handsome: large, dark eyes and curly hair cut very short. He spoke to Lodo's sister-in-law on his left, then to

Sandra, both of whom nodded and smiled easily in return.

As the man continued his conversation with Sandra, Brunetti saw Gonzalo place his palms on either side of his plate and start to rise, but almost immediately he relaxed back into his chair and picked up his knife and fork. He looked at his plate, his face without expression. Even through the obstacle of the flowers, Brunetti saw the tension in it. Gonzalo leaned forward and looked to his right, at the man on the opposite side of the older woman. '*Buonasera*,' Gonzalo said, still looking towards the newly seated man. A waiter was clearing the plate from in front of Margherita, who stopped speaking while he did it. Gonzalo's voice was tentative, and Brunetti turned away from the sound of it.

The younger man turned towards Gonzalo and met his glance. Three seconds passed – Brunetti counted them – before he nodded and directed a blazing smile at the older man.

'Sorry I'm late,' he said, as if Gonzalo were the host and thus the person who deserved an apology for his lateness.

The decades Brunetti had spent observing and pondering human behaviour made him consider this brief exchange. The apology demanded a response, and the only response the younger man expected – Brunetti was certain – was submission, and that could be acknowledged only by the other person saying that the lateness didn't matter in the least.

Gonzalo smiled from a face that was relaxed and renewed. 'So long as you got here,' he said and picked up his fork.

The other man's laugh brought an answering smile to Gonzalo's face. As Brunetti watched Gonzalo eat, he saw him sit up straighter; his shoulders seemed to better fill his jacket, and his voice lost all sign of age and grew deep and sonorous, as Brunetti remembered it had once been.

He and the younger man did not speak directly to one another more than a few times during the rest of the meal, but the way they spoke left no question that there was a bond between them. Brunetti's view of both was obstructed by the flowers, but he saw how Gonzalo inclined his head towards the other man whenever they spoke, although the other did not bother to turn to catch Gonzalo's eye when he answered.

Margherita, seeing how little interest Brunetti took in her details of evidence and witness statements, turned and spoke to Paola for a while.

The waiter appeared at Margherita's left and served something that Brunetti didn't bother to glance at. He heard the play of emotions in Margherita's voice as she repeated to Paola her description of the dead worker's family, but he paid far more attention to the play of emotions on the portion of Gonzalo's face he could see as the older man leaned forward and looked down the table towards the younger man.

Conversation on both sides of the table, from

what Brunetti was able to hear, was chiefly about films, the topic no doubt originated by the director of the festival. Brunetti believed this topic prevailed at so many dinners because, in recent years, it had become increasingly dangerous to discuss politics or immigration or, indeed, almost any major topic; even comments on the politics in neighbouring countries could lead to trouble. Brunetti had nothing to contribute to a discussion of cinema because he had little free time and begrudged the watching of movies. Those few times he was cajoled into going, he invariably returned home grumbling about the waste of time: he could have been reading.

Dessert came, then coffee, and then some magnificent apricot schnapps a friend of Lodo in Val Venosta sent him every year. Few people showed any desire to linger after the schnapps. Most gave their thanks and took their leave by eleven.

Gonzalo had not noticed Brunetti, or at least not acknowledged him, though he had spoken to Paola, it seemed with great affection. Brunetti lingered behind, not wanting to force a meeting, thanking Lodo and his wife until everyone else had left.

'Well?' Lodo asked as he and his wife accompanied Paola and Brunetti to the door.

'It was a wonderful dinner, Lodo,' Paola said, thus cutting off the possibility of any conversation regarding Gonzalo, the younger man, or her father. 'I hadn't seen Margherita in such a long time,' she continued, driving a second nail into the coffin of discussion of Gonzalo and his young friend. 'She really looks wonderful, and she seems so happy, proud of her job.'

'She is that,' Lodo agreed, thus acknowledging that there would be no embarrassing talk about his client, Paola's father's friend. So, discussing Margherita's professional success, they continued to the door of the apartment, where there was a flurry of kisses and wishes of thanks and goodwill.

As they turned toward the Accademia Bridge, Brunetti asked, 'Well?'

'You're not asking what I thought of the food, are you?' Paola answered.

'If I were a clever man, I'd say I spent more time paying attention to the bait than the food.'

'If you're talking about Gonzalo,' Paola answered as they entered Campo Santo Stefano, 'I'd say he took the bait a long time ago and is safely and securely hooked and landed.'

'That's the impression I had,' Brunetti agreed, 'but you were sitting closer to him and probably heard more of what went on.'

'I heard a fair bit.' She stopped and looked at the moon, visible above Palazzo Franchetti. She didn't call his attention to it in any way, merely stood and observed the disc in the sky. When they had had enough of that, they continued across the *campo*, towards the new bridge.

'And,' Brunetti prompted.

'And il Marchese Attilio thinks Quentin Tarantino is a genius.'

'And I'm Galileo Galilei,' Brunetti said. 'Did they spend the whole dinner talking about cinema?'

'I'm afraid so. You would have screamed. I almost did.'

'Why? I thought you liked films.'

'I do. I just don't like having to listen to people talk about them. Most people talk rubbish about film. Worse, it's pretentious rubbish.'

Before she could continue, Brunetti asked, 'What did you think?'

'I think Gonzalo is in love, and I think il Marchese is taking care that he stays that way.'

'Hummm,' was the best answer Brunetti could come up with.

'He has shark's eyes,' Paola said.

'Il Marchese?'

'No. Gonzalo.'

'Excuse me?' Brunetti said.

'Remember when we met and you decided you liked me?'

'You've always been given to understatement,' Brunetti said. 'It's because you were educated in England, I think.'

Ignoring what he said, Paola went on. 'For a time, you had shark's eyes. I've seen them in men all my life. It happens when they're overcome by passion and can't control it.'

'Me?' Brunetti asked in a peeping voice.

'You. For about a week. And then you began to like me, and then you realized you loved me, and your eyes stopped being shark's eyes and went back to being your eyes.'

Brunetti decided not to pursue this and asked, 'And Gonzalo has shark's eyes?'

'Or else I'm Galileo Galilei,' Paola said, and they started to cross the bridge.

CHAPTER 9

The person who brought him coffee at eight the next morning set the cup and saucer on the table next to him and bent to kiss his left ear. 'Coffee,' she said.

Still not free from sleep, he mumbled, 'Paola?'

'No,' she said brightly and slipped into French. 'It's Catherine Deneuve, and I've left everything behind to come to you, my darling.' She bent and used both hands to pump the mattress up and down a few times, then switched back to Italian to say, 'You told me to wake you up at eight because Patta wanted to talk to you.'

Brunetti turned and hauled himself up against the headboard. He reached for the coffee and drank it in three quick sips. He shook his head. 'I'll never forgive him for this.'

'For what?' she asked, confused.

'That I had Catherine Deneuve in my bedroom but had to tell her I couldn't stay because I had a meeting with my boss.'

She smiled and turned towards the door. 'I told you you'd lost your shark's eyes.'

She was gone before he could throw a pillow at her.

Patta did indeed want to speak to Brunetti, Signorina Elettra informed him, but not until after eleven. This gave Brunetti more than an hour to wait. Back in his office, his mind returned to the events of last night, but then they wandered off to consider adoption as a means to take a family name forward in time. Caesar had done it and given the Roman world his nephew Octavian, who had rebranded himself as Augustus and ruled in relative peace for forty years. But then had quickly come trouble: Tiberius, Caligula and Nero.

Brunetti was trying to remember the exact succession of the emperors when his phone rang, and Signorina Elettra told him the Vice-Questore was free. Downstairs, he found the door to Patta's office open, walked silently past Signorina Elettra and entered, saying, '*Buondì*, Vice-Questore.' He was about to ask in what way he could be helpful that morning but, remembering Vianello's warning, realized how servile it would make him sound, and so said no more.

Patta was behind his desk, his silver hair freshly cut, a bit shorter than usual at the sides, as though he had chosen to imitate so many of the young men they arrested these days and thus would soon arrive with his hair shaved to the level of his ears, a long crest running from the front to the back of his head. On a head that noble, atop a face so handsome, it might well work and propel Patta to the cutting edge of fashion.

'Ah, good morning, Commissario. Please have a seat, there's something I'd like to discuss with you,' Patta said, giving a toothy smile that set Brunetti's own teeth on edge.

'Yes, Vice-Questore?' Brunetti inquired neutrally.

'Actually,' Patta began, his teeth now hidden behind his lips, perhaps being sharpened for their next appearance. 'It's about my . . . it's about my wife.'

'Ah,' was all Brunetti would permit himself. He decided it would be best to seek shelter, so placed a look of mild concern on his face and hid behind that.

'There was a . . . a disturbance at my home last night,' Patta began. Brunetti sensed, but did not see, the force it took his superior to remain calm as he spoke.

Brunetti nodded.

'You've heard about it?' Patta asked, fear mixed with anger. 'Already?'

'No, Dottore,' Brunetti said. 'I merely nodded to show I'd heard what you said.'

'Are you lying to me, Brunetti?' the old Patta demanded.

'No, Signore. I swear it.'

'All right, all right,' Patta said quickly. 'There's no way you could have, I suppose.' He lapsed into silence and stared at the surface of his desk, perhaps looking for the cue cards that would show him how to tell this story.

Brunetti, who had met Patta's wife once or twice but never done more than shake her hand and nod his pleasure at meeting her, said nothing. He remembered a woman taller than Patta, with a small nose and a broad face, who had a general air of eagerness, as if she were waiting to be shown the next thing to enjoy. He had done nothing more than exchange names with her, but he had liked her, not least because of Patta's devotion to her, the sincerity of which had always pulled him back from the brink of any attempt to dismiss the possibility of Patta's humanity.

Patta glanced at the small crossed flags of Italy and the European Union planted in the brass penholder on his desk, and as he stared at it, Brunetti saw desolation cross Patta's face. His first thought was illness, but Patta would not want to see him if that were the case; in matters concerning his family, the Vice-Questore was usually a private person.

Patta's eyes rose and met his. 'You're Venetian,' he said and stopped.

'Sì, Signore,' Brunetti answered.

'So you understand them?' Patta asked, as though he were speaking of Hottentots or Pygmies.

'Venetians, sir?'

'Yes. Who else were we talking about?' he said with his more usual tone.

'If you give me a bit more information, sir, I

might be able to be of help.' Brunetti followed this with a smile he was careful to make seem entirely natural.

'Yes, of course,' Patta said in a softer tone. He leaned forward and ran his fingers through his hair but pulled them away in surprise as soon as they touched the short stubble at the sides. He latched his hands together and set them on the desk in front of him where they could not cause him any more trouble.

'We have neighbours,' Patta said. Brunetti nodded and resisted the impulse to remark that many people did. 'They're Venetian.' This time Brunetti did not remark that, in recent times, many people's neighbours no longer were. Instead, he nodded again.

'We've had trouble with them,' Patta said, leaving Brunetti no choice but to offer up in sacrifice to the Madonna of Medjugorje his request for her help in maintaining silence in the face of this Occasion of Sin. With her aid, Brunetti refrained from saying he was not surprised and, instead, made a small humming noise that was enough to encourage Patta to add, 'Recently.'

'I'm sorry to hear that, Dottore,' Brunetti said and surprised himself with the realization that he meant it. Few crosses were heavier to bear than that of bad neighbours. Only incidents of domestic violence were worse to respond to in terms of the aggression and calculated nastiness that the police might encounter.

Before Brunetti could ask where these people were in relation to Patta's apartment – directly above or next door were the worst because of the noise – Patta added, 'They're below us.' Bad luck. Brunetti knew because of the water: if it came from above, it was their fault, and no discussion. Burst pipe, forgotten bath, coming initially from the roof: it made no difference to the damage it would do, and water was the worst.

While Brunetti was considering this, Patta hastened to add, 'It was never a question of water. There's never been a leak, not in all these years.'

'Then what is it, sir? If I might ask.'

'Their son insulted my wife,' Patta said. Then he added, before Brunetti could say anything, 'More than once.'

It passed through Brunetti's mind to ask if he was going to spend the rest of his career taking care of family problems. Into Patta's continuing silence, he chose to say, 'I hope the parents did something.'

Patta laughed, though not with amusement. 'They did nothing. They told my wife she was inventing it, and their son was an angel.' The snort of disgust Patta gave told Brunetti how ridiculous he believed the claim to be.

'How long ago was this, Signore?'

'Seven months ago, just after the beginning of the school year.'

'How old is the child?'

'He's eight.'

'Can you tell me what he said, Signore?'

Patta looked up, and then away. Brunetti waited for him to answer.

Finally Patta said, 'He said she was a filthy whore.' He watched Brunetti raise his eyebrows in surprise and added, 'I'm not sure he knows what it means, except that it's something he shouldn't say to a woman.'

Because 'porca puttana' was so often said in response to disappointment or surprise, Brunetti asked, 'Was he speaking directly to your wife when he said it?'

'You mean, was he saying "porca puttana" because he tripped on the steps and not calling my wife "una sporca puttana"?'

'Yes.'

'My wife said she was coming down the stairs and met the boy at the front door. When he saw her, he stopped and looked at her and said, "Tu sei una sporca puttana." So there was no linguistic confusion, Commissario: he meant to say it to her.'

Brunetti no longer recalled when he had first understood what a puttana was, but he did know that if either of his parents had found out he'd said it to a woman, any woman, the consequences would have been swift, physical, and unpleasant. Times had changed, so it was no longer unthinkable that a child would also use the familiar 'tu' with an adult: in his case, it would have doubled the offence.

'Did your wife speak to the parents?' Brunetti asked.

'That evening. She went down to see them before dinner and when the mother answered the door, she told her what her son had said.'

'And the mother?'

'She closed the door in her face.'

'And then?'

'My wife told me about it when I got home, and I went down and asked to speak to the father. He came to the door – I was standing on the landing – and said his wife had told him what mine had said, and he thought my wife was crazy.'

'What did you do?'

'There was nothing I could do, was there?' Patta said.

'This was seven months ago?' Brunetti asked. At Patta's nod, he continued, 'What's happened since then, Signore?'

'We've met occasionally on the steps, but we haven't spoken. The parents, that is. If my wife passed the boy on the steps, and they were alone, he made noises at her, but he never said anything. Then, about two months ago, when my wife came home and had got as far as the first landing, she heard someone running down the steps, so she stopped on the landing to move out of the way of whoever it was. When the boy got to the landing, he switched his schoolbag to his other hand and banged it into my wife's legs.' Patta seemed to have finished, but then added, 'He was gone before she could do anything,

93

not that there was anything she could have done. Not to a child.'

Taking courage from Patta's confidences, Brunetti asked, 'And last night, sir?'

'It was the same: he was coming down the stairs, and when he saw my wife coming up, he stood in front of her and refused to move, saying the stairs were his and he got to say who went up and down them. She had two bags of groceries and she set them down beside her.' As Patta approached what Brunetti thought might be the crucial moment, he thought of Oedipus and Laius confronting one another at the crossroads: this way trouble comes.

'She said they stared at one another for a long time, and then he jumped down two steps and landed on one of the bags, then kicked everything in it down the stairs.' Patta's voice grew so tight that Brunetti was glad his superior had not been a witness to the scene.

'What did your wife do?'

Patta took a few deep breaths, as if to expel some of his anger. 'She grabbed him by his arm and started to pull him up the stairs. He kicked at her, she said, so she grabbed him by both arms and shook him until he stopped. And then she walked him up to his apartment and rang the bell.

'When his mother came, my wife told her what the boy had done and told her she was free to go downstairs and see her bags on the stairs.'

'And the other woman?'

'She grabbed the boy and pulled him inside and slammed the door. My wife could hear him screaming for the next half-hour.' Patta stopped as if that was all he had to tell.

He picked up a pen and started to draw rectangles on the border of a letter that bore what looked like the letterhead and seal of the Ministry of the Interior.

'After dinner, his father came up and said he knew I was a policeman, and so he had no chance of winning any case he might bring against my wife for having assaulted their son.' He looked at Brunetti to measure his reaction to this, and in the face of Brunetti's failure to give any reaction at all, he added, 'He said that this was the sort of thing that happened once they let Southerners live in the building.'

'Ah,' Brunetti let escape his lips.

'Then he said that if my wife continued to cause his wife and son trouble, he'd have no choice but to speak to his father.'

'Who is?' Brunetti asked.

Patta grimaced as at a bitter taste and said, 'Umberto Rullo.'

A dark fin broke the waters of Brunetti's memory and disappeared without a sound, leaving a few concentric rings expanding.

When the circles stopped, Brunetti repeated the name and asked, 'How is he involved?'

'He's the managing director of the company

95

where Roberto works. They make fertilizers.'
Another flash and then the memory.

'Your younger son?'

Patta nodded.

No stranger to the modern age, Brunetti asked,
'What sort of contract does he have?'

'Temporary,' Patta said, adding with a voice as
bleak as his expression, 'He's had a temporary
contract for five years. They renew it twice a year.'
He ran his fingers along the hair on the sides of
his head. 'Five years getting a degree in Economia
e Commercio, and he's got a contract that lasts
six months.'

He looked at Brunetti, a father who had no
important connections, not in the North, to use
in order to find a better job for his son. 'If he loses
this job, he'll never find another one. Not up here,
at least.' He raised his hands in a gesture of hope-
lessness. 'And there's no work at home.' Brunetti
knew Patta meant Palermo and not Venice.

Brunetti sat quietly, thinking of the ease with
which both of his children were sure to find jobs
when they finished their studies. It didn't matter
at all what they chose to study: from Archaeology
to Zoology, the name Falier, lurking in their background, was sure to win them entry anywhere.

Sounding suddenly tired, Patta said, 'That's why
I wanted to talk to you. I'd like you to help me.'

'I'd be happy to, sir,' Brunetti answered, relieved
that Patta had not dressed this up with talk of
making it a 'special assignment'.

'I'd like you to ask Signorina Elettra to try to find out if there's something wrong with the boy.'

'Signorina Elettra, sir?'

'Of course. Who else can find out these things?'

So much for their elaborate manoeuvres to keep Patta from knowing what was going on in his own office; so much for their quiet sense of superiority to the dullard from the South who had no idea of what was going on and how things really worked at the Questura.

'If you'll write down the parents' names and the boy's, and their address, I'm sure she'd take a look, sir,' Brunetti said.

'Good,' Patta said. He opened the drawer of his desk and pulled out a sheet of paper. Quickly, he wrote the names and the address on it, then looked up at Brunetti, who was leaning forward to take it. 'And,' Patta began, paper still under his hand, 'if it turns out there's nothing wrong with the boy – that he has no real problems – then would you ask her to have a look at the parents?' In response to Brunetti's evident surprise, Patta said, 'If there's a problem with the boy, then I don't want to cause them more trouble.'

'And if there isn't?' Brunetti asked.

'Then I'd be very interested in getting something I can use to threaten them with,' Patta explained. In an even more severe voice, he added, 'He can't do that to my wife.'

Brunetti, in response said, 'I can't remember the name of the company Rullo's the director of.'

Patta looked up at him sharply, unable to erase the suspicion from his face. 'Why do you want the name?'

'It might be profitable for her to have a look at everything while she's at it.'

Patta picked up the pen again and stared at Brunetti for a long time, then lowered his head and wrote the name of the company on the paper. He slid it across his desk.

Brunetti took it but did not look at it. He wished his superior good morning and went out into Signorina Elettra's office to ask her if she would be willing to do Vice-Questore Patta a favour.

CHAPTER 10

Signorina Elettra seemed pleased to be asked to help the Vice-Questore, but when Brunetti gave her the sheet of paper, she said, very softly, 'Umberto Rullo? I know the name.' She bent the fingers of her right hand and pressed them to her face for a moment, then sat in quiet consideration. 'Umberto Rullo,' she repeated.

Years ago, Brunetti had seen a painting – he could no longer remember who had painted it – of Santa Caterina di Siena in Contemplation of the Divine Essence of God. She too was seated, her right hand to her cheek, as she stared out of a window. Beyond her the Divine Essence was to be sought in the gentle hills of Tuscany. Signorina Elettra, however, contemplated nothing more than the façade of an apparently deserted building on the other side of Rio di San Lorenzo. Santa Caterina had been draped in the tasteful black and white of the Dominicans. Signorina Elettra, coincidentally, had that day chosen the same colours, a voluminous white silk shirt with black tuxedo studs as buttons, tucked into a pair of slender black cashmere toreador slacks.

Santa Caterina had carried what looked like a handbag, a touch that Brunetti, at the time, had thought made the painting look very modern. Only later did he learn that it was made of the skin of the dragon she was believed to have vanquished. Signorina Elettra's bag hung on a thin leather strap from the back of her chair. Brunetti restrained his curiosity as to the origin of the leather: Signorina Elettra would never purchase anything made from the skin of an endangered species.

She broke out of her trance and asked, 'Wasn't he involved in the bankruptcy of that plastics factory? Ten years ago? Fifteen?'

Of course, that was where Brunetti had read the name: the factory up near Udine. Children in the area with contaminated blood – he couldn't remember the name of the chemical in the drinking water. And something about doctors being able to wash their blood clean? Barrels of contaminated waste buried near the factory. And when the Guardia di Finanza went in and sequestered their accounts, they found that the owner was a Panamanian company with an office in Luxembourg that was itself owned by a Nigerian company based in the British West Indies, which in turn . . . Ultimately they failed to find an owner. Rullo claimed, and then proved, that he was the manager, received a salary just as everyone else did, and knew nothing about who owned the company. He was an insignificant cog who did his job in seeing that orders were filled and employees paid.

The judges bought it. Or were bought themselves. The abandoned factory stood in the middle of a fenced-off field, and the water in at least twenty nearby towns was contaminated and unfit for human consumption.

And now Rullo was again in charge of a company that worked with chemicals.

'His son and his family live below the Vice-Questore,' Brunetti said. Signorina Elettra gave a slow shake of her head, as if receiving bad news. 'Their little boy's been insulting the Vice-Questore's wife for months, even hit her with his schoolbag.'

Signorina Elettra failed to hide her astonishment at this. 'But she's a sweet woman,' she said indignantly.

Although surprised to hear her say this, Brunetti had no evidence that it was not true.

'It's probably better to start with the boy,' he suggested. 'If there's something seriously wrong with him, the Vice-Questore told me he wouldn't proceed.'

'Why ever not?' Signorina Elettra asked.

Brunetti formulated an answer that would not be too shocking to her. 'Perhaps he believes the boy's sufficient trouble for them to have to deal with.'

He watched her as understanding dawned. 'Good heavens,' she finally said. She looked over at the door to Patta's office, quite as if she'd never seen it standing there in the wall, and asked, 'Whoever would have thought it?'

101

Brunetti believed it unseemly to comment and thus answered, 'I'll leave you to it, then.'

He had no idea what power Umberto Rullo might wield: apparently he had enough to have slipped free of any accusations – well, condemnation – relating to the factory near Udine. Rullo Junior certainly invested his father's name with magic powers sufficient to quell a mere Vice-Questore di Polizia, and a Southerner at that. Brunetti was surprised at how offensive this abuse of power was to him, as if his profession, his honour, his life had been called into question by nothing more than a veiled threat by some fool who thought he had access to power superior to that at the disposal of Dottore Patta.

He stopped short in the middle of the flight of stairs, startled by the power of his response, especially after his own rush of relief – he could admit this at least to himself – at the knowledge of what power the Falier name could wield. What was it his friend Giulio always said in Neapolitan? '*Votta 'a petrella e annasconne 'a manella.*' Throw the stone and then hide the hand. Indeed.

On his desk, Brunetti found the scheduling rosters for the next month and spent an hour looking them over and making changes, some to keep men who disliked one another from being on patrol together, twice to place women officers in charge of patrols, rather than leaving them in the Questura to push papers around, and once to cancel a disciplinary measure against one of the pilots, who had used his police launch to take a tourist to the hospital when he saw her lying on the pavement, her husband waving to him for help. She'd tripped on the pavement and dislodged, not broken, her ankle, but there was no way the pilot could have known that, and so Brunetti countermanded the measure and then noticed with delight that it had been initiated by Lieutenant Scarpa.

It was Thursday, and so the children were at lunch at their grandparents' home. Paola had taken that opportunity to organize a tutorial session with the only doctoral candidate she had that year. Brunetti went downstairs to ask Vianello if he wanted to go to lunch.

It was an uncommonly warm day, the third in a series of uncommonly warm days, and they decided to walk down to the *campo* in front of the entrance to the Arsenale to see if they could have lunch outside. On the way, he told Vianello about Patta's request and his concern that the parents not be further burdened if the son were in some way . . .

'Special?' Vianello supplied the word.

'If he has serious problems, yes,' Brunetti confirmed.

They passed the church of San Martino and found themselves in front of the lions that guarded the entrance to the Arsenale. Brunetti stopped in front of them, as he had been doing since he was a boy. They looked the same as ever, two of them quite respectable and the one on the far right still looking guilty about having eaten a Christian. It had done him precious little good, so thin was he. The one lounging on the lintel above the door looked more robust: he'd have to be; his wings alone did not look strong enough to have carried him up there.

'What do you think?' Vianello asked, stopping at one of the outdoor tables. Brunetti noticed that there were no tablecloths and, even stranger, no tourists.

'Inside,' Brunetti said. They were here, and since they were on duty all day long, the Ministry of the Interior would pay for their lunch.

Brunetti pushed open the door and entered and found people sitting at six tables.

The owner, Luca, came out of the kitchen, saw them, and stopped. A strange look passed across his round face, something more than surprise, almost disappointment at the sight of a pair of regular guests with one of whom he was on a first-name basis. For the first time in the years since he'd known him, Brunetti noticed the horizontal lines of age on Luca's forehead.

'*Ciao*, Luca,' Vianello said, removing his hat and looking round. Brunetti smiled and made for the far corner, where they usually sat. Vianello passed a menu to Brunetti. It was a show gesture and meaningless: Brunetti always ate *paccheri* with tuna, olives and *pomodorini*, and Vianello always asked for *pasta alla Norma*.

Luca came to their table with small steps, a towel held in both his hands.

'*Buondí, signori,*' he said as he approached, failing to call Vianello by his first name. Luca usually went through the formality of writing down their order, but he had brought no pad with him. He stood beside the table, trying to strangle the towel, and shifted his weight a few times but said nothing more.

Finally Brunetti asked, 'What's wrong, Luca?' Then, hoping to ease the situation with a joke, he added, 'We're not here to arrest you. Don't worry.'

Luca's face did not move, but he stopped trying to throttle the towel.

This time, Vianello asked, 'What's wrong, Luca? Has something happened?'

'You don't know?' the owner finally asked. 'Didn't you read *Il Gazzettino* today?'

'No,' Brunetti answered. He looked across the table and raised his chin to Vianello.

Vianello shook his head.

Luca shifted his weight a few more times. Finally he said, 'It's in the kitchen; let me get it.' He turned and walked to the kitchen, pushed open the door, and disappeared.

The men exchanged confused looks and Vianello said, 'I hope they didn't catch him not giving a receipt.'

'No, he always gives them to clients,' Brunetti said, however strange that was in a restaurant.

In a moment, the doors swung open and Luca

reappeared, bearing the second, local, section, with the famous dark blue masthead.

He handed Brunetti the paper. Brunetti spread it flat on the table between him and Vianello so that both could read the headlines. Brunetti, attracted by the largest headline, began to read about the possible failure of yet another bank but was distracted by Vianello's whispered '*Oddio.*'

Brunetti looked at his friend, who pointed to a headline reading, '*La Questura non paga trenta mila Euro.*' And then, in smaller letters: '*Ristorante non accetta la Polizia.*' He read on. The owner of a restaurant in Chioggia where the local police were in the habit of taking their midday meal, which the police paid for those in service, was owed more than thirty thousand Euros by the Questura and had refused to accept any more police as guests unless they paid for the meal themselves. He told the reporter that the officers were free to take the bills to the Questura themselves and ask for payment, but he was having no more of it.

Brunetti looked up at Luca, then at Vianello. 'We'll pay, Luca. Don't worry.'

'It's not you, Commissario,' he began and then, as if afraid he'd offended Vianello, 'or you, Lorenzo. It's the others. They come in and think they can still eat here and not bother to pay. This isn't a kitchen run by Caritas,' he said, then, as if realizing what he must sound like, he added, voice growing stronger with each sentence, 'I'm owed more than fifteen thousand Euros. That's enough. No more.'

Vianello put his hand on the man's arm and said his name. 'Don't worry. We'll pay you. And when we get back, we'll report to the Vice-Questore what the new rules are.' Either his touch or his words managed to quiet the other man, but to be certain, Vianello added, 'All right, Luca?'

The owner picked up the newspaper, folded it, and nodded. 'One paccheri and one Norma, right?'

'And a bottle of still mineral water,' Vianello added and patted Luca's arm again. The owner tucked the newspaper away and headed to another table where a woman was signalling him to bring the bill.

While they were waiting for their lunch, Vianello said, 'I hope the boy turns out not to have problems. Serious ones.' He tore open a package of breadsticks and broke one into four or five pieces, which he placed in a row beside his fork, then ignored. 'It must be terrible.' He pushed two of the breadstick pieces a bit to the right, then put his forefinger on the bottom of one of them and tipped the other end up from the table. Letting it fall back down, he continued, 'To have a child you know is bad, really bad, not just high-spirited and a pest.' There was a long pause.

'Have you ever known one?' Brunetti asked, for he had not.

Vianello nodded and prised the second piece of breadstick into the air, then let it drop immediately. 'A boy in the house opposite ours when I was growing up,' he said. 'No one liked him, not even his parents, at least not all that much.'

Luca approached and set the water on the table and said it would be a few more minutes until their pasta was ready. Brunetti glanced at his face and noticed that the horizontal lines were less evident. 'What became of him?' he asked Vianello.

'I don't know. They moved away when he was about fifteen, and I never saw him again.' Vianello poured them each a glass of water and pulled out another breadstick. He ate this one.

Luca returned with their pasta, said he hoped they'd like it, and went back to the kitchen. Brunetti speared one of the paccheri, added a cube of tuna, and tried it. Maybe a little too salty this time, but still wonderful.

'With some kids,' Vianello continued, 'especially little boys, it's hard to tell. Most of them grow up to be normal people, but some don't, I guess.' He ate some pasta then set his fork down. He looked across at his friend. 'After all, the people we work with – the ones we arrest – they have to come from somewhere, don't they? I mean, they have to start to be bad. Or something has to affect them.'

'I've started to think that maybe they're born that way,' Brunetti said, his own fork suspended in the air over his plate. 'I wonder if that's what the Calvinists meant when they talked about predestination. It's just a question of what a society thinks. We want physical reasons for everything, and they wanted spiritual ones, so they said you were born saved or damned, and there was nothing you could do about it.' He shrugged and set his fork down on his plate, drank some more water, wiped his lips.

When Vianello demonstrated no desire to discuss the varieties of religious experience, Brunetti thought he'd take further advantage of his friend's good sense and said, 'I'd like to have your opinion about something else, Lorenzo,' using his first name and thus signalling that this was a personal matter.

Had Vianello been a deer grazing in a forest, he could have been no more alert to the change in the normal sounds around him. He raised his head quickly from what he was eating, set his fork down, and gave his attention to his friend.

'It's about a man I know, a friend, someone I've known for years,' Brunetti began. He gave a quick tilt of his head to acknowledge how vague this sounded. 'He's really a friend of my father-in-law: his oldest friend; Spanish by birth. He's about the same age, gay, and wants to adopt a younger man – much younger.' He stopped to assess Vianello's reaction, waiting long enough to give him a chance to respond.

'How much difference in age?' Vianello asked.

Brunetti looked down at the sauce left on his plate and was reminded of how much he disliked having plates from which he'd finished eating sitting in front of him.

'At least forty years,' he answered.

'You said he's a friend of your father-in-law?'

Brunetti nodded.

'Same class?'

'He's from an aristocratic family, wealthy. And he seems to be very wealthy himself.'

'Where'd the money come from?' Vianello asked.

'He made a lot of money in South America, but he left and came back to Europe and became an art dealer.'

'And the man he wants to adopt?'

'I saw him once, at a dinner, but didn't speak to him.'

Vianello turned away, but it was only to signal Luca and ask him to bring them two coffees. When he turned back to Brunetti, he asked, 'Do you think it's his class, as well as his age?'

'That makes him want to adopt instead of marry?'

Brunetti rubbed at his cheek and found a small spot he had missed while shaving that morning. Luca arrived with coffee; Brunetti put sugar into his and stirred it around to give himself something to do while he thought of how to answer Vianello's question. Finally he said, 'Yes, I'd say.' He listened to the echo of that and added, 'I don't understand them, the people my father-in-law knows, the people of his class. Some of them seem to do whatever they want and never give it a thought, but others act as though everyone and their dog is paying attention to all that they do.'

'Just like us peasants,' Vianello said, laughed, and called over to Luca to ask him to bring the bill.

CHAPTER 11

O n their way back to the Questura, Brunetti
explained that he'd asked Signorina Elettra
if she could find time to fill in some of the
gaps between the few events he knew in Gonzalo's
life. Vianello reminded him that tomorrow was her
last day in the office before her vacation, and she
might not have time to do anything 'private'.

Vianello's comment made Brunetti realize to
what degree he had blocked from his mind the
fact that Signorina Elettra would not be there for
three weeks. He knew himself incapable of doing
the research and would not ask anyone else, not
even Vianello, to take on something that was, as
Signorina Elettra observed, 'private'.

Neither of them spoke again until they reached
the Questura, where, still silent, they separated,
each returning to his own office. Brunetti spent
the rest of the afternoon reading through the files
that had arrived on his desk that morning.
Rizzardi, the chief pathologist, confirmed that a
tourist who had been found three days before in
what was described as a 'lake of blood' by the
chambermaid in the hotel where he was staying

111

had indeed bled to death after a varicose vein in his leg exploded. The man had been drinking heavily and apparently had been unconscious when the vein burst. Brunetti chose not to look at the photos taken by the team sent to the man's hotel room.

A Bangladeshi cook had been attacked and beaten while walking home from his job in a restaurant on Lista di Spagna. No attempt had been made to rob him; his attackers spoke Italian. A bomb had exploded in a Bancomat in front of one of the banks in Campo San Luca two nights before, but the blast had failed to open the machine. A video camera above it had recorded both the planting of the bomb and its premature explosion, which had wounded one of the men. Both of them were identified by the first police to view the video, and one was arrested the following day. Within an hour of the explosion, the other had presented himself at Pronto Soccorso with blast wounds and third-degree burns on his right hand and arm and was arrested when he emerged from the surgery that had removed what remained of three of his fingers. Two still photos of the men from the video camera were attached to the report: Brunetti recognized both of them, petty criminals to whom the judicial system had become a recycling centre.

He went out for a coffee, came back to the Questura and went up to Griffoni's office but found it empty. Finally, not long after six, he decided he had had enough, so left his office and the Questura. It was still light outside, a flash of delight at the end of a tedious day.

Traces of red in the sky to the west were reflected in some low-lying clouds, and Brunetti regretted not having chosen to walk along by the water at least as far as the Basilica. By the time he got to Rialto, the red was gone, the clouds returned to light grey shreds.

As he passed what used to be Biancat, he thought about no longer being able to stop and get flowers on his way home. No sooner had he registered his regret than he told himself not to think of it, not to complain about it, not to whine. Biancat was gone, and now there were cheap purses and belts, and that was that.

Upstairs, all was silent in the apartment. He walked down to the bedroom, passing Paola's empty study on the way, and hung up his jacket, replacing it with a thick brown sweater he had been given for Christmas by a not-disinterested Raffi. He went back to Paola's study and placed himself in front of the shelves that held his books. He studied the titles on the spines, uncertain what he wanted to read. Recently he'd been reading the Greek tragedies he'd not looked at since he was a student and now wanted to continue with them because, reading them after so many years, he found them new and revelatory. He heard himself grunt softly as his eyes passed over the possibilities. He still wasn't ready to read *Medea* again, and *Agamemnon* was too unforgiving. What about *The Trojan Women*? He remembered his Greek professor throwing up his hands in disgust when none of them could think of a contemporary parallel with the story. Oh, had Professore De Palma been living now, Brunetti thought, the parallels would rain down upon him: the seas around Italy were filled with boatloads of Trojan Women. The brothels of Europe were bursting with the living spoils of war in the East.

He took the book from the shelf and went back to the living room and began to read. A half-hour later, when Paola came home, he had read only a few pages and had stopped at Poseidon's words: 'What fools men are to raze a city, destroying tombs, and temples, and sacred places, when they are so soon to die themselves.' He wondered how many wise people had said the same over the millennia, yet here we are, still sending in the helmeted men in search of revenge. And loot.

Brunetti wasn't aware of Paola's arrival until she called his name. He closed and set the book aside and got to his feet. He went over and kissed her cheek, fighting down the impulse to wrap her in his protective arms and promise that he would keep her safe.

Unaware that she might need her husband's protection, Paola hooked her jacket on the rack beside the door and bent to pick up the shopping bags at her feet. He took them from her, telling himself that, even if he could not save her from the wrath of Menelaus, he could at least carry the groceries into the kitchen.

One bag was much heavier than the other. He hefted it a few times and asked, 'What's in here?'

She turned at the door and looked at the bag. 'Ah, a kilo of asparagus and a kilo of new peas. I think we should eat as much of them as we can while they're in season, so I want to see if they'd work together in a risotto.'

'Not just peas?' he asked. Venetian to the marrow, he'd grown up on *risi e bisi* and loved it. 'Perhaps we could have the asparagus first?'

'Do I hear the pleading of an addict?' she asked.

'You know I love *risi e bisi*.'

'You have no culinary curiosity, Guido.'

'I do,' he insisted, putting the bags on the counter and his hand on his heart. 'It's just that I love *risi e bisi.*'

'You're worse than the kids. At least they're willing to try new things.'

'So am I,' he insisted. 'But I thought it would be nice if we could have . . .' He let his voice fade away and then added a few whimpering hiccups. In an attempt to placate his daughter, he added, 'Besides, serving us local vegetables will make up for the *vitello tonnato.*'

Paola had been unpacking the vegetables, and poked him on the arm with the bunch of asparagus. 'All right, all right, all right. Go back to your book and leave me alone.'

When he moved towards the refrigerator, she

said, 'There's a bottle of Gewürztraminer in there. Why don't you open it so I can add some to the risotto?'

Brunetti did as ordered, ever obedient to the voice of good sense.

When he returned to his place and to his book, he paused before opening it again and took a sip of his wine, and then another. This was the point, he knew, when he could put the book back and choose something less threatening. He knew what was going to come, but he had forgotten how most of the characters reacted to their destinies, those caused by the whims of the gods or those of man.

He set his glass on the table and picked up the book.

He heard the kids come home. Chiara came in and kissed the top of his head and disappeared without saying a word. Occasionally a noise or a voice filtered through to him, and he was relieved, in the midst of what he was reading, to hear the sounds of life.

When Paola came to the door to call him to dinner, he had succeeded in reading only five more pages and was glad of her summons, for it freed him – at least for the moment – from hearing Cassandra's prophecies of the murderous consequences of her rape. He set the book aside again, for he knew what would befall the mad princess and the women captured with her. But what of the moment's many rapes, in boats, on beaches, in trucks and cars, as more Trojan Women were cast from their homes into the arms of the men who had placed a bid on them or been promised them as part of the loot?

Brunetti stopped in the doorway of the kitchen and shook himself free of the play's encirclement, but not before he accepted that what had to happen, would.

The others looked up when he came in, each of them happy at the sight of him. In the centre of the table stood a porcelain bowl of risotto with peas, its creamy surface all but undulating to him in welcome. He took his place, Paola spooned steaming risotto on to his plate, and passed it to him. Then the children, then herself.

Chiara pushed herself up from her seat in a spontaneous demonstration of delight. '*Risi bisi, risi bisi,*' she said, not hiding her joy.

Brunetti breathed his silent hope – had he been a believer, he would have called it a prayer – to something about which he knew nothing and in which he probably didn't believe, that Chiara would have endless seasons in which to take such delight in peas. To do so would help her have a happy life: he believed that without understanding why.

'*Papà,*' she asked tentatively, when her first hunger was sated, 'is it true that Zio Gonzalo is trying to adopt someone?'

Luckily, Brunetti had just begun to eat, so he could delay a moment while he formulated an answer. By way of response, he asked, 'Where did you hear that?' He glanced towards Paola and saw her nod of approval at the calm with which he'd responded.

'Nonno said it at lunch today, and then he kept talking about it, even when Nonna asked him to stop.'

'What did he say?' Paola interrupted to ask.

Chiara cast a glance at her brother, who had been with her at their grandparents' for lunch, but Raffi continued eating, seeming to pay little attention to the conversation.

'Oh, the usual stuff,' she answered.

'What usual stuff?' Brunetti asked.

Chiara set her fork down and looked at her father. 'That it was a mistake.'

Brunetti, who was pretty much of that opinion himself, asked, 'Did he say what kind of a mistake?'

'Kind?'

'Yes. Was it because he had a family already or because he was too old to take on new responsibilities, or did Nonno have some objection to the person?'

This brought Raffi into the conversation. 'He didn't explain it. He said that Gonzalo shouldn't do it, and that was that.' Raffi waited a moment until he saw how his parents had digested this, then added, 'It's not like Nonno to be so close-minded, is it?' This sounded to Brunetti like a rhetorical question, so he gave Paola the chance to answer it: il Conte was her father, after all.

118

It was not until all three of them were looking at her that Paola finally said, 'I'd guess it's because his idea of family might be different from Gonzalo's.'

'Family?' Chiara asked. 'Isn't Zio Gonzalo's in Spain?'

Paola nodded.

'Then why should it bother them if he adopts someone here?' she asked, honestly puzzled.

Raffi broke in to say, 'He has us as family here, doesn't he?' Seeing their expressions, he added, 'Well, sort of family.'

Paola looked at Raffi and gave a small smile. 'Your grandfather doesn't think of family as something that can be "sort of" anything. Either it is or it isn't.'

'What does "family" mean to him, then?' Chiara asked in a strangely adult tone. '"Family" because of what?'

'Blood, I think he'd say,' Paola answered.

'Then what about Bartolomeo?' Chiara asked instantly, naming the adopted son of a colleague of Paola's.

'Maybe it's different because he was adopted when he was a child,' Brunetti suggested.

'What's the cut-off age?' Chiara shot back.

Momentarily confused, Brunetti asked, 'Age for what?'

'For when the adoption works and you really become the child of the people who adopt you? Is there an age?' There was a touch of something

119

– mischief, not sarcasm – in the way she asked her question.

Chiara was often put on the defensive, Brunetti knew, when her remarks were not treated seriously, but this time she remained entirely calm and continued, 'I'm just trying to find out what the rules are that let you become part of a family.'

Oh, the clever girl, Brunetti thought in silent pride.

'Did Nonno know how old this person is?' Paola asked. To make it absolutely clear, she added, 'The one Gonzalo wants to adopt?'

'From what he said before Nonna managed to stop him,' Chiara said with the merest suggestion of a smile, 'I'd guess he's old.'

Raffi looked at his sister and said, 'I have a feeling that someone at this table is going to ask you what you mean by "old".'

Chiara gave him the long-suffering glance of a person beset by obstacles and said, 'I think he's about forty.'

Instead of asking how she had discovered that, Brunetti nodded and agreed, 'Old.' He wondered how long it would take for Chiara to ask if there were a limit at the other end of the age scale for adoption, but she did not.

She turned to her parents and said, 'You said that Nonno might object to the person.' She ate a bit more risotto then placed her fork across what remained on the plate and said, 'He never said who it was, but I got the impression that Nonno knew him and didn't like him.'

'Did he say that?' Paola asked.

'No, but you know Nonno doesn't need a reason to think something.'

Had Chiara's remark been made as anything other than the simple observation of a truth known to everyone taking part in the conversation, one of her parents would have reproved her. As it was, it passed uncommented and thus agreed upon.

'Besides,' she continued, 'we've all heard Zio Gonzalo talk about his family over the years. The only one he can stand is his sister, the doctor. So why shouldn't he decide to start his own family?' She looked around the table, but no one said anything. 'It's what he'd do if he got married, isn't it?' she asked, a quaver of uncertainty in her voice.

Paola looked at Brunetti and signalled that this was a question he might better answer than she. Chiara turned to him and tilted her head in inquiry.

With legal dispassion, Brunetti began, 'It's a bit more, I think. If he adopts, then his adopted son will inherit everything; a wife gets only her portion.'

Chiara interrupted immediately. 'I'm not talking about money, *Papà*. I'm talking about love.'

No one spoke. The silence spread out until Paola got to her feet and started to collect the plates. Mutely, they all handed them to her, careful to see that the forks did not fall. She was quickly back with a large serving dish of chicken with cherry tomatoes and olives, which she placed in the centre of the table, then went back to the counter and brought Chiara a plate of assorted cheeses.

Brunetti waited until Paola was seated again before he continued. 'I'm afraid the law can't say anything accurate about love, Chiara. It can't be measured, or evaluated, or even recognized. So when lawyers talk about things like adoption, they have to talk about the things that are certain, and that means they can talk only about the laws, and the laws are concerned with money and objects and what people can and cannot do.'

Her plate forgotten in front of her, Chiara kept her eyes on her father.

'I can't speak for your grandfather or about why he doesn't approve of what Gonzalo wants to do, but I think I can explain why he is . . . uncomfortable . . . with the idea.'

'Is it because Gonzalo's gay?' Chiara asked hesitantly.

'No,' Brunetti said without a moment's hesitation. 'That's not important to your grandfather.'

'Then why is he making such a big thing about this?' Chiara asked. 'I really don't understand.'

'I think it's because he believes Gonzalo hasn't given it enough thought,' Brunetti said, realizing that this might well be the truth. 'The law makes it certain what a father's obligations to his son are: he has to support him, and then he has to leave his estate to him, and because Gonzalo doesn't have a wife, it will go to his adopted son. Once the adoption is concluded, he can't back out.' Chiara nodded in understanding.

'But going the other way,' Brunetti went on,

'from the son to the father, there's no legal protection. He has no obligation towards the father, nor to love him nor to feel grateful to him.' This time it was some time before Chiara nodded.

'And so perhaps that's why your grandfather is worried about what his best friend wants to do.'

Paola suddenly surprised them all by saying, 'I'd like us not to talk about this any more, please. It's not our business.' Then, before anyone could comment, she added, 'To the degree that we love Gonzalo, we can be concerned for him. But we cannot gossip about him, at least not at this table.'

CHAPTER 12

The mood of the meal could not be lightened, even by Paola's reminder that half of a date and almond cake waited in the refrigerator: not even Raffi was interested. She sent them all out of the kitchen and washed the dishes. Brunetti, who was in the living room, was conscious of how very quietly she worked that evening, entirely without the clacks and thuds that were a part of the process when she had a final comment to make on something that had been said over the meal.

He chose to listen to the noise she was making rather than return to the Trojan Women. He sat on the sofa and mused about this: these fictive people and what happened to them were much more upsettingly real to him than what he read in even the most graphic police reports. Himself no writer, a man who had no special ability with words, Brunetti found in their power traces of what he was embarrassed to call the divine.

Paola came to the door and asked, 'Coffee?'

'Yes, please.'

He heard her steps fade back towards the kitchen. What would it be to be herded on to a beach by the strange and violent men who had exterminated your family, your city, your past, and held there until they could decide to which of their friends you would be given? Nothing left of what you'd had than the clothes you wore. No rights, no possessions, no power to say no to anything. They had killed everything; the only freedom left to you, really, was to kill yourself. The gods had taken your sacrifices for years and then had washed their hands of you and gone over to the other side. And you were there, on the beach. Perhaps the swollen corpses of the familiar dead still washed up and back in the surf at your feet; behind you were the crashed-down towers, the shattered gates, and only devastation to be seen, with a slow rain of greasy ash to fall on you and everyone else with grim, slithery equality. You were a person without country and, more horrific, without family.

'Guido?' he heard, and looked up to see his wife standing and holding a cup and saucer towards him.

'Ah, thank you, my dear,' he said and took them from her.

'Are you all right?' she asked, sitting on the low table that faced him, setting her cup and saucer to one side.

'Yes. I was just thinking.'

'About what?'

'About how a writer can make even the most awful things . . .' Brunetti didn't want to say 'beautiful', but that was what he meant. 'Can make

125

them powerful,' he chose, instead. It wasn't the same, but it was also true.

She surprised him by saying, 'I've never understood why you studied law.' She picked up her coffee and took a sip.

'I'm not sure I do, either.'

'Do you regret it?'

He shook his head. 'No. The law is beautiful. It's like building a cathedral.'

'You've lost me,' Paola said with a smile.

'You want to make something that will last and that will give shelter, so you have to make it hold together, with no weak places. You have to think of all the problems that could arise if one part is weak or badly planned. You have to try, at least, to make it perfect.'

'That certainly sounds fine and noble,' she said. She leaned forward and placed both of her palms on his knees. 'But it doesn't do those things, does it?'

He shook his head and turned to tap the cover of the book that lay beside him. 'Perhaps that's why I've abandoned history for tragedy,' he said.

'Why?'

'Because the writers don't have to worry about giving an accurate record of events.'

'What do you think they want to do?' Paola asked.

'Forget about the facts and tell us the truth,' Brunetti said with the certainty of a person who has come lately to a belief.

This time Paola laughed. 'I've been telling you that for years, my dear.' She picked up her coffee but, finding it cold, set the cup and saucer back on the table.

Later, when she'd moved over to sit next to him, they spoke of Chiara's growing willingness to form her own judgements, even if they didn't agree with them. 'Even about Gonzalo?' Brunetti asked.

Paola shrugged. 'She sees him only through love's eyes, Guido.'

'You think that makes a difference?' Brunetti asked.

'I should hope so, Guido,' she said, then with a slight shrug, 'We've done what we can.' If Brunetti expected more than that, he was disappointed: Paola picked up the cups and saucers and took them back to the kitchen.

Later, when Paola had come back with a book to sit next to him and read, Brunetti asked her, 'Can you think of anyone who might know more about his . . . feelings?'

Paola gave him a long look, as if surprised to find that word on his lips. 'The only one of his friends I ever knew well was Rudy. And he's gone.' After a minimal pause, she added, voice grown more sombre, 'I wish he could find a way to be happy. He's been in my life for as long as I can remember.'

She picked up Brunetti's hand and stroked the back of his fingers. 'You really have beautiful hands. Did I ever tell you that?'

'Six hundred and twelve times, I think, though I lost count during our honeymoon.'

Tossing his hand away, she said, 'You are such a fool, Guido.'

Surprised by a realization, Brunetti asked, 'But why don't we know any of his friends any more?'

'Should I consider this police harassment?' she asked.

'No, that's when I tell you that if you don't answer my questions, we'll torture your husband.'

'Oh, yes sir, please sir, please, please, please.'

'It's not right that we don't know anything about his life or anyone who might tell us.'

She threw herself against the back of the sofa and muttered, 'I'm married to a lunatic.'

'Do you . . .'

Paola cut him off by saying, 'Dami.'

'Excuse me?'

'Padovani,' she said. 'He's back here for a sabbatical. I saw him two weeks ago.'

'And you didn't tell me?' Brunetti said.

'Jealous?' Paola asked and smiled. Her university classmate was one of the leading art critics in the country: talented, acerbic, funny, and flamboyantly gay.

'If he's still as clever as he was, then yes.'

'If anyone knows the art world, it's Dami, and Gonzalo was part of it for years,' Paola said.

'When can I see him?'

Instead of answering, Paola got up and went down to her study. When she came back, she had her *telefonino* in her hand. She plunked herself down next to him, punched in a number and, when it began to ring, handed him the phone and moved towards the kitchen.

The phone rang four times before it was answered by a deep voice, asking, 'Paola?'

'No, Dami, it's Guido.'

'Ah,' Padovani said and sighed deeply, then cleared his throat, quite as if he were preparing to play a different character from the one that gave the sigh. 'What a pleasure to hear your voice after all these years, Guido.'

'Paola said you were back here on a sabbatical.'

'You can call it that. In fact, I can call it that.'

'Isn't it?'

'Not really.'

'Then what is it?'

'An American foundation has asked me to write a book.'

'About what?'

'A painter who lived here for some time.'

'Who?'

'No one you would have heard of, believe me, Guido. He had no talent but masses of money. He lived in Palazzo Giustinian for three years and painted about seventy portraits of his dog. He was a very sweet man, convinced of his talent, and good to his friends.'

'And how is it that you're writing the book? Did you know him?'

'I did meet him once, about fifteen years ago, at a dinner.'

'And was that enough to make you want to write the book?'

Padovani burst into laughter. 'Oh, no, no, no.' And then he was gone for a while in laughter. When he stopped, he said, in an entirely serious voice, 'I imagine you called to ask me about something else.'

'You have no faith in my motives, Dami.'

'Quite the opposite, Guido. I have every faith in them. Only they're often motives I don't understand.'

'Right, well . . .' Brunetti began. 'There is someone I'd like to talk to you about, if you'd be willing, and assuming that you know him.'

'Who is it?'

'Gonzalo Rodríguez . . .' Brunetti began, only to have Padovani join him in a duet for 'de Tejeda'.

'Ah, then you do know him,' Brunetti said.

'There was a time when it seemed that everyone in Christendom – or at least in Rome – knew Gonzalo.'

'Is that a compliment?' Brunetti asked.

'Yes.'

'Do you know him?'

'Am I a Christian?' Dami asked with a short laugh, then continued, 'Yes, I know him, or knew him, at least during the time he lived in Rome. I haven't seen him in a few years, but I do hear from him from time to time.'

'Will you talk to me about him?'

Padovani took a moment before he answered. 'Only if you know in advance how highly I think of him,' he surprised Brunetti by saying.

'Tomorrow?' Brunetti tried to think of a place to invite Padovani, a place suitable to discuss Gonzalo Rodríguez de Tejeda. 'Florian's at ten?'

'*Oddio*, you must have heard how much I'm being paid to write this book. If I come, will you let me talk about my painter?'

'I'm paying, so you don't get to talk about him.'

'I'm desperate to find someone who will listen. It's the only way I might think of something to write.'

'That bad?' Brunetti asked.

'Worse,' Padovani said and was gone.

CHAPTER 13

Brunetti called the Questura at nine and told the officer at the switchboard to please inform the Vice-Questore – but only if he inquired – that he would be in later because he had to interview a witness. He waded through the tourists in Piazza San Marco and got to Florian's at 9.45. He asked if he could be seated in one of the back rooms. The waiter nodded and led him past the bar, turned left and into a small room. He told Brunetti he could choose any of the tables he wanted: it was unlikely there would be any other guests for at least half an hour.

Brunetti thanked him and said he'd order when his friend arrived. He thought of describing Padovani so that the waiter could direct him to this room, but it had been so long since he'd seen the journalist that he did not know what he looked like. 'His name is Padovani,' he said.

'Of course, Signore. Il Dottore has often been our guest.' From the man's smile, Brunetti realized that Dami's charm had not lessened. Nor, he imagined, the size of his tips.

He sat and saw himself in the mirrored wall in

front of him, then shifted to a seat that looked across the room, telling himself it was so that he could see who came through the door. He picked up the menu and had a look at the things on offer. He could have a coffee with whipped cream if he chose: the idea sickened him faintly. A different waiter came into the room, and Brunetti again said he'd order when his friend arrived.

He had not thought to bring a newspaper, so he read all of the menu and then glanced around the room to see if anyone had left a newspaper there.

'Guido?' he heard a man's voice ask.

He turned and stood and saw Dami at the door, looking much as he had the last time they'd met. The journalist had the same stocky build and flattened nose, and although his hair was white, the rest of him seemed younger. His beard and paunch had disappeared and the white hair was brushed back from his forehead, creating an effect not of age but of vitality. Brunetti remembered a more – what was the word? – indolent? Yes, a more indolent appearance: this man could well have been the tennis doubles champion of a private club in Milano.

Suddenly recalling how much he had liked Dami, Brunetti walked to the door and embraced him. The old Padovani would have turned this into a coy joke, but this one seemed to have outgrown his former manner and did nothing more than pat Brunetti's shoulder a few times and trap his hand in both of his. 'How nice to see you, Guido, after all this time.' He stepped back and took a better look. He smiled and said, a bit of his old self peeking out, 'If you'll tell me I look the same, I'll tell you you do, too.'

With almost funereal sincerity, Brunetti intoned, 'You look just the same.'

Padovani poked him in the ribs and moved towards the table where Brunetti had been seated. 'Why ever are we sitting back here where no one can see us?'

'Because back here no one can hear us,' Brunetti replied neutrally.

'Ah, of course,' Padovani said amiably. 'Are we here to plot something?'

'Perhaps,' Brunetti said.

'Not against Gonzalo, I warn you,' Padovani said seriously, with no echo of the frivolity that Brunetti had found so appealing in his conversation in the past.

Brunetti shook his head. 'If anything, I'd like it to be in aid of him.'

'Oh no,' Padovani said in sudden alarm. All smiles stopped together, and he asked, 'What's happened to him?'

The original waiter appeared at the door and came over to their table. Both ordered coffee, and Padovani, putting on an amiable expression, asked for a brioche, as well.

When the waiter was gone, the journalist asked, 'What's wrong?'

'Nothing,' Brunetti said in a voice he tried to make reassuring. 'Gonzalo wants to adopt a son.'

Padovani closed his eyes for a moment and shook his head. The temperature of his voice dropped when he asked, 'Could it by any chance be a younger man? A good-looking one?'

'Do you know him?' Brunetti asked.

'I know the type.' There was contempt in his tone, perhaps something stronger, but Brunetti had no idea who the target might be: Gonzalo? The other man? Himself?

Padovani asked, 'Have you met him? He's been around for some time, and I've been told he spends a lot of it with Gonzalo now.'

'Do you know who he is?' Brunetti asked. 'We're curious to learn something about him,' he added, choosing to make no mention of his father-in-law's original prompting.

The waiter came in and, pretending to be invisible, set two coffees on the table, then a small plate with one brioche. He went back to the door but did not pass through it. Brunetti looked over and saw a young Japanese couple standing on the threshold, peering around either side of the waiter, who blocked their way. The waiter bowed, the two young people bowed, and all three disappeared.

'The one I'm thinking of is called Attilio Circetti di Torrebardo,' Dami said, pronouncing the name as though he were a television presenter introducing his guest. Then he added, 'Marchese di Torrebardo.'

'Wherever that is,' Brunetti said, leaving it to

Padovani to infer that he was already familiar with the name.

Brunetti picked up an envelope of sugar and poured it into his coffee, stirred it around for far longer than necessary, and then asked, 'What else have you heard about him?'

Padovani leaned forward and added sugar to his own coffee, then took a small sip, set the cup back on the saucer, and picked up the brioche. After two bites, he set it back on the plate, then finished his coffee. Only then did he say, 'He's an art historian. Well, he studied art history in Rome. And he's been nibbling at the edges of the art world since then, about ten, fifteen years.'

'Nibbling how?'

'Doing the research for books by other people. Writing the books, for all I know. Writing catalogues for art exhibitions, reviewing art shows on-line, writing a blog. Since he's been living in Venice, he's occasionally given talks at the Accademia or taken people around the museum.'

'Doesn't sound like steady work.'

'It's not,' Padovani agreed. 'But it's a job where the chief requirement is charm, and he's got plenty of that.' He took another bite of his brioche and set it back on the plate.

Brunetti hesitated but then dared to risk it. 'Am I to believe you're speaking from experience?'

'Good heavens,' Padovani said, smiling broadly, 'living with Paola all these years has turned you into an insightful boy, hasn't it just?'

136

Brunetti laughed. 'I hope her having kept me around will help you believe you can trust me,' he said and waited for Padovani's reaction. After a moment's hesitation, the journalist smiled.

'I was very impressed by him when I met him,' he said coolly.

'But no longer?'

'No,' Padovani said. 'At first, I was charmed by him: he's bright, very well mannered – that still counts a great deal with me – and seemed to be a generous person. But after a time, I began to see that it was a generosity of words: he never spoke badly of other people; I'll grant him that. It's a pleasant relief in the world I live in. But he never actually did anything for anyone, and I seldom knew him to pay for his own dinner.'

Padovani sighed. 'It's a very common type. Dresses well, knows the names of people in the art world, is always seen at dinners or parties, has a string of elderly contessas he can call and visit or take to the opera or dinner.' He considered what he had just said, and amended the last to, 'Be taken to the opera or to dinner, that is.'

He reached for the glass of water that had come with the coffee and drained it, then pushed himself back from the table; the delicate chair squealed in protest; Padovani jumped in surprise. He landed back on the chair and took a quick look under it, where he must have seen nothing strange; then returned his attention to Brunetti.

'It's fake.' He held up a hand as if to prevent

Brunetti from moving. 'There's little real kindness in him. He'll be charming and affable and pay you a lot of attention, but what he's doing is looking for a way to profit from you. Every second of every minute he's with you.'

'What happened when you realized this?'

'I called him one day and cancelled a dinner I'd invited him to. I don't know why: I'd simply had enough of him. He called me a few days later, but I was busy, I said. And then when he called again, I was busy again. And that was that. No more calls.'

'It sounds like you got off cheaply,' Brunetti said. What he did not say was that his list of Torrebardo's offences could as easily be the plaint of a spurned lover as the dispassionate assessment of a man's serious flaws. Freeloading off the rich was a way of life in Venice, not a crime.

'I did.'

'And Gonzalo?'

Padovani gave a shrug. 'It sounds as if Attilio's moved on to greener pastures.' After a pause, he added, 'It's the normal trajectory for a man like him.'

'From what to what?' Brunetti asked.

'From a journalist with a modest amount of money to a man who has a great deal.'

'Is that certain?'

'That my fortune is modest, yes,' Padovani said and laughed with pure delight when he saw Brunetti's embarrassment. He reached across the

138

table and patted Brunetti's arm. 'It doesn't matter, Guido.' He laughed again and said, 'But about Gonzalo, there's little doubt about his fortune. He's certainly considered a very rich person, and he lives like one.' As though surprised by what he had just said, he paused to listen for the echo, then added, 'I've never lived in a city where so many people are trying to seem richer than they are, or with so many people trying to seem poorer.' He laughed again, the laughter given to the revelation of surprising truths. 'You Venetians have strange ideas about money.'

Brunetti thought for a moment and decided that the venality or not of Venetians was on the list of things he no longer had the patience to talk about, so he changed the subject and asked, 'Were you familiar with his collection?'

Padovani shrugged. 'Yes. He has excellent taste, bought a lot of good paintings years ago.' He tilted his head and looked into the distance for a moment, then glanced at Brunetti and said, 'He's got a small Bronzino – unattributed, unfortunately – of a young courtier. It's so beautiful, I still dream about it. And a complete first edition of *I Carceri*. In perfect condition. I've never seen anything like them.'

Padovani gave a small shake and said, 'Most of the other things are of the same quality, so to answer your question, yes, he did very well by the gallery. Galleries.'

Brunetti picked up his coffee and took a sip, but

it was cold. He set it down and asked, 'Has he ever done this before, fallen in love and tried to wrap the person up in his money or the promise of his money?'

Padovani's mouth turned up in a humourless grin. 'Is it that obvious?'

Brunetti stopped himself from smiling. 'I've spent much of my life living with a woman who's in love with Henry James and who reads his novels repeatedly: you think I haven't learned anything about the ways people make use of one another?'

Obviously uncomfortable with the drift the conversation had taken, Padovani lightened his tone and said, 'I've never read him, but I know enough about him to be able to pretend I have.'

As if still talking about literature, Brunetti said, 'James is interested in predation, but with soft voices and afternoon tea.'

Padovani's face hardened, perhaps at the word 'predation'. 'Makes it worse, somehow, when it's done with a cold heart.' Then, after a long pause, he added, 'It shouldn't happen to someone like Gonzalo.'

He picked up his empty cup and tried to nurse a few more drops from it. Failing, he replaced it in the saucer. He looked across at Brunetti, who held his glance until the waiter appeared to ask if they'd like something else.

Both ordered another coffee.

Again Padovani let some time pass before he said, 'He was one of the first people I met when

140

I began my career. We met . . . well, it doesn't matter where or how we met, but we met, and we liked one another. Perhaps because we both liked to laugh or because neither of us took the world we were living in then – the world of art dealing – at all seriously. Gonzalo even less than I.'

Brunetti pushed himself back from the table to cross his legs, and his chair let out a squeal even more hysterical than the one Padovani's chair had made earlier. Both men ignored the sound.

The waiter appeared with two more coffees and two more small glasses of water on a silver salver and placed them on the table, discreetly removing all sign of the others.

When he was gone, Padovani continued. 'Gonzalo taught me about modern art, and contemporary art, taught me how to distinguish between the good and the bad and between what would and would not sell. He told me which agents to flatter, which artists to promote, when to praise a young genius, and when to stay clear of writing about someone whose career was soon going to end.'

He broke off and took a sip of coffee, and Brunetti took the opportunity to remark, 'You make it sound like a confidence game.'

'It is. It's as fake as soccer: they're both decided in rooms, not on the field. Agents decide who goes up and who goes down, who wins and who loses. Occasionally there's a genius who simply ignores it all and paints or sculpts or takes photographs, and nothing they do can touch him. Or her. But in most cases, it's the agent who does the real creative work and who transforms a mediocre painting into a masterpiece.'

'And a mediocre painter into a genius?' Brunetti asked.

Padovani leaned forward and said, 'And I became a good writer about bad art.'

He laughed at his own remark and finished his coffee. When it seemed that Padovani was finished speaking, Brunetti asked, 'And?'

'Gonzalo taught me how to survive in this world, and soon I was famous. Well, as famous as a journalist ever becomes.' He paused, making it obvious he still had something to say. He shifted his cup and saucer slightly to the left, glanced at Brunetti, and continued. 'He's the most generous person I've ever known, Guido. Generous with his wealth, but lots of people are. He's generous with what he knows, and most people aren't.' Again, Padovani stopped speaking, but this time Brunetti wasn't sure if he'd finished. He waited, and at last Padovani said, 'This means that much of what I say is probably the result of my shame that I treated him so badly and that he had the generosity to continue to treat me well.'

'What happened?' Brunetti asked, for the cadence of Padovani's story had taken on a decidedly last-chapter rhythm.

'I found someone else, or someone else found me, and that part of it was over.'

'And then?'

'We remained friends, thank God. Or thank Gonzalo. He was still generous with information and help, kept making contacts for me, and he had suddenly become avuncular – if that's the word – towards me. We were friends, and he was older and protective.' He stopped as if he'd just thought of something clever to say. 'But time passes, and now he's even older, but I'm the one who's become protective.'

'I see,' Brunetti said, and they lapsed into silence.

Brunetti felt himself at a loss how to phrase what he wanted to ask Padovani. 'Do you fear the worst?' seemed archaic and exaggerated, but that was precisely what he wanted to know. Instead, he settled for the much more prosaic, 'Do you worry about him?'

Padovani's eyes grew serious. 'Yes, and now that you've told me what you have, I'll worry even more.'

Brunetti could think of nothing to say. He sat silent for some time and then asked, 'Where does he come from, Torrebardo?'

'Piemonte, but I don't know where.'

'Have you been in their company?'

'You mean his and Gonzalo's?'

Brunetti nodded, and when Padovani failed to answer, asked, 'Well?'

Padovani started to respond but was interrupted by the return of the waiter, who led six Chinese tourists into the small room but was careful to seat them at the table farthest from Brunetti and

Padovani. He handed out six menus and said he'd be back soon to take their orders. The tourists opened them and set to talking quietly among themselves.

Padovani picked up his menu and tapped Brunetti on the back of the hand with it. Smiling, he said, 'No, I've never seen them together.' His smile appeared for a moment, then vanished. 'I don't know why I'm being so unpleasant about this.' An awkward replica of his smile flashed for a second, and then he said, 'Remember, I'm hardly a neutral witness.' He tossed the menu back on the table and said, 'Besides, if Attilio is good to him and takes care of him, what's wrong with that?'

'That's not how you sounded a moment ago,' Brunetti said.

'I told you I wasn't a reliable witness.' The journalist moved uncomfortably in his chair, shot back his sleeve to take a look at his watch, and then looked across at Brunetti. He pressed his lips together and shook his head. 'I can't say he's a bad person. He's selfish and greedy, but so are many of the people in that world. He's interested in living a comfortable life but, for that fact' – he paused and gave a small puff of air – 'so am I.'

'You've switched over to the defence,' Brunetti observed, 'just in case you hadn't noticed.' He smiled as he said it, but Padovani failed to return the smile.

'It's called mixed feelings, Guido.'

To save time, Brunetti asked, 'Would you trust Torrebardo?'

'With what?'

'A secret?'

'If I told him it was not to be repeated, yes.'

'Money?'

'No,' Padovani answered without hesitation. 'He wants it too much, wants the things it will give him or let him have.' He thought about this for a moment, shrugged, and added, 'He's still young. Well, seen from my age, he's young. He still thinks that way.'

'Most people do, whether they're young or not,' Brunetti said, adding, 'And it usually doesn't change when they get older.'

'I know that,' Padovani said and tried to smile. 'But one does so like to believe that, just once, things will be different.'

'And someone will love us for who we are, not for what we own?' Brunetti asked.

'Something like that,' Padovani said, peeking down at the sugar dissolved in his cup.

'You never knew my mother,' Brunetti began, causing Padovani to stare across at him in confusion.

'After my father died, I asked if she believed.' When he saw that Padovani's confusion remained, Brunetti added, 'She'd always gone to Mass and always dragged me and my brother along with her. But she'd treated God like a distant relative, and I'd never known what she really believed. So

145

I asked her if she believed our father was with God.'

He stopped but Padovani said nothing: Brunetti waited until the other man finally asked, 'What did she say?'

'"It would be nice."'

CHAPTER 14

They spent another quarter-hour talking of many things but not returning to Torrebardo, nor to Gonzalo. The room gradually filled, and Brunetti decided they had occupied the table long enough. He caught the waiter's attention and feigned writing in the air. The waiter was soon back and handed the bill to Brunetti, ignoring Padovani's upraised hand.

Brunetti saw that they had been given the lower rate that was given to locals: he paid the waiter and added a tip that would do Padovani proud the next time he came. They emerged into the Piazza to feel that springtime had scampered back down south, leaving them with damp air and a breeze that must have passed through Siberia on the way to Venice.

'We just have to get through the next few weeks,' Brunetti said, 'and the weather will come to its senses.'

Padovani stopped and said, in a surprisingly serious voice, 'I think the weather's lost its senses.' He sounded remarkably like Chiara. The journalist shook Brunetti's hand and walked off in the direction of the Accademia.

When Brunetti reached the Questura, the guard at the door stopped him, saying, 'Commissario, there's a man upstairs in your office, waiting for you.'

The officer was young and new to the force, so Brunetti used a moderate tone to ask, 'Who is he?' wondering what magistrate or official might have come to talk to him.

The man looked down to inspect his boots and mumbled something.

'Excuse me, Coltro, I didn't hear that.'

Still attentive to his boots, the officer said, 'He wouldn't say, sir.'

'And you let him into my office?'

'Well, sir, he's a man of a certain age, and he's dressed very well.'

'That's all it takes to get into my office?' Brunetti asked, trying to remember what files had been on his desk, the desk he never bothered to lock.

'He walked right past me, Commissario, and started up the stairs, and I had to get the key from my desk and lock the front door before I went after him, and by the time I got to him, he was going up to the second floor, but he was leaning over the railing and looked awful. He was gasping from the climb. His face was white and covered with sweat.'

Telling himself to speak normally, Brunetti asked, 'What did you do?'

'Rugoletto was coming down the stairs, and we sort of helped him – really, sir, it was more like we carried him – up to your office. I'm afraid we couldn't think of anything else to do.'

'Is he still there?'

'I think so, sir. It was only a few minutes ago. Rugoletto went to his office to get him a glass of water, and I had to come back to open the entrance door. That's when you came in.'

'I see,' Brunetti said and turned away. He walked to the steps and started up. At the first landing, he turned to Coltro and waved him back into his room. He continued up the stairs, walking quickly but taking the steps one at a time.

When he was halfway up, he heard loud footsteps pounding up the stairs behind him and turned to see Rugoletto leaping up two at a time. He was carrying a bottle of mineral water and a glass. When he reached Brunetti, the young officer stopped and held the glass up in a semi-salute. 'Coltro told you, sir?' he asked.

'Yes,' Brunetti answered.

'Do you want me to come along, sir?'

'No, I'll go and talk to him.' Brunetti took the bottle and glass from the other man, thanked him, and continued up the stairs. At the door to his office he stuck his head inside to see who it was.

Gonzalo Rodríguez de Tejeda sat in one of the two chairs in front of Brunetti's desk, elbow propped on one of the arms, head supported by his hand, the other hand hanging limp in his lap. A crumpled white handkerchief lay on the floor at his feet.

'Ah, Gonzalo,' Brunetti said in his most casual voice. 'How nice of you to come and visit. It's been too long since we've had a chance to talk.' He set the bottle and glass on the desk and moved papers around for a moment, then turned to the seated Gonzalo and patted him a few times on the shoulder. 'Let me get another glass,' he said in his best housekeeping voice and went over to his bookcase, where he moved things around slowly until he found a glass and came back with it.

When Brunetti returned, Gonzalo was sitting upright, hands on the arms of his chair; there was no sign of the handkerchief.

'May I give you a glass of water?' Brunetti asked.

'Yes, please, Guido,' the older man said.

Brunetti filled a glass and handed it to him, then poured another one and set it on the desk in front of the second chair. He bent over Gonzalo, resting his hand on his shoulder for a moment, then shifted the second chair to face the older man's, and sat. 'I'm sorry I wasn't here when you arrived, Gonzalo. I was having a coffee with an old friend I haven't seen in years.' He closed his eyes at the memory. 'He was at university with me and Paola.'

Sitting so much closer to Gonzalo now, and without any obstruction, he noticed how much his friend had aged in the time since their meeting in Campo Santi Apostoli. The smudges under his eyes had turned into ripples of dry skin. His lips had tightened and looked as though they would cave in, had his teeth not been there to offer

150

resistance. His eyes had faded and grown faintly cloudy. But he sat up straight, no matter the effort it took him, had even managed to cross his legs in a decidedly casual manner.

'How long has it been since you saw one another?' Gonzalo asked, managing to make it sound as though he were really interested in casual conversation and catching up on what had happened to each of them since their last meeting. There was a new, exaggerated sibilance in his speech, a sound Brunetti associated with dentures, as he did the white perfection of Gonzalo's smile.

'I can't remember exactly, but more than fifteen years. Paola keeps in touch with him.'

Setting his glass on the desk, Gonzalo said, 'It can be a good thing, to stay in touch with old friends.'

Deciding not to take this as a reproach, Brunetti told himself to display no curiosity about why Gonzalo was there, to behave as though it were the most normal thing in the world for him to drop in to talk about the value of maintaining old friendships.

Seeing that Gonzalo's glass was empty, Brunetti drank the rest of the water in his own and refilled them both. When in doubt, talk about the weather, he knew. 'It's wonderful to have the feeling the warm weather is coming back,' he said. When Gonzalo made no response, Brunetti added, 'And that it stays light an hour later.' Having exhausted his interest in things meteorological, he stopped talking and drank some more water, determined to let Gonzalo speak when he wanted to.

The older man leaned forward and placed his empty glass on the desk with a loud clack, having misjudged the distance. Brunetti started at the sound, but Gonzalo seemed not to have noticed it. He put his hands on the arms of his chair, extended the forefinger of his right hand and began to rub it back and forth across the wood. After a moment, his middle finger joined it, and together they rubbed away at the surface. Brunetti tightened his grip on the arms of his own chair and told himself not to speak.

Time passed. The room was so quiet that Brunetti thought he could hear the faint rubbing sound of Gonzalo's fingers, though he knew that was impossible. Brunetti began to count to four and then to four again, something he had done at the beginning of his career to make the hours of surveillance pass, waiting for someone to leave a building or return to it at night. Doing so had never speeded things up, he recalled, but it had relieved some of the anxiety he felt at the need to endure nothingness.

Gonzalo gave in and broke the silence first. 'I've come to ask you to do me a favour, Guido,' he said in a firm voice. 'It's about Orazio.'

'Yes?' Brunetti asked neutrally.

'It seems he's going around the city asking questions about me.' Brunetti heard the undercurrent of anger in the older man's voice and saw it in the hands now anchored on the arms of his chair.

'What is he asking questions about?' Brunetti asked.

Gonzalo looked at him, making no attempt to hide his surprise. 'If you weren't Paola's husband, I'd get up and leave,' he said roughly. Then, accusingly, "He talked to you, too, didn't he?" The anger took a few steps closer to Brunetti.

'Yes, he did: he asked me when I'd seen you last and how you were.' Brunetti decided that this was how he'd remember the conversation with il Conte, for both of these things had happened.

'Did he speak about a young man?'

With no hesitation, Brunetti answered, 'Yes, he did.'

'Did he ask if you'd seen us together?'

Brunetti let out a puff of air to suggest exasperation, something that occasionally happened when he dealt with the children. 'I saw a young man at the dinner at Lodo's, and I noticed that you spoke to him, but I didn't pay it any special attention. I wasn't introduced to him, and we never spoke.'

Gonzalo closed his eyes for long enough to allow Brunetti to refill both of their glasses. When he opened them, his face had grown calmer. 'You and Paola were both there, I know, but we didn't have time to talk. I'm sorry,' he said.

Brunetti leaned towards him and patted the back of his hand. 'We're talking now, aren't we, Gonzalo?'

Gonzalo pulled his lower lip inside his mouth. When he released it, Brunetti saw the marks his teeth had left. Gonzalo took the handkerchief from the pocket of his jacket and wiped it across his face before replacing it. He looked back at Brunetti and, with no introduction, said, 'We'd had an argument. Before dinner.'

'You and this young man?' Brunetti asked, believing that Gonzalo lacked the energy to continue without being prodded into doing so. Gonzalo nodded.

'What about?' Brunetti asked, knowing it would lead him into a discussion he wanted to avoid.

'Money,' the older man said.

'Ah,' Brunetti sighed.

'I was trying to persuade him to take a job as a researcher. I've been out of the art world for some time, and I haven't stayed in touch with the people in it. I haven't kept an eye on the market, well, not seriously, so I don't know who's up and who's down.' He paused to give Brunetti a chance to show that he was following. While Brunetti considered what to say, the older man's eyes moved across the room, stopped at the government-issue print on the far wall, and quickly veered away.

Brunetti said, 'I see,' and Gonzalo picked up where he had left off.

'I need someone who knows how to work a computer and can find the hammer prices in important auctions and tell me what sold in Hong Kong and at Art Basel and for how much. Unless I can get a sense of what's happening, it would be a mistake even to think of getting involved again.'

Then why, Brunetti wondered, did he want to

154

get involved again? Brunetti had little familiarity with the art business, but he suspected that no price list, however long or detailed, would provide sufficient information from which to launch Gonzalo's re-entry into the art world. His understanding was that this world was much like any other cult: people talked to fellow believers in the language of belief, and dogma changed to follow the market. Both were about faith in winning entrance to Paradise, either final or fiscal.

'You want to go back to working in that world?' Brunetti asked, trying to pump enthusiasm into his voice.

Gonzalo gave one of his old full-power smiles. Even with the new teeth and the old face, it radiated the energy and charm that Brunetti had always seen in it. 'It's the only thing I ever knew much about,' Gonzalo said and then, with the sense of timing that was so much a part of his humour, added, 'except cattle farming, and I don't see much of a future for that in Venice.'

Brunetti laughed, and the tension between them eased. 'Did you go ahead with the plan?' he asked, thinking this a better question to ask Gonzalo than whether he was going to disrupt his life with a rash decision only to give this young man a job.

Gonzalo shook his head. 'He – Attilio – suggested I call around to my friends who still worked in the business and ask what they thought of the idea.' His voice drifted away from this sentence and from whatever would have followed it.

'Did you?'

Gonzalo nodded and said, shortly, 'They told me not to do it.'

'Ah,' was all Brunetti managed to say. Like a dog jumping up to protect the home at the sound of the doorbell, his conversational feet slipped repeatedly on the polished marble floor of his mind, scratching back and forth, finding no purchase. 'Perhaps better,' he risked. 'If your friends told you.' How could he sound interested but not invasive?

As if he sympathized with Brunetti's discomfort, Gonzalo said, 'So I'll remain a retired gentleman, and Attilio will not work for me.'

Brunetti could think of nothing to do but nod and smile, as if in approval.

Then, unsolicited, unasked, Gonzalo said the thing that dragged Brunetti, nails still leaving marks on the polish, to the opening of the door. 'So I decided to find a better way to help him.'

'I beg your pardon?' Brunetti yipped out.

'To adopt him.'

'Is that possible?'

Gonzalo considered this for some time before he answered. 'With the right lawyers, yes.'

'Ah,' Brunetti managed to say again. Then, 'Why are you telling me this, Gonzalo?'

The older man, surprised by the question, answered without thinking, 'Because Orazio loves you and trusts you, so he might listen to you.'

'If I said what?' Brunetti asked, though he knew, he knew.

'That it's too late to stop me,' Gonzalo began, his voice growing stronger with every word, though his face remained that of a tired old man. 'He can stop asking my friends to try to dissuade me and stop trying to find evidence that I've lost my mind or that I've fallen into bad hands.'

Did this mean, Brunetti wondered, that Gonzalo had already adopted Attilio or that his decision would not be changed? He pressed his palms together and held them to his mouth. Releasing them, he asked, 'Can't you tell him yourself?' then added, in an amiable, reasonable tone, 'You've been friends for longer than I've been alive, after all.'

Gonzalo turned suddenly cold eyes on Brunetti. 'Don't try to discourage me, please, Guido.'

'That's not my intention, nor is it my business,' Brunetti said instantly. 'I simply don't want to get involved in this.'

'Well, you are involved in it,' Gonzalo said coolly.

Brunetti had learned early in his life that the best way to defend a weak position was to attack. 'What's that supposed to mean?' he asked, releasing all of the irritation this situation was causing him.

'That you're related to Orazio – by law and by love – and you have a chance to stop him from doing something foolish, something he'll regret.'

Brunetti resisted the temptation to tell this old man that neither he nor his friend Orazio had enough life left to risk soiling and spoiling it with something like this. Paola was forever telling him that every interchange men had was about power and who had more of it, and here was more evidence.

Thoroughly out of patience, he said, 'This is not my business, Gonzalo. I assume you're doing this in order to ensure this man inherits everything from you, rather than providing him with only a part of it.' Gonzalo held up a hand in protest, but Brunetti's feet were on the carpet now, and he had more than enough traction to take himself wherever he wanted to go. 'You could simply start giving him whatever you want. Now. Just take it from wherever you keep it and give it to him, and name him as the heir of whatever portion the law allows you to give him in your will. If anything happens that makes you change your mind about him, then you can change your will. Until then, you simply liquidate any assets you want and give it to him. In cash. No tax. No traces.'

Gonzalo leaned forward then and said in a tight voice, 'And this from the man who said he didn't want to get involved.' Then, almost with disdain, 'But who conveniently has it all worked out already.' He raised his hands and made a brushing gesture with his fingers that removed Brunetti from his life.

'If I tell you what your lawyer would tell you . . .' Brunetti began, pulling himself back from anger. When he saw the flash of uneasiness in Gonzalo's eyes, he added, 'and probably has already told you, I'm not getting involved; I'm merely giving you the advice any lawyer would give you.'

It was obvious from the way Gonzalo stared that he had not expected to hear this from Brunetti. He was surprised at the source, Brunetti was convinced, not at the remarks.

Deciding to spare Gonzalo nothing, he went on. 'Once you adopt him – or anyone – there's no going back, Gonzalo. You can't open the door and offer everything you own to a person, then change your mind and close it in his face.'

Brunetti's anger dissipated as soon as he stopped speaking, and he felt guilty about the way he'd spoken to this old man, slapping him in the face with the law. He was ashamed of his own cowardice in not admitting to Gonzalo that he knew far more than he seemed to know or would admit to knowing. And what did it matter to him, anyway, where Gonzalo's money went, whether he left it to this young man or let it go to his brother and sisters? Or lost it on the slot machines, as so many retired people did every month?

Brunetti looked at Gonzalo's face then and saw him nod, then try to speak. A noise, but no words, emerged. He held up a hand, asking Brunetti to be patient, and cleared his throat a few times. Finally, he said, 'That's all right, Guido. I know your heart.' Brunetti thought he said something else, but he couldn't make it out.

'Excuse me, Gonzalo. I didn't hear.'

The older man looked at him directly. 'It's because you can't understand, Guido,' he said. Then, almost as though he were afraid of having offended him, he placed his veined hand on Brunetti's and said, 'It's because you're surrounded by love, Guido. You swim in it. You have Paola, and Chiara, and Raffi; you even have Orazio and Donatella, who love you, too. You have so much of it,' he began and then broke into a smile, 'that you probably don't even notice it.'

Gonzalo stopped, and Brunetti sat, mute, resisting the impulse to take his hand away or, worse, make a joke. He waited.

'I miss it, Guido. Being loved. I had it in the past, so I know what's gone from my life.' He gave Brunetti's hand a pat and then released it. Brunetti pulled his hand back and put it in his lap with the other.

'I'm thirsty for someone to love,' Gonzalo said. And then he added, 'And I've found him.'

'Are you sure?' Brunetti couldn't stop himself from asking.

Gonzalo looked across at him again and said, 'Don't pity me, Guido. The pity of the people we love is worse than the pity of strangers.'

'I don't pity you, Gonzalo,' Brunetti said, telling the truth. 'I'm merely worried that this is fake.' There. He'd said it, delivered his warning. But he felt no better.

Gonzalo raised his chin and put his hand over his heart, both gestures that spoke of exaggeration. 'But what *I* feel isn't fake, Guido.'

Brunetti sat, unable for a minute to speak. Finally he said, 'I'm sorry, Gonzalo. This is none of my business, and I should keep my mouth shut. It's your right to do whatever will make you happy.'

The lines on Gonzalo's face seemed to have deepened in the last half-hour; his mouth seemed set in sad resignation. 'That's what's wrong, that's what I don't know.'

'What?'

'What will make me happy.'

CHAPTER 15

It flashed through Brunetti's mind that it was a bit late in the game for Gonzalo to be saying this. *Il Gazzettino* had recently printed a story about the trouble many women carers from the East had with their male employers or patients. Many of these old gaffers, some of them in their nineties, made sexual advances to the women – almost all of whom were young – threatening to accuse them of theft or mistreatment if they did not make the concessions the old men demanded. Sexual access to these women would no doubt make them happy, but that hardly turned their happiness into a Holy Grail before which all must bow.

'Do you know what will make *him* happy?' Brunetti risked asking, regretting it as soon as he'd said it. He wanted to stay out of this, regardless of his friendship, or Orazio's friendship, with Gonzalo.

'He says it makes him happy to be with me and learn about art and the art market, who the people in it are, who the artists are.'

Gonzalo must have read Brunetti's face when he heard this, for he quickly added, 'But not only

162

that: he wants to understand why some painters are better than others. In artistic terms, not in terms of sales.'

Or so he says, Brunetti caught himself thinking, then asked himself why he had taken a stand against this man to whom he had never spoken. Padovani himself had at least admitted he was not a neutral witness.

Gonzalo, his gaze fixed on the floor, began to speak again. 'He's so much like the way I was when I was his age. Clever, curious, eager to learn. I want him to be able to . . .' Failing to bring the sentence to an end, he raised his head and looked at Brunetti. He smiled, but there was no happiness in it; quite the contrary. 'To be able to love . . .' he began before Brunetti saw pride slam the door of his mouth.

No, Brunetti realized, Gonzalo didn't want the young man to learn or have an opportunity to study art. He wanted him to feel grateful to him and love him because of that. He had no idea whether to laugh or weep at this old man's near-confession, for that's what it had been. Gonzalo must somewhere be aware of his illusions. Brunetti excluded any other interpretation of events or motivation. The young man was merely another of the bright young things, men and women both, making compromises on their way down the long road towards success. Gonzalo had known many, Brunetti was sure, but now time's wingèd chariot was hurrying near.

'There's something else,' Gonzalo said in a tired voice.

'What is that, Gonzalo?' Brunetti asked in a tone he fought to make sound interested.

Gonzalo took his handkerchief and wiped his mouth again, then put it back in his pocket. 'It's hard to explain.'

Brunetti sat, a statue.

'My things,' Gonzalo said. 'I don't know what to do with them.'

'Which things?' Brunetti asked.

It took Gonzalo a long time to answer: Brunetti thought he might be preparing a list.

Finally the old man said, 'All of them. Everything.'

'I'm afraid I don't understand,' Brunetti said.

Time passed. Gonzalo looked out the window. Finally he turned, looked at Brunetti, and said, 'Think of that Canaletto you have.'

'The one in the kitchen?' Brunetti asked, utterly lost.

Gonzalo nodded and uncrossed his legs. 'You've told me for years that Chiara loves it.'

'Yes, she does,' Brunetti responded. He didn't understand why Chiara loved the painting or why Gonzalo remembered that she did.

'That's just it,' Gonzalo said, his voice suddenly grown eager with the desire to explain. 'She loves it, so you and Paola know what to do with it: you can give it to her.' He looked at Brunetti and, seeing he didn't understand, said, 'It's something you love, and you know it will go to someone who loves it.'

When Brunetti didn't speak, Gonzalo leaned forward in his chair to move closer. 'Guido, I've spent a lifetime collecting beautiful things, and I love them. But now I don't know where any of them will go. They'll be divided up among my brother and sisters, or be sent to auction and sold to strangers who won't feel anything for them.'

There was nothing Brunetti could say.

Gonzalo sat back in his chair and re-crossed his legs. 'You thought I was going to call them my children, didn't you?' he asked lightly in the whimsical voice Brunetti remembered.

'No, I didn't think that,' Brunetti answered, hiding his uncertainty.

'I'm not that far gone yet, Guido,' the old Gonzalo said. Then, calmly, 'They're beautiful, and I'd like them to go to someone who will appreciate the beauty in them.'

'If he doesn't?' Brunetti asked.

Gonzalo gave a one-sided grin and said, 'Then I've been a silly old queen and given it all away.'

'Instead of?' Brunetti inquired.

'Instead of being someone who collected beautiful things and made a good choice about passing them on.'

'Is that better?' Brunetti asked, knowing he shouldn't. He had, he realized, come to the end of his patience. He put his hand on Gonzalo's arm and gave it a brief squeeze. 'I think it might be better if you went home, Gonzalo. This conversation has upset us both.' The older man nodded in

165

agreement and he seemed to soften and sink into the chair.

'Is someone at home, Gonzalo?'

The older man nodded again. 'Maria Grazia. You know her.'

Brunetti recalled the woman, from Umbria, wintry in aspect, dedicated to her *padrone*. 'Of course,' he said. 'Could you give me her number?' He punched it into his phone as Gonzalo recited it. When a woman answered with no more than '*Pronto*,' Brunetti asked if this were the home of Signor Rodríguez de Tejeda, and she said it was and asked who was calling.

Brunetti explained that he was Signor Brunetti, an old friend of Signor Gonzalo, and that he was sending him home in a boat and wanted to be sure that someone was there to meet it. The woman sounded relieved to hear this and asked to speak to *il Signore*. Brunetti passed the phone to Gonzalo.

Even if the old man still looked limp and shattered, his voice was firm and almost bold when he said he'd be home in twenty minutes and hoped she'd gone out to get the papers so he'd have something to read when he got there. The woman's relief, though not her words, was audible even to Brunetti, and then the conversation was over. Gonzalo placed the phone in Brunetti's extended palm but held on to it and lifted his other hand to support Brunetti's from beneath. He pressed on it with both of his by way of thanks.

Brunetti called Rugoletto and asked if he'd mind

coming to his office for a moment, then called Foa and asked if he could do him a favour and take a friend of his to his home in Cannaregio.

'Ah, how convenient, Commissario. I've been hearing a strange thudding in the motor all morning, and I wanted to take it over to the mechanic – who just happens to be in Cannaregio – before lunch to have him take a look at it. Sure, your friend can come along: I can ask him to listen to the noise and tell me what he thinks it might be.'

'He'd be delighted, Foa. And what a happy coincidence that your mechanic is in Cannaregio.'

'Indeed it is, isn't it, Commissario?' With a laugh, the pilot was gone. Brunetti imagined Foa had mechanic friends conveniently located in every *sestiere* of the city, just in case he was asked to give someone a ride home.

When Rugoletto arrived, the young officer came over and took Gonzalo's left arm; Brunetti took the right, and together they went with him out to the hallway and down the stairs. Gonzalo made a number of grunting sounds and pulled in a few sharp gasps, but he made it down the stairs. At the bottom, he freed his arms and thanked them for their help, then said, 'I've never liked stairs; always been afraid of falling.' He straightened up and walked unaided to the door, Brunetti following behind. Outside, Brunetti helped him on to the boat, and then he and Foa helped him down the steps and into the cabin.

'Would you like me to come along with you,

Gonzalo?' Brunetti asked when the older man was seated near the door.

'Of course not, Guido. Your captain here can easily take me home. And María Grazia and Jérôme are probably already at the door – pair of old fools – waiting for the boat.'

'Fine, then,' Brunetti said and leaned down to kiss Gonzalo on both cheeks. 'I'm happy to have seen you again.'

'It was too long,' Gonzalo said, but Brunetti was already on the point of leaving and wasn't sure if Gonzalo meant the time they hadn't seen one another or the time they'd spent talking so he didn't turn to ask.

The twin doors swung closed behind him. He jumped from the boat; Foa revved the motor and swung the boat around towards Rio San Giovanni Laterano. And then, from the cabin, Gonzalo was waving at him. Brunetti waved back with both arms and watched them until the boat turned to the right and disappeared, on its way to the *laguna* and then left towards Cannaregio.

As he went back to his office, Brunetti reminded himself that, had Gonzalo been interested in a woman forty years younger and wanted to marry her, few people would have questioned his desire. The good sense of it, perhaps, but not the desire itself. He was a man, after all, and they were entitled to what they could afford. But because the person he'd chosen was a man, and Gonzalo's desire was to adopt, this would be viewed in a

168

different light, for what could a man in his prime want from a man so much older but his wealth? Regardless of whether this was true or not, Brunetti did not question that it was likely to be common belief. Nor did he question that most would believe it was natural for a woman to sell herself for money, although not for a man.

When Brunetti got to his computer, he called up the laws regarding the adoption of an adult and read through them, then read them again carefully.

If a childless person wanted to keep his or her fortune flowing in a straight, lightly taxed line, he or she had only to convince his or her spouse to agree to adopt the most acceptable person, so long as this person was at least eighteen years younger. The fact that the parents of the person to be adopted were still alive presented no impediment, so long as the natural parents gave their consent. Once adopted, the son or daughter was attached to the new parent or parents like a limpet to a rock and had most of the rights of a legitimate or illegitimate child. The new parent had the legal obligation to maintain the adopted person financially for as long as they were unable – or unwilling – to do it themselves.

Brunetti could not hypothesize the situation which would induce a shoemaker, for example, to adopt an adult nor understand why an adult would want to be adopted by the greengrocer. But to keep the treasure of the Duca of this or the

Contessa of that from being devoured by the less worthy heirs or by the fees of the lawyers hired to fight for their clients' shares, how much wiser to choose the best of the new generation and leave it all to him, or to her. No need, thus, to fight over the tapestries and villas, the bank accounts hidden here and there, and no indecorous revelations about the origin – or, more shocking, the extent – of the wealth. Adopt an adult and everything can remain the same, with few inconvenient demands made by the state. And now, in democratic times, the law applied to all, so anyone could adopt.

People of many other countries, Brunetti knew, could do with their money what they wanted: leave it to orphans and widows, to their mistresses, to their cat; even – if they chose – pile it on a Viking ship, set it ablaze, and shove it out to be carried off by the tide. But he, and all other Italians, had to follow a blueprint and leave an appointed share to their relatives in legally mandated percentages. The remainder was for squandering or for following the laws of love, not those of the state.

Brunetti had, upon his mother's death, inherited €712, half of the savings in her bank account. Thus he had a measure of difficulty in understanding the concern others felt about seeing that their fortunes went to the right person or people. He knew that his wife would some day become an heiress, and his children would eventually be rich. He thought it far more important that both were already concerned with the environment, and Chiara had no goal other than saving the planet. Could one's child have a grander dream?

He looked around, startled to find himself still at his desk. He refused to call Foa to ask if someone had been there to meet Gonzalo. Surely, the pilot would have called if there had been any trouble. He looked at his watch, saw that it was past one, and decided to go and get something to eat. When he arrived at the bar, he saw only tourists there, so he asked Bambola, the Senegalese barman, for a coffee and two *tramezzini*, slid that day's *Gazzettino* across the counter and looked at the front page while he waited for what he had decided he was going to call lunch.

When it arrived, Brunetti thanked Bambola and remained at the counter to page through the newspaper. Known for the shock value of its headlines – often followed by factual accounts that ran counter to their insinuations – the paper today did not disappoint. The murderer who had left the dismembered body of a woman in a forest to the north of Verona had, the newspaper opined, hoped that the local wild boars would dispose of the corpse for him.

'I think that's enough,' Brunetti said under his breath and folded the newspaper closed. He moved down the bar towards the cash register. '*Come va?*' he asked the barman.

The smile of a joyful Cheshire cat revealed teeth

no whiter, though they were perhaps wider. 'Fine, Dottore,' Bambola said. 'My wife and daughter are coming.' He paused for a moment, as if uncertain whether he should say more, then added, 'Dottoressa Griffoni, she wrote some letters for me. And she called a friend of hers in Rome. And then the papers came.' Overwhelmed by his emotions, he braced his arms on the counter and looked down at it. Brunetti thought he saw tears in the man's eyes. 'I haven't seen them for two years,' he said in a voice that jagged in and out of a whisper.

'How old is she now?' Brunetti asked, hoping that banality would help the other man regain his composure. 'When you showed me the photo, she was just a tiny little girl.'

Bambola lifted his head and stared at him. 'You remember the photo?'

'Your daughter was just like mine when she was that age. What was she then, three?' Brunetti asked. At the other man's nod, he continued. 'She stood just the same way, legs all twisted around one another, her hand in her mother's, and just the littlest smile on her face, as if she couldn't decide whether she was happy or afraid.'

Then, suddenly serious, Brunetti said, 'I'm sorry you've lost these years, Bambola.' After a moment's thought, he added, 'But she's still a little girl, and there's nothing more beautiful in the world. And soon she'll be here.' He reached across the counter and put his hand on the other man's shoulder. 'I hope the days pass quickly, and I hope we get to see them all here very soon.'

Keeping his head lowered to see the coins, Bambola slid the three Euro across the counter and put them in the cash register, ringing up the sale. He looked at Brunetti, smiled, and said, 'I'll have a reason to live again.'

'There's no better one,' Brunetti answered and turned towards the door.

How could a man bear that? Brunetti asked himself as he went back to the Questura. Without his family for two years, called by a name some Italian invented because his real one was too difficult to pronounce. All the years Brunetti had known him, Bambola had worn his djellaba, each day radiantly white and freshly washed and ironed. Was this the way he clung to who he was?

He went up to Griffoni's office and found her at a document-covered desk, one hand shifting a messy pile from left to right. She grunted in greeting and reached for another pile of documents.

'You wrote letters for Bambola?'

She nodded but didn't bother to look up.

'And called someone in Rome?'

'I have a friend who works in the Ministry of the Interior,' she said, still shifting papers around.

'To get his family here?'

'No, Guido, to see if I could get him a job as Undersecretary to the Minister,' she shot back. Then, looking up at him, 'Of course to get his

173

family here. You don't expect him to go on living like that, do you?'

'Did he ask you?' Brunetti wanted to know.

'It's none of your business,' she said in a voice that was no longer very friendly. But then she clarified by adding, 'The only thing he's ever asked me, other than how I am that day, is whether I'd like a coffee.'

'When you wrote those letters, you had to use his real name, didn't you?'

Removing the vocal gloves, Griffoni said, 'Yes. Of course. The Ministry would hardly give a residence permit to the wife and daughter of someone called Bambola, would they?'

Ignoring her tone, Brunetti asked, 'What is it? His real name?'

'Bamba Diome.'

'Thank you.'

To admit to curiosity did not come easily to Griffoni, so it took her some time to ask, 'And?'

'And I can start calling him by his right name.'

Griffoni nodded and added, 'His wife's name is Diambal, and his daughter is Pauline.'

'Pauline?'

'Yes. She's five.'

'Good,' Brunetti said, and then, 'Thank you.'

'You're welcome,' Griffoni answered and returned to moving papers around on her desk. Brunetti went back to his office.

CHAPTER 16

About an hour later, Signorina Elettra came into Brunetti's office to say goodbye. He lacked the courage to ask her where she was going and contented himself with nothing more than to wish her '*Buone vacanze.*' She failed even to suggest she'd be in touch during the next three weeks, and he did not presume to ask if she would be reachable by SMS. He thought of going over to the door to shake her hand but did not. Impervious to his awkwardness, she gave a small wave and wished him '*Buon lavoro.*'

As if crime had decided to take advantage of her absence, towards the end of the first week, thieves managed to remove three pieces of jewellery on exhibition in the Palazzo Ducale from under the amiable gaze of one of the video cameras set up to protect the objects. The video from one surveillance camera showed the two thieves idly gazing at the cabinets, keeping close attention on the other people in the room. Then, when they were alone, a camera on the other side of the room showed one of them opening the display case with surprisingly little effort, slipping the three pieces into his pocket, and following his accomplice from the room. They ambled to the main exit and mingled with the other visitors, hands in their pockets – calm, calm, calm – even when the alarms began to sound.

The personnel at the Palazzo shut some of the exits and tried to stop the flood of tourists from leaving the building. This all served no good: the two men and the three objects were gone, subsumed into the crowds of tourists strolling along the Riva degli Schiavoni or pushing their way through the crowds of other tourists on their way to the Rialto, or to the Accademia, or down to Florian's for a coffee.

Vianello and Pucetti took charge of all communication and exchange of information with the staff of the Palazzo. Within hours, they had photos of the missing pieces, photo stills of the two thieves taken from the video cameras trained on all of the display cases, and copies of the provenance and insurance documentation for every object in the show. They worked in the officers' staff room, no one daring to use Signorina Elettra's desk. Her computer sat abandoned, and a rumour circulated that she had extracted the hard disk before she left, although no one could be found to admit to knowing this for a fact. Nor was anyone willing to approach her desk to check, far less to seek a way to insert their hand into the side of her computer to verify the presence or absence of the hard disk; and of course there were those like Brunetti who would not have recognized it had it appeared in a vision and spoken to them. The investigation, handed over entirely to experts from the Art Fraud squad in Rome, continued; it did not advance.

The third week was to bring death, but apparently not crime. Usually, at least in fiction, death comes in the middle of the night, waking people from sleep that is always heavy or troubled or deep. The news of the death of Gonzalo Rodríguez de Tejeda reached Brunetti on his *telefonino* at eleven-fifteen in the morning of the last day of Signorina Elettra's vacation. Like everyone else at the Questura, he had taken to marking dates by how long it was until her return, and so it was in this manner that he would in future recall and refer to it.

It was his father-in-law who relayed the news to Brunetti, having received it from Gonzalo's sister, Elena, who '. . . called me this morning. He was there to visit, and they were on their way to the Thyssen, when he fell forward on to the pavement. Just like that, she said. One second he was walking beside her, saying how much he wanted to see the Goyas again, and the next he was on the pavement, dead.'

'She's the retired doctor, isn't she?' Brunetti asked.

'Yes,' his father-in-law answered. 'By the time she understood what had happened and knelt down to try to do CPR, there was nothing to do. In seconds,' il Conte said, voice trailing off, as if he'd just then realized how short those seconds were, and how close they could be. 'She thinks it was a cerebral haemorrhage.'

'This morning?' Brunetti asked.

'Yes. She called me a half-hour ago.'

'What's going to happen?' Brunetti asked. 'Will they do an autopsy? And the funeral?' He was trying to think of those things one never thought of during an emergency, shock still spinning through the brain, the veins, the heart.

'She didn't say anything,' il Conte said. 'She was still at the hospital.'

'Poor woman,' Brunetti whispered, meaning it.

'She said she'd call me, but I have no idea when that will be.'

'Will you go?' Brunetti asked.

Il Conte made no answer; Brunetti said nothing, determined to wait him out. 'That depends on Elena, I suppose,' he finally answered.

'If she invites you?' Brunetti asked in confusion.

'No, I'm waiting to hear whether she thinks Gonzalo would have wanted me to come.'

Without thinking, Brunetti asked, 'Was it that bad?'

'Was what so bad?' il Conte asked angrily. 'He fell down and died.' Brunetti heard the other man take in a heavy breath, forcing himself to calm down.

'I wasn't clear, Orazio,' Brunetti said. 'I meant your last meeting with him. You told me he left you in the restaurant.'

'Ah,' il Conte said, extending the exhalation for

what seemed a long time. 'I forgot I told you that.' Brunetti listened to the other man breathing for some time, and then il Conte finally said, 'No, it wasn't so bad. We'd had arguments before, far worse ones, but I was afraid of what he might have said to her about me while he was there, that I was spying on him.'

'She called you, didn't she?' Brunetti asked. 'Certainly that means a lot.'

'I hadn't thought of that,' il Conte said, then was silent. He finally continued, a certain tightness gone from his voice. 'She must still think of me as his best friend.'

'Well, you were, weren't you?' Brunetti asked.

Instead of answering him, il Conte said, 'I'll go, then.'

'And Donatella?'

'She'll come. Gonzalo was her friend as much as mine.'

Brunetti and his father-in-law exchanged some further remarks, then Brunetti ended the call by suggesting that il Conte keep his line free to receive any information Gonzalo's sister might want to give him.

After they hung up, Brunetti went to the window and glanced down at the Canale di San Lorenzo: it would be too symmetrical if the tide were going out. He saw a red plastic bag floating on the surface and watched it until he saw that it was going to the left, past the old people's home. The tide was coming in. So much for symmetry.

He called Paola, who was at the university, and told her. 'Ah, the poor man,' was her response, then she asked how her father had taken the news.

'Badly. They'll go to the funeral.'

'Ah,' was all she found to say.

'Will you be back for lunch?' he asked, knowing this was her day to spend an hour in her office, seeing students.

'I'll put a sign on the door.'

'Good. I'll see you at home, then,' Brunetti said and replaced the phone. For no reason he could understand, he was swept with the desire to read the final scenes of *The Trojan Women*. Gonzalo's life had been put a stop to, like a door slammed in his face: the people who loved him had had no time to prepare themselves for loss. Brunetti thought he remembered what was going to happen to those women and hoped that advance warning would make learning their fates easier to bear. Not bothering to tell anyone where he was going, he left his office, left the Questura, left it all and went home.

It took him an hour to finish reading the play, so dense did he find the text. Hecuba, Queen of Troy, is to become a slave of Odysseus, 'that vile lying man', 'a monstrous beast'. Andromache's son is taken from her to be cast to his death from the walls of Troy, and she is led from the scene to be raped and enslaved by Agamemnon. In the third relentless blow of fate, her child's battered corpse is given to his grandmother, Hecuba, who can do nothing but provide burial for him, even though, in her ruin, she has realized that 'the dead care little about burial. It is the vanity of the living.' Then she is taken from the stage, now the slave of Odysseus, a man she knows to be 'as false in hate as in love'. There, below, the Greek ships wait.

He closed the book and set it aside. Paola was always banging on about how vital to our spirits the reading of the classics is because they use beautiful language to tell us important things. Because he was reading the text in translation, he had no idea of how beautiful the original language was: the Italian read easily, with the occasional wondrous phrase, but was that Euripides' or the translator's merit?

He thought for a moment about what the important things might be. War and greed drag in the innocent and kill or maim them. Men go off and play at being heroes; women get raped and widowed and see their children die, or are murdered on a whim and tossed aside. Men ride off to battle and fame; women stay home and wait. We've been reading and listening to that for two and a half millennia, Brunetti thought, and still we run whooping off to war

He got to his feet and went into the kitchen to get himself a glass of wine before lunch.

The news of Zio Gonzalo's death troubled the kids when they learned of it at dinner that evening. Chiara still had the teddy bear he'd given her when

181

she was seven, and Raffi still had his first book in English, *Treasure Island*, which Gonzalo had sent him from London for his eleventh birthday. Both of them were shocked by the terrible suddenness of it: one moment walking, next moment dead. It ran counter to everything life had shown them so far. Life was not meant to be merciless. They hadn't lived long enough to understand what grace it was to die in an instant and not to linger.

When they were alone in the living room, night in full possession of the city, Brunetti sat for a long time after drinking his coffee before he asked Paola, 'Did you speak to your father?'

'They fly to Madrid tomorrow. The funeral's the next day, and they'll come back on Monday afternoon.'

'I wish . . .' Brunetti began and then stopped speaking, not sure what he wanted to say.

'Wish what?' Paola asked.

'That I had listened to Gonzalo the last time I saw him or had the courage to ask if he'd already adopted him.'

'Do you think he could have?'

'He said it was too late for your father to stop him, but I chose to believe that meant he'd made up his mind, and there would be no changing it. But it could just as easily mean he had already done it.'

'Is there any way you can find out?' she asked.

'I suppose I could, once Signorina Elettra's back: have her check the files in the Tribunale and see if he made the request and if it was granted,' he said.

'Will you?'

Brunetti considered this for some time and finally said, 'There's no sense to it, is there?'

Paola raised her eyebrows, so he continued, 'Either he adopted him or he didn't. Either he'll inherit or Gonzalo's brother and sisters will . . .'

'Maybe my father could . . .' Paola said.

'Don't ask him, Paola. Your father wouldn't think it decent to stick his nose into this.' His voice was sharper than he had intended it to be.

Paola was seldom embarrassed to be called out for what she said, but this time she looked away, perhaps to hide her blush, and then nodded a few times. 'You're right, Guido.' After a moment's reflection, she added, 'Besides, if Gonzalo's estate passes to this young man, the whole city will know about it soon enough.' He saw her listening to her own conclusion, after hearing which, she added, 'And after that, the city will talk about it for days.'

Brunetti thought of Gonzalo and what a gentleman he had been and how fine his sense of privacy, and that prompted him to add, 'Poor Gonzalo: he'd hate this.'

Seeing Paola's confusion, he explained. 'Being gossiped about. Just think what they'll make of this,' he said, not believing it necessary to name the friends and well-wishers who had accepted Gonzalo's invitations and dined at his table for years.

'"Foolish old man, ready to do anything to satisfy his lover." "Ageing queen, having to pay for sex."' Brunetti tried to put into his voice the disgust he knew some people would use when speaking of Gonzalo's life, but his heart wasn't in it. He stopped and took a few breaths then went on, more calmly, '"Blessed are the merciful."'

'In a city where gossip is the lymph that travels through the body politic,' Paola said, 'there's not a lot of mercy lying around to be picked up from the streets.'

Brunetti started to get up, and his copy of *The Trojan Women* fell from the sofa to the floor. He bent and picked it up, saying, 'I finished it.' Then, almost sulking, 'Now I don't have anything to read.'

Paola smiled up at him. 'You've got three long shelves in my study, Guido. Surely there's something to read there.'

He nodded. 'I know. It's really that I don't know what I want to read.'

'Go and take a look,' she said, adding, 'Perhaps something light.'

'Light?'

Paola pulled her book down from the arm of the sofa and her glasses down from on top of her head. Peering over the top of them, she smiled and said, '*Sturmtruppen*, for example. I found the copy I had at university a few days ago and had a look. It's still very funny. It's on my desk.'

He remembered the comics from his student days. Hell, why not *Sturmtruppen*?

Two hours later, his face was tired from smiling, even laughing, at this absurdist vision of the military. Ordinary soldiers suffered and died under the command of various incompetents, speaking in their broken German-Italian about putting things in their '*tasken*', suffering under the abuse of the *Sergenten* and the even worse *Uffizialen Superioren*, who added senility to their uselessness. Even the *Eroiken Portaferiten*, the medics, were too busy looting the bodies of the dead and nearly dead to be of any use to the wounded or dying.

He took it to bed and laughed until he turned out the light. It was only then he realized that, in its own light way, *Sturmtruppen* was as strong an anti-war book as was *The Trojan Women*.

CHAPTER 17

The weekend passed quietly, interrupted by two phone calls from Paola's parents in Madrid. The first was to say they had attended the funeral Mass and were invited by Elena to a family dinner to be held in a restaurant that evening for relatives and close friends. It was the Contessa who called, explaining that Paola's father had been overcome by tears during the Mass and had suggested they go back to the hotel to have a rest.

'Rest?' was all Brunetti heard Paola say to her mother, after which she listened to a long explanation, told her mother she loved them both and asked her to call, if she could, when they got home; the time didn't matter.

'Have a rest?' Brunetti asked.

'My father wanted to go back to the hotel and rest after the funeral.'

Brunetti stared at her, uncertain he had heard her clearly. 'Your father?'

'He was very upset,' Paola explained. 'There's a family dinner tonight. They're invited.'

Brunetti said, the first thing that came into his head, 'I think we should go for a walk.'

'Good idea,' Paola said, getting to her feet. 'We can go over to the Zattere and walk in the sun.' They did exactly that, going first to San Basilio, which meant they had to cut through Campo Santa Margherita and then weave their way through the back reaches of Dorsoduro to emerge on to the Canale della Giudecca. The sunlight lashed them; Paola even brought her hand up to shade her eyes and regretted she'd forgotten her sunglasses.

They turned left, the sun behind them, and started down towards the Gesuati, surprised by the number of *gelaterie* that had opened in the last year. Brunetti wondered if ice cream and pizza were now the two most common foods in Italy. In the world? An enormous navy blue yacht was moored just before the pizzeria, surely blocking the view to the other side of the canal for most of the residents of the buildings in front of which it floated.

They looked across the canal to the Giudecca, draped in shadow and looking low and foreboding: Brunetti had no great affection for the place, nor – had he been forced to confess it – for the Giudecchini. Most of the ones he'd known had been foul-mouthed and loud, given to boasting and acts of violence, large and small. It was, however, a wonderful place from which to look across at the city and see – especially near the end of it, up near the Zitelle – its full glory.

He reached over and slipped his arm under Paola's, pulled her close, and shortened his step to match hers. Ahead of them, a woman held, with considerable difficulty, the leash of what looked like a Great Dane that was squirming to break loose. It was only when they drew closer that Brunetti identified it as an Irish Wolfhound.

He tightened his grip on Paola's arm to capture her attention. 'What in God's name is she doing with a dog that size?' he asked.

'Maybe her children ride it,' suggested an ever-practical Paola.

Brunetti laughed, looked off to San Giorgio, battered by the afternoon's light, and thought of what a wondrous life he had.

When il Conte called Brunetti's *telefonino*, it was close to midnight. Brunetti and Paola were still in her study, reading, waiting for the call. He took the receiver and shifted closer to Paola, switching the phone to loudspeaker so they could both listen.

'They made us part of the family,' was the first thing il Conte said. 'In a way, Elena's my long-distance sister. We didn't know the others well, but Elena's always talked about them so much, we felt as if we already knew them.'

He broke off for a moment, and Brunetti could hear him talking to his wife, his voice calm. 'Donatella sends love,' he said and returned to talking about the evening. 'Even Rudy was there. He arrived yesterday. He said that when he read about Gonzalo's death in the papers – no one thought to call him – he went to the airport and took the first flight to Madrid.'

'How is he?' Brunetti asked.

'He's in good health, but Gonzalo's death has upset him terribly. He couldn't stop crying at the funeral.' Il Conte's voice trailed off, then came back to say, 'It's a pity . . .'

'Did you know anyone else there?' Brunetti asked, to change the subject.

'One or two of his friends that I'd met over the years, but Rudy and Elena were the only ones . . . Well, the only ones I really knew.'

Paola waved her hand to get Brunetti's attention and mouthed, 'Tomorrow?'

'What will you do tomorrow?' Brunetti asked.

'Tell Paola,' il Conte said with his usual uncanny ability to read his daughter's mind, 'that her mother said it would be nice to go to the Prado and then have a walk. It's very warm here, really springtime.'

'Good, good,' Brunetti muttered, at a loss for what to say.

Paola had just raised her hand and started moving an invisible fork towards her mouth when her father said, 'I think it would be better if we had dinner together on Tuesday. We'll both be tired when we get there, I think.'

'Paola will call you.'

Brunetti heard the Contessa's voice, and il Conte added, 'Bring the children, if they want to come.'

Brunetti agreed, happy at the possibility that the meal would be spent talking about something other than the trip to Madrid. 'Thanks for calling,' was the only thing he could think of to say to bring the conversation to a close.

He lowered the phone and rested the back of his hand on his knee. 'Well?' he asked, staring at the lights beyond the window.

'I think it's time to go to bed,' Paola said, getting to her feet. She left the room without saying anything further and went down the corridor towards the bedroom. Brunetti followed her from the room, switching off the lights as he went, then walked back to the front of the house to see that the lights were off and the door locked. That done, he joined his wife in their bedroom.

Monday morning brought the return of Signorina Elettra Zorzi to the Questura. There was no panoply, no trumpets sounded from the windows as she stepped from Foa's launch, arms filled with bouquets of flowers that must have been bought from one of the usual florists and not at the Rialto Market. The armed officers failed to raise their pistols and fire off a celebratory round or two when she walked through the front door.

There was, however, general rejoicing to be observed, had one the eye to detect it. Vianello had placed four vases on the windowsill, already filled with water for the flowers. Pucetti had made a mixture of vinegar and distilled water and cleaned the screen of her computer since Signorina Elettra objected to the use of chemical fluids. Vice-Questore Patta had asked Lieutenant Scarpa to stop at Mascari for a gift basket of dried fruit and chocolates, which now stood at the side of her desk.

Brunetti had chosen a less obvious route and stood at his office window at nine to wait for the police launch to pull up at the dock below his window. He suspected that more than a few people had been drawn to the windows of their offices by the triple beep of Foa's horn as they passed under the Ponte dei Greci.

No one threw palm fronds on the ground at her feet, but surely the sight of such a display would have surprised no one.

Thinking it seemly to delay his arrival, Brunetti went back to his desk and glanced through that month's staffing schedule. At best, these lists alerted the uniformed officers to the days and shifts when they were to be on duty: the higher ranks viewed their assignments as suggestions, so often did the vagaries and uncertainties of crime force them to work longer hours, indeed, some-times days on end.

He glanced at his watch and, seeing that it was almost ten, decided he could mosey on down the stairs to say hello to Signorina Elettra, newly returned from no one knew where. He stacked the papers and put them in his out-tray. He was wearing a new white shirt and the dark grey suit, half silk and half wool, he'd had made in Naples: he realized he'd dressed for her return.

There was no line outside her office, nor did the sound of voices filter into the corridor. He rapped twice on the frame of her door and went into the office. Two full vases remained, one on her desk and one on the windowsill: that meant she'd used the others to decorate Vice-Questore Patta's office. She was at her desk, her computer apparently restraining whatever desire it had to purr at her return to work. 'Ah, Commissario,' she said when she looked up at the sound of his steps, 'how very nice to see you again.'

'We missed you,' Brunetti said, only then realizing how true that was.

'I trust that everything proceeded as usual while I was away,' she said with mendacious humility.

'Things have a way of not changing here, Signorina, or so I have observed.'

'A very mirror of the country, one might say,' she replied with a smile, and then asked, 'Was there a great deal of talk and activity during my absence?'

'A great deal of talk, and a great deal of activity. And not much change.'

Her smile blossomed. 'I rest my case, Your Honour,' she said. Then, suddenly more serious, she asked, 'Shall I continue with what I was working on when I left, Signore?'

Obviously, then, no one had told her.

'No, I'm afraid that won't be necessary, Signorina. Signor Rodríguez de Tejeda died while you were on vacation.'

She was surprised and made no attempt to disguise it. 'Oh, I'm sorry, sir. I know he was a friend of yours.' Then, her voice growing softer, she asked, 'Can you talk about it?'

'He was in Spain, with his sister, on their way to a museum; he fell forward with what his post-mortem examination confirmed was a cerebral haemorrhage. He died instantly.' This was the first time since Gonzalo's death that Brunetti had described it at length. He was surprised that it was so difficult to do. He took a deep breath and fingered the petals of a pink tulip.

'And the adoption?' she inquired.

'I've no idea,' Brunetti said. 'It doesn't matter any more.'

She paused the way she did before saying something she thought might not be well received, then said, 'It might matter to his family.'

Brunetti nodded to acknowledge that she was right. 'I meant it doesn't matter whether we know about it or not. The law will step in and decide what happens.'

'Exactly,' she responded, not smiling. 'The law will determine who the heirs are, and that's why I asked about the adoption.'

'It's not our concern, Signorina,' Brunetti said, speaking in what he thought was an amiable voice.

'Perhaps it never was.' He did not want to sound melodramatic, so he did not say that Gonzalo was far beyond being able to care about this any longer.

'Then what shall I do with what I found before I left? Or with whatever might have come in while I was away?'

'I'd like you to leave it alone, if you would, Signorina. Put it all in a file somewhere, and then we can decide about it . . .' he began, incapable of thinking about when this might happen. '. . . later,' he concluded.

Signorina Elettra tilted her head to one side as she considered what he had just said. She glanced at the screen of her computer, which Brunetti noticed was blank. Then she nodded a few times, more to herself than to acknowledge having heard him, and said, 'All right, Commissario. I'll open a file and put everything in it, and then when this is less painful for you, you can decide what to do with it.'

'That seems wise,' Brunetti said and reminded her that they were still waiting for information about the Vice-Questore's downstairs neighbours. He thanked her for her concern, remembered he had not formally welcomed her back, and did so. He added that he was happy to see her looking so rested, then left her office, and went back up to his own.

CHAPTER 18

Brunetti told himself that it would be best to act in accordance with what he had told Signorina Elettra: leave it alone. The press would surely get hold of the story of Gonzalo's death: after all, he had owned a famous gallery in the city for many years and thus could be presented as someone who was 'well-known in artistic circles'. They'd cover his death in the back pages of local news for a day or two, until something more interesting came along or some other notable person died.

A few days passed. *Il Gazzettino* finally discovered Gonzalo's death and surprised Brunetti by publishing a characteristically decorous obituary in which Gonzalo was praised as having been a benefactor of the city as well as a successful art dealer. It was noted, as well, that he had chosen, twenty years before, to renounce his Spanish citizenship and had become an Italian. His survivors were listed – no names given – as two sisters, a brother, and an adopted son.

So there it was. Gonzalo had gone ahead and done it before it was too late. He had found a

195

lawyer who would organize it for him, or else Lodo Costantini had agreed to do it and had kept his mouth closed.

After dinner that same night, Brunetti told Paola about the obituary and how he now felt that the city – at least the voice of the city – had done Gonzalo justice.

'And the adoption?' Paola asked.

'It's not my business what happens to Gonzalo's money,' he said brusquely. 'If that's what he wanted to do with it, then it was his decision, and that's that.' Brunetti thought back over his friend's life and said, 'He gave people the chance to live with beautiful objects. I know it's old-fashioned to think this, but I believe it enriches the lives of people who do.'

'I agree,' she said and added what Brunetti heard as an epitaph of his dead friend. 'Besides, he was funny and generous and never said a bad word about people, even those who had cheated him. He was honest and kind and kept his word.' Then she rolled it up into one ball and said, 'He was a gentleman.'

A week later, Brunetti had a call at home. When the caller identified himself as 'Rudy', Brunetti was caught unprepared and started to run names through his memory, hunting for a 'Rudy'.

'Rudy Adler, Gonzalo's friend,' the caller added, and everything slipped into place.

'Of course. Rudy. I'm sorry, but I wasn't expecting

to hear from you.' This, Brunetti realized, was the simple truth. 'Orazio said he saw you last week,' he added, leaving it to the other man to decide whether he wanted to talk about the funeral.

'Yes. It was good to see him again, after all these years. I'm sorry you and Paola couldn't come, but Orazio explained.' Silence lay between them until Rudy picked up the conversation and said, 'It's probably good you didn't come.'

'Why?'

'His family is very religious, so there was a lot of that sort of thing.'

'Orazio didn't mention it.'

'That was kind of him,' Rudy said, then permitted himself to add, 'It was more than a little grotesque.' He waited a second and added, 'Gonzalo would have hated it.'

'I'm sorry to hear that,' Brunetti said. Then, remembering conversations he and Gonzalo had had, he said, 'I never knew anyone more allergic to the Church.'

'Aren't you forgetting your wife?' Rudy asked with a laugh. 'I remember one dinner at our place when you got up and left the table while she and Gonzalo ganged up on a Jesuit.'

Brunetti recalled the dinner and was still glad he had chosen to leave and walk home alone. 'At least, if I remember correctly, the priest was giving as good as he got,' he said.

'The Jesuits are meant to be the intellectuals of the Church, aren't they?' Rudy asked. Rudy was,

Brunetti recalled, from Bremen, so he was likely to be a Protestant and thus no doubt possessed some mistaken ideas about the Order of Jesus.

'"Intellectuals"?' Brunetti repeated. 'I think it's more true to say they're the cartographers of the Flat Earth Society.'

Rudy laughed again and then said, in a more sober voice, 'I didn't call to talk about old times, Guido, but to tell you we'll be there tomorrow.'

'Tomorrow?' Brunetti repeated in confusion. 'Whatever for?' He did not inquire as to the use of the plural.

'It's a kind of exploratory mission,' Rudy said, then stopped. 'That is, umm, we'd like to arrange a memorial service for Gonzalo, really a dinner for his closest friends where people who knew him, and loved him, could say a few words to the others, perhaps reminding us all of why we loved him as much as we did. And do.' He paused to give Brunetti the opportunity to say something, but he chose not to, curious to learn who was invited and then to see who came.

'It was Orazio's idea, I think,' Rudy continued. 'Or mine. It doesn't matter: we were talking at the funeral, and one of us said how sad it was that several of his friends in Venice probably didn't come to Madrid because they were too old to make the trip.'

Not only the old were unwilling to go, Brunetti confessed to himself. But all he said was, 'It's a good idea. Whom will you invite?'

Without hesitation, Rudy answered, 'He and Donatella and you and Paola are the Venetians he cared for most. There are two people who worked in the gallery and stayed in touch after it closed; the professor at the University who wrote his catalogues; some of his clients and two antiquarians who became friends. And then some of the people I met with him over the years.' It seemed a short enough list to Brunetti, who had remained with the idea that Gonzalo knew everyone in the city.

'I hope,' Rudy began but stopped. 'I hope I have the most important ones. Gonzalo and I didn't . . . have much contact during the last four years, so my list might be – er – out of date.' Brunetti wondered if he was simply being polite and didn't want to suggest that other people might also have broken with Gonzalo in the last years.

Gonzalo had walked out on a meal with il Conte, Brunetti remembered. Who knows with how many other people he might have done the same? If so, they might still want the chance to speak of him with love, as it had been in old times, before offence had been given or taken.

Brunetti ran his memory over the time he'd spent with Gonzalo recently and could remember no one Gonzalo had mentioned save for a doctor from Cremona who was interested in some Renaissance bronzes that he had for sale. The host of friends Rudy recalled seemed to have vanished in the last years. Brunetti didn't know if the newcomer, Attilio, was on the list, nor did he want to ask.

'I'm sorry, Rudy, but I can't think of anyone you wouldn't know already.' As he said it, Brunetti realized that he was himself among those who had seen less and less of the ageing man, as if each year that was added to Gonzalo's life subtracted from the interest younger people could possibly take in him.

In an entirely different voice, Rudy said, sounding very pleased to be able to say it, 'At least you'll finally get to meet Gonzalo's best friend.'

Without hesitation, Brunetti said, 'I thought that was Orazio.'

'That's his male friend, his buddy. Berta is his best friend, ever. They've known each other since he was in Chile. That's who's coming with me.'

Brunetti didn't think it correct to quibble by pointing out that Gonzalo had met Orazio before he went to Chile and, instead, asked, 'Berta?'

'Alberta. Alberta Dodson.'

'It doesn't sound like a very Chilean name to me,' Brunetti observed.

'She married an Englishman and went to live in an enormous castle in Yorkshire. He raises cattle.'

'Well,' Brunetti interrupted, 'that certainly sounds Chilean.'

Rudy laughed, probably with relief that this was turning into a normal conversation, and went on, 'No, it's those shaggy ones with the long horns that grow out to the sides. Mean as snakes, apparently; at least that's what Berta always says about them. But beautiful, like something out of a Minoan fresco.'

'A woman living in a castle in Yorkshire hardly sounds like the sort of person who would be Gonzalo's friend, let alone his best friend.'

'Oh, but she is. They met in Santiago when he was first there. Apparently her family took him in, and Berta became his baby sister. He made his first fortune and left at about the same time she did, and he stayed in touch with her. Always.'

'You know her?'

'Of course. She came to see Gonzalo twice when . . . when we were together. It was a constant celebration. Gifts and champagne, puns and jokes in Spanish. Once some English friends came with her for Christmas, and they put on a real Christmas pantomime.'

'At your place?' Brunetti asked. Certainly Gonzalo's place could accommodate a show.

'Yes. She always stayed in a hotel, but she spent all of her time with us. She'd call her husband six times a day and spend the rest of the time gossiping with Gonzalo.' Rudy stopped talking for a moment; Brunetti heard him take a few deep breaths. 'They fought all the time: politics, religion, economics – she'd been a communist and then a socialist, and then I lost track.' He drew a final deep breath and then gave a small laugh. 'In fact, they sounded at times like an old married couple.'

'And the one she lives with?' Brunetti asked, emphasizing the verb.

'He adores her and has for twenty years. The word "Tory" is embroidered on his underwear, but he listens to everything she says about politics, then smiles, and nods.'

'Yes, that sounds like a real marriage,' Brunetti observed. 'Well, one that's survived twenty years.'

All the time he was listening to Rudy, he wondered again why he had never heard even the smallest anecdote about someone named 'Berta'. Orazio had never mentioned her: had he been jealous of the person Rudy considered Gonzalo's best friend?

When he switched his attention back to the conversation, Rudy was just saying, 'We get in on Thursday, a bit after one.'

An idea came to Brunetti. It was a crime, and it was called 'Abuse of Official Powers', but it was a way to make up to Rudy for having been distant from him in recent years. 'Tell me your flight, and I'll meet your plane.'

The crime took place on Thursday at 1.23 in the afternoon at the airport of Marco Polo, where Brunetti was standing outside the just-landed plane from London as its door was pushed open. Beside him stood a uniformed police officer who saluted the first people to emerge from the plane, a tall man and a small woman. The officer leaned forward and took their hand luggage before turning crisply on his heel and starting down the long tunnel that led from the plane to the terminal.

Brunetti stopped just inside the entrance to the terminal and took a closer look at his guests. Rudy had not aged, he observed, though his hair was now a lighter shade of brown. The woman beside him had short grey hair cut in a boyish cap that just managed to cover her ears. Her skin was fine and without age marks, although horizontal lines radiated out from the corners of her eyes. Her nose was arched and thin, her mouth a strong red. Her face seemed to be the result of nature's slow advance and nothing more. She could have been sixty; she could have been older. She wore a brown woollen dress and a beige coat draped over her shoulders and held a dark brown leather handbag in her left hand. Brunetti, deciding to treat their arrival in proper fashion, bent and kissed the air a few millimetres above her extended hand.

'You must be Commissario Brunetti,' she said in very English English that had an element of Mediterranean light in the vowels. 'I'm Berta Dodson.' Her voice grew warm as she added, 'Rudy's told me you were a friend of Gonzalo's.'

'Yes, we were friends for a long time.' Then, as if that needed explanation, he added, 'Orazio Falier is my father-in-law.' He turned to Rudy and shook his hand, then, moved by the grief sneaking out from Rudy's smile, embraced him and held him for a moment.

Stepping back from Rudy, Brunetti turned again to the woman. She smiled and showed teeth as perfect as her skin and of equally natural provenance.

'Ah, how Gonzalo loved Orazio. Far more than he loved his own dreadful brother,' she added, falling into step beside Brunetti.

They walked through the terminal, Brunetti sweeping them past the motionless, still-empty luggage carousels. The same policeman stood at the terminal exit and opened the door for them. When they were outside, he hurried past them and opened the back door on the passenger side of a dark blue car. Once the woman was seated, the officer walked to the other side and held the door for Rudy, then came back and opened the door for Brunetti before taking his place behind the wheel and putting the car in motion.

'And our luggage?' Rudy asked.

'It's being taken to the boat,' Brunetti answered.

The driver pulled out after the number five bus and followed it to the first traffic circle, where the car turned away from the bus and then to the right. It stopped at the beginning of the long wooden landing dock, where a police launch was moored. Seeing them, Foa jumped down from the deck and approached the car. He saluted Brunetti, who had got out, and opened the door for the woman. 'This way, Signora,' he said, turning back towards the boat.

As though Berta were a meringue in the form of a human, the pilot helped her on to the boat and, giving her his arm, helped her down to the cabin. While Brunetti and Rudy were boarding, a second blue car pulled up behind them, and a man in a grey uniform got down from the passenger side. He took two suitcases from the back of the car, walked to the boat and lifted them down to Foa, who stored them on deck to his left.

'Was that one of your famous Auto Blu?' Berta asked when Brunetti was seated opposite her.

'Yes.'

'They're for politicians and ministers, aren't they?'

'For important people,' Brunetti said with a broad smile and a wave in her direction.

'How many of them are there?' she asked, ignoring the flattery.

'It's difficult to get a precise number, Signora,' Brunetti responded, 'but the number that's often given is around ninety thousand.' He let that sink in and then added, 'Unless you believe the other number that is often given: six hundred thousand.'

'I suddenly feel less honoured,' she said, but the last word was drowned out by the bark of the motor as Foa started to reverse from their parking space.

'How did you manage to get it, Guido?' Rudy asked.

'I lied,' Brunetti answered easily. 'I said two people who were coming from the United States to give secret testimony were arriving, but coming from London to guarantee their safety, and it would be better if we could keep them from being seen by too many people.'

'Whom did you ask?'

'Someone I know at the Ministry of the Interior.'

'And he believed you?' Rudy asked in open surprise.

'We Italians are always ready to believe there's a secret reason behind everything.'

Alberta Dodson took a list from her handbag and passed it to Brunetti, saying, 'These are the people from Venice Rudy and I would like to invite to the memorial service.'

Brunetti asked where they planned to have the dinner, hoping it would not be one of the ultra-chic new restaurants catering to wealthy tourists.

'Antico Martini has promised us a room to ourselves,' Rudy said, much to Brunetti's relief.

Brunetti looked out the window on his side and saw that Foa had turned into the Canale di Cannaregio. That meant they'd get the full show and be taken up the Grand Canal to the hotel where they were staying, a newly converted *palazzo* not far from the Rialto Bridge.

Brunetti had no idea of their plans for the rest of the day and tomorrow morning and so had no idea what to ask them or to suggest. 'If there's anything I can do to be of use to either of you, please tell me,' he said. He told them his *telefonino* number and waited while they keyed it into their phones.

Signora Dodson smiled and placed a hand on his wrist. 'Gonzalo always said you were a kind man.' She looked away after saying that, and when she turned back to him, there were tears in her eyes. 'He was a good man.' Then, as though the words had been fighting to escape her lips, she said, 'He saved my life.'

Rudy broke in to say, 'I've heard you say that before, Berta, but you never said what happened.'

She brightened and turned to the other man. 'I suppose I'm exaggerating, Rudy. It wasn't bandits or a lunatic with a knife.' She waved her hand in dismissal and looked out the window and sighed. Leaning closer to the glass, she touched Brunetti's arm with Latin ease. 'What's that *palazzo*?'

Glancing to the left, Brunetti said, 'Ca' d'Oro. It's a museum now.'

'And over there, up ahead?'

'It's the Tribunale,' Brunetti answered. 'The courthouse, I suppose you'd call it in English.'

'It's hard to imagine that anyone would commit a crime in a place so beautiful,' she said with childlike wonder, and Brunetti thought she believed it. He nodded and chose not to comment.

Rudy filled in the silence. 'I have to reserve some more rooms at the hotel for people who are coming from abroad, and then I'm going to the restaurant to see the room and talk about the dinner.'

This was news to Brunetti, who had heard nothing about foreign guests. He contented himself with making an inquisitive noise.

'Family,' Berta said. 'There are two nephews – with their wives – coming from Madrid. And his sister Elena.' And the rest of the family? Brunetti wondered. Were they excluded or did they refuse to come? These were questions he preferred not to ask, so he returned his attention to Signora Dodson.

'And then there's someone I want to meet and talk to this afternoon,' she added.

'If . . .' Brunetti started to say, but she held up her hand.

'And in the evening, English friends of mine are at the Cipriani, and they've invited me for dinner.' Brunetti smiled and nodded, thinking it might be easier to meet British friends for dinner somewhere closer to home. When she saw his expression, she said, 'I've really just come along to keep Rudy company and see he doesn't get too upset by all of this.'

'Oh, don't be a sentimental fool, Berta,' Rudy said but placed his hand on hers for a moment after he said it. She looked up at Brunetti and smiled, and he was aware of how men would have been dazzled by her in former years.

The launch passed under the Rialto Bridge and continued for a while until Foa began to slow the motor, and soon they began to veer a bit to the right and towards the dock of the hotel. 'Oh, this is so beautiful,' Berta said, and this time her voice wavered. When she saw Brunetti looking at her with concern, she explained, 'My husband and I always wanted to come here, but we always delayed it because of work or some other reason. And now I'm here on my own.' She turned away and pressed her nose against the window as they approached the hotel. As the motor slowed and they headed for the dock, she clapped her hands together to banish such thoughts and turned to Brunetti. 'Would you like to join us for a late lunch?' She pushed up her sleeve and saw the time and so added, in descending tones, 'Very late lunch.'

Brunetti smiled and said, 'It's as if I'd accepted, but I do have to get back to work.' When Rudy gave a sceptical humph, Brunetti said, 'They might miss the boat.'

That settled it, and Brunetti waited while two bellhops approached the boat: one jumped down to get the luggage, and the other stood on the dock, waiting to help Berta on to the quay. First, however, she went over to Foa at the wheel and said, in Italian spoken with a heavy Spanish accent, 'Capitano, I want to thank you for your help. It's the most beautiful ride I've ever had.' Then, acting like anything but a proper English lady, she took Foa's hand and pressed it between both of hers, saying, 'There's no way I could ever thank you enough.' She gave his hand one last squeeze and turned to the steps. The bellhop took her arm, long practice allowing him to make it look as though the person needed no help, only assurance, as he all but lifted her up the steps.

Rudy waved the bellhop away and pulled himself up the steps. Brunetti followed. There, smiling and saying nice things to one another, they parted. The two older people went into the hotel, and Brunetti and Foa returned to the Questura.

CHAPTER 19

That evening after dinner, Brunetti decided to ask Paola if he should speak to her father about Signora Dodson, who surely must have been at the funeral in Madrid. Raffi had gone to a friend's house to study with him, while Chiara was in her room, trying to do research about the connection between air pollution and Alzheimer's.

Brunetti and Paola sat facing one another, he in an easy chair, she on the sofa, two coffees on the table in front of them. 'It's strange,' Brunetti said, 'that in all these years, I've never heard Orazio mention her.' He thought back to his conversation with Signora Dodson and realized she had never said she knew Orazio, only that Gonzalo loved him. He wondered if any of Gonzalo's friends, aside from Rudy, knew her.

Paola did not seem to find this particularly strange. 'Lots of us have different spheres of friends, and many of them never meet the other set, sometimes don't even know about them.' She finished her coffee and replaced the cup, then said, 'It's one of the reasons funerals are so interesting: you see people show up you'd never expect to see there. It's as if the dead person had lived in two separate worlds. Or three.'

'But they're both friends from the early part of his life,' Brunetti said, as though this should make things different, unite them somehow.

'They're also friends from different continents, if I might remind you.'

'I know,' Brunetti said in that voice he used when he wasn't persuaded and was merely stalling. His own life and background were entirely different: he and his friends had met as children and lived the major part of their lives in Venice. He'd been stationed in other cities, but they had been brief periods, none more than two years.

Brunetti's close friends – the ones with the rights of family members – were all Venetian, and they all knew one another. The only exception was Griffoni, but she fell into the category of work-related friends.

The thought of Griffoni made him wonder if he'd got it wrong and perhaps it was entirely ordinary for people to have bulkheads between the compartments in which they kept their different friendships: school friends here; work friends there; friends they almost never saw. So, yes, it was possible that Gonzalo had never mentioned his best friend to his best friend.

Paola interrupted his thoughts by asking, 'What's she like?'

'Attractive,' he said almost without thinking. 'She's quick-witted and has a sense of humour.

She must once have been a great beauty. She's got the bones.' He thought about this for a while and said, 'I get the feeling that she doesn't mind that her beauty's . . . not gone, but fading. She's still someone you'd turn to look at again.'

'You liked her?'

'Very much. She embraced Foa's hand and thanked him for the ride up the Grand Canal. On the way back to the Questura, Foa said he'd never had anyone thank him like that: like they really meant it and were grateful to him for what he'd done.'

'She's lived in England so long, perhaps she's acquired their politeness,' Paola said.

Brunetti laughed and tried to provoke her by saying, 'I thought we Italians were the polite ones.'

'Good heavens no,' Paola said, sounding really surprised. 'We're gracious and charming, but the English are polite.'

'I don't understand the difference,' Brunetti said.

'That's because you didn't spend six years in a private girls' school in England, Guido. Believe me, the English are polite.'

Brunetti realized he didn't want to argue the point and so picked up his copy of *Sturmtruppen*, telling himself this one was definitely going to be the last in the series he would read. And knowing he was lying.

They had been sitting like that for some time, he entranced by his comic book and Paola captured by *The Princess Casamassima*, when his *telefonino* rang. It must be Raffi, Brunetti thought, calling to say he was still with his friend. Paternal radar had detected noise from the other end of the house, so Chiara was safe at home.

The number had an English prefix. Well, it was an hour earlier there, so it wasn't really a late-night call.

'Brunetti,' he answered.

'Guido?' a man's voice asked, terror badly disguised.

'Yes. Who is it?'

'It's me. Rudy.' Then, as if Brunetti were going to ask for further identification, 'Rudy Adler.'

'What's wrong, Rudy?' Brunetti asked in a voice stripped of any sign of suspicion or authority.

'It's Berta,' he said and made some soft, choking noises. 'She's dead, Guido.'

Paola had set down her book when she heard Brunetti's question and now, at the sight of his face, she leaned across the table and put her hand on his knee.

'Tell me what happened, Rudy,' Brunetti said in a toneless voice.

'I don't know. I have no idea. They're letting me make one call.'

'Who is?'

'The police.'

'Tell me why.'

'It's absurd,' Rudy said, voice veering higher at the end of the short protest.

'Tell me what happened, Rudy.'

213

'We had connecting suites. We always travelled like that when we went anywhere together. We always left the connecting door unlocked. It was a habit from when Gonzalo and I travelled with her.' He stopped abruptly, then said, 'I'm babbling, aren't I?'

'It doesn't matter, Rudy. Take your time and tell me what happened.'

'That's what's wrong. I don't know.'

Brunetti was familiar with the stunned confusion of people suddenly exposed to the vast reality of death. In many cases, it pummelled them to silence; other times, it squeezed speech from them in a constant stream, as if to cease talking would allow death to sneak back at them.

He remained silent, certain that, sooner or later, Rudy would tell him. The silence expanded, and Brunetti thought of the information he had to get: where was Rudy calling from? Why were the police with him? What had happened to Berta? And why was he being allowed only one call?

Suddenly, Rudy started to speak again. 'I came back from dinner a half-hour ago, stopped at the desk and asked if Signora Dodson was in her room. They told me she was, and I went up and knocked at her door. When she didn't answer, I assumed she had gone to bed, and so I went to my own room and let myself in.' He stopped, like a car with a sudden electrical failure.

A key turned in Rudy's mind, and he began to speak again. 'Berta was on the floor in my room, near the connecting door.' He stopped talking and took a few rasping breaths. 'I thought she'd fainted or collapsed or something, so I went over to her, but as soon as I got closer – I don't know why I thought this – I knew she was dead.' He started to sob, great, racking sounds that came through the phone so loudly that Paola could hear them.

'Rudy,' Brunetti shouted. 'Rudy. Rudy.' The fourth time, Rudy came back and choked out, 'What?'

'Give the phone to one of the policemen.' When Rudy started to ask, 'Wha—' Brunetti said, even louder, 'Give the phone to one of the policemen.'

He heard some fumbling and then a man's voice said, 'It's Tomasini, Commissario.'

'The man with you speaks some Italian, so please speak to me in Veneziano and talk very quickly. Tell me what's going on.'

Tomasini took off like a rocket: 'The desk called us, said there was a dead woman, looked suspicious. We came on a boat.'

'Who?'

'Me, Alvise, and Pucetti. We're on night duty this week. The two men on patrol in San Polo are on the way.'

'What happened to the woman?'

'The crime crew's on the way. So's Rizzardi. I know you prefer him.'

'What does it look like, Tomasini?'

'I'd say someone choked her until she died. But that's just what it looks like to me. Her neck.'

'Take the man downstairs and put him in one of the salons.' Brunetti thought of whom he could have stay with Rudy: Alvise was an idiot; Pucetti was bright and would notice things. 'You stay downstairs with him until I get there, and—'

'You need a boat, Commissario?' Tomasini interrupted to ask.

'No, it's faster if I walk.'

'All right, sir.' A pause and then he asked, 'Should I block access to the rooms?' For the love of God, that meant he hadn't done it already.

Very calmly, Brunetti said, 'Yes. Both rooms. Put Alvise and Pucetti in front of the two doors and tell them that no one – and I mean no one – goes into those rooms until the crime squad gets there.'

'Yes, sir. Anything else?'

'No,' Brunetti said and broke the connection. He turned to Paola. 'You heard?'

'If the crime squad is going, then the poor woman's dead, and if the police are at what I think must be her hotel, then it wasn't an accident.'

He nodded. 'She was found in Rudy's room. At least that's what I think he said.' He stood and dropped the comic on the table, embarrassed to have been reading such a thing when Rudy called.

'I'll go over there now,' he said. 'Poor woman. To come here and have this happen.'

'It's no more terrible that it should happen here than anywhere else, Guido,' Paola said, then immediately asked, 'This will take a long time, won't it?'

'Yes. Go to bed. I'll wake you up when I come

in,' Brunetti said, knowing that, if waking Paola had been the thirteenth labour of Hercules, even the hero could not have done it once she was asleep.

He kissed her goodbye, put on a light overcoat, and let himself out of the apartment.

Because the hotel where Rudy and Signora Dodson had booked rooms was on his side of the Grand Canal, it took Brunetti less than ten minutes to reach it. When he approached the entrance, at the end of a narrow *calle*, he saw two uniformed officers standing outside the main door. They both saluted. 'Any sign of the boys from the lab?' he asked.

'They'd come up the Grand Canal,' one of them said, 'and dock at their *porta d'acqua*. Maybe we'd hear them coming, but we can't see them from here.'

Brunetti nodded and asked, 'Have people gone in or come out?'

'Two couples came in, sir. We went to the desk with them and made sure they were staying in the hotel.'

'Anyone leaving?' Brunetti asked.

'No one that we've seen, sir,' the same man answered. 'Not since we got here. About ten minutes ago.'

'Thank you,' Brunetti said. 'Stay here until I send someone down to tell you . . .' he began but realized he didn't know when their shift ended.

'. . . when you can leave,' he concluded and entered the hotel.

A man in a dark grey suit stood behind the front desk. Brunetti gave his name and showed his warrant card. He'd seen the man at his barber's a number of times and nodded to him. His nametag said he was Walter Rezzante.

'Could you tell me where my men are?' Brunetti asked.

'Room 417, Signore.'

'Thank you,' he answered, not moving from his place in front of the desk. 'And Signor Adler?'

'He's in the club lounge, sir. One of your men is outside the door,' Rezzante said in a voice so low it was sure not to travel beyond Brunetti's hearing.

Brunetti nodded. 'Signor Adler and the lady arrived about two. I'm curious about what they did after they got here.'

'After I checked them in,' Rezzante said, 'Signor Adler went up to his room with the bellhop and then came down and spoke to me about reserving rooms for three people next month. As well as the two rooms he and Signora Dodson . . .' Brunetti watched him run into the wall presented by the need to choose a tense for the verb. '. . . reserved,' he chose to say, avoiding the problem. Then, perhaps from the habit of always speaking for the hotel, he added, 'It wasn't easy, but I found them rooms; the hotel might be new, but it's already become quite well known.'

Brunetti nodded as if this were common knowledge. 'And the lady?' he asked. 'Did she leave the
hotel?'

'I assume so, sir. She asked me for a map, and
when I gave it to her, she asked me for the
shortest way to get to Campo Santa Margherita.
I showed her on the map,' he said and looked at
Brunetti as if to suggest how meaningless a map
is to anyone unfamiliar with the city. 'She spoke
passable Italian, so I told her she could easily ask
people on the street.'

Brunetti nodded.

'Did you see her again?'

'No, sir. We don't have actual keys here, so there's
no need for people to come back to the desk. The
guests are given their key cards when they register.'
He looked at Brunetti, as if asking him to understand. 'People seem to like the greater privacy this
offers. They can come and go as they please.'

'Of course,' Brunetti said, though he preferred
the old system of leaving the key at the desk.

'Could she have had dinner here?'

'That's unlikely, sir. We had a birthday dinner in
the hotel tonight, for forty people, so the restaurant
was closed, even to guests.' Rezzante thought of
something and held up his hand to signal Brunetti
to be patient. He punched some keys on his
computer, then more. The screen blinked a few
times, then he said, 'There's no sign that she used
room service, so if she ate anything, she didn't eat
in the hotel.' Brunetti stopped himself from saying

that Rizzardi would find what she had eaten and wished he could have stopped himself from thinking it.

'Because of the dinner, it was very busy here tonight, sir.' Rezzante's voice grew warmer, almost confiding. 'We're short-staffed too: the night clerk is down with flu, so we're all working twelve-hour shifts.'

'Did you see Mr Adler come in?' Brunetti asked.

'Yes, sir. Shortly before midnight. He used the stairs,' Rezzante added, as if noting unusual behaviour he thought might somehow prove important to the investigation. 'A few minutes later, he called me on the house phone, sounding entirely out of control. He kept saying, "She's dead. She's dead."'

'I thought at first that he might have had too much to drink, but then I remembered how he was when he came in: completely calm and in control of himself. And then I thought maybe he'd had a phone call and been told of someone's death. I asked him that.'

The man's face had grown more and more agitated as he spoke and was now covered with a film of perspiration. Brunetti wondered if he had gone up and seen what had happened but knew this was not the time to ask him. Rezzante needed to talk his way free of the worst of it before Brunetti could ask him about it.

The man sighed deeply. 'He said, no, it was there, in his room. His friend was there, and he thought she was dead. He asked me what he should do, and I told him I'd come up.'

'You didn't think to call 118?' Brunetti asked.

'No, sir,' Rezzante answered. 'Not before I saw what had happened. I didn't want any unnecessary disturbance at the hotel.' When Brunetti nodded, he continued, saying, 'You can imagine how our guests would react to an ambulance coming up the Grand Canal with its siren blaring.'

Brunetti was left with no response. 'And then?' he asked.

'Luckily, there was still someone in the kitchen, cleaning up from the dinner, so I called Franca and asked her to cover the desk for me. Then I went upstairs. 'The door to his room was open. Signor Adler was standing beside it. He had one hand braced against the wall as if he were afraid of falling.' He stopped.

'And then?' Brunetti said softly.

'I went into the room and saw the woman lying on the floor.' Rezzante looked at Brunetti and gave an awkward smile that showed a smoker's teeth. 'I knew she was dead, but the sight of her still shocked me. So I took my *telefonino* and called the police.'

'Did you touch her? Go near her?'

'No, sir.' He sounded almost offended by Brunetti's question and explained in a serious voice, 'I watch a lot of television, sir, and I know you're not supposed to go near to dead people until the police have seen them.' He spoke as if in reproof of a careless Brunetti.

221

'That was very wise of you, Signore,' Brunetti said, making it sound like real praise. The man nodded as at a compliment, and Brunetti asked, 'How long was it before our men got here?'

'It must have been twenty minutes.'

'And did you stay there?'

'Yes, sir. I did. First I called Franca and asked her to stay there. I told her the police would be coming.'

'And what did you do until they got here?'

'I stayed in the room with Mr Adler.'

'What did he do?'

'At one point, sir, he sat down on the floor, sort of slid down the wall before I got to him. I asked if I should call a doctor, but he told me no, that he just had to sit down.'

'Did he say anything else?'

'No, sir. He sat there and I stood by the door until your men arrived.'

'And then?'

'When they arrived, one of them – he was young but he seemed to be in charge – thanked me for calling and asked me to tell him what happened. After I did, he said he'd take care of everything and I could go back to the desk.'

'And then?'

The man seemed confused by the question.

'Then what did you do?' Brunetti repeated.

'I came back down here and told Franca she could go back to the kitchen,' Rezzante said and then remained silent for some time. 'It's always strange when there's a death in a hotel, sir. None of us likes it.' When Brunetti did not comment or ask a question, he added, 'It's because they're often alone when they die, sir. And that shouldn't happen to anyone.'

Brunetti thanked him, asked for the home address and phone number of the dead woman, and when he had it, went over to the staircase.

CHAPTER 20

At the top of the stairs, Brunetti turned to the right, towards the two rooms. He saw the officers: Alvise standing stiff in front of the door at the end of the hallway, Pucetti in front of the one before it. Alvise snapped out a salute, and Pucetti raised his hand towards his forehead, then let it drop.

Brunetti looked at his watch: it was just after 1 a.m. He approached Pucetti. 'Are they here yet?'

'*Sì, Signore,*' Pucetti answered. 'Bocchese is with them.'

'How many?'

'Bocchese and two technicians.'

Brunetti turned to Alvise, not wanting him to be offended. 'Good evening, Alvise,' he said.

Alvise saluted again but said nothing.

Brunetti saw that the door behind Pucetti was ajar and nudged it with his foot. Across the room, Bocchese, white-suited, gloved, booted, stood at the door leading to the other room, his nose only a few centimetres from the handle as he dusted it and the surrounding wood. Without turning, the chief technician said, 'Good evening, Guido.'

Brunetti was distracted from answering by the presence of two other white-suited men standing over something on the floor, their legs partially blocking his sight of it. One of them stepped back a bit, the better to photograph an angle of what lay there, and Brunetti saw the short grey hair he'd noted that afternoon, though this time he saw only the back of her head, for she lay facing away from him.

'Can I come in, Bocchese?' he asked.

'Of course,' the technician answered, still busy with his brush.

Brunetti walked to a place in the room from which he could see the dead woman. Stripped of vitality, stripped of energy, she looked smaller, and he saw her thinness and fragility.

'I had a look,' Bocchese said. He turned towards the woman, as if she deserved the respect of his attention as he spoke about her. 'I'd say she was strangled.'

'By hand or with something else?' Brunetti asked, aware of how strange that sounded. Things were made by hand, built by hand, not meant to be killed by hand.

'Oh,' Bocchese said. 'I don't know. I didn't want to look closely. That's for Rizzardi.' He shook his head, perhaps as a sign of pity for the woman who lay on the floor. 'Her fingernails are blue.'

Brunetti nodded. He'd seen it before.

'Good evening, gentlemen,' a man's voice said from the doorway. Brunetti turned and saw Ettore

225

Rizzardi, the chief *medico legale* of the city and a man he considered a friend. He wore a sober blue suit. A light camel overcoat was draped over one arm. He held a black leather bag.

'Tomasini said you'd be here,' Rizzardi added.

'I knew the victim.'

'I'm sorry,' Rizzardi said, then asked, 'Can you tell me anything?'

'I met her for the first time this afternoon,' Brunetti said. 'She's an old friend of a friend of mine. She was here to plan a memorial service for him. The man at the desk wasn't sure of her movements this evening, only that her friend, whose room this is, came in just before midnight and found her.' He thought of anything else he should add. He didn't mention Bocchese's remark about her fingernails: Rizzardi was the pathologist, after all.

Rizzardi moved towards a chair but stopped and gave a questioning glance to one of the technicians. At his nod, the doctor draped his coat over the back of a chair and walked over to the dead woman.

He went down on one knee and leaned over her body. Bracing one palm on the floor, he leaned farther over her and brought his face closer to her neck. He pushed himself to his feet and moved to the other side of her body, then knelt again. He reached back to his bag, opened it, and pulled out a packet of disposable plastic gloves. After handing another package to Brunetti, he stripped his open and removed the gloves, stuffed the empty package in his bag, and put the gloves on.

Leaning over the woman again, he stuck one finger inside the collar of her dress, to give himself a better view of her neck, then let it fall back into place. He looked up at the technicians. 'You finished with the photos?' he asked.

'Yes, Doctor,' one of them said.

'Guido?' Rizzardi asked, and Brunetti was left with no choice but to kneel down on the other side of the body and help Rizzardi shift her onto her back. He saw the bruising then, straight across her throat. He looked at that, not at her face, and saw that there was no sign of the stronger pressure points caused by fingers, and then he looked away.

Rizzardi got to his feet and pulled off the gloves, dropped them into his bag. Looking down at the woman, he said, 'She's been strangled, probably with some sort of cloth.' He glanced at his watch to make sure of the time so as to enter it on his report.

He turned to Brunetti to ask, 'Was she wearing a scarf when you saw her this afternoon?'

Brunetti remembered seeing her get off the plane, walk ahead of him to the exit, arm in arm with Rudy. Then on the boat, then here at the hotel. 'I don't think so,' he said.

'There might be something under her finger-nails,' Rizzardi said and turned to the technicians. The men nodded without a word.

Rizzardi picked up his bag and coat. 'I'll do it

tomorrow morning, but I don't think there'll be much to find. Only if she managed to scratch his hands or his clothing.'

Brunetti felt no surprise at Rizzardi's use of 'his'. Women didn't often strangle, and when they did, it was not other women, but too often their own children. What a horrible piece of information to have floating in his mind, he realized.

Rizzardi moved towards the door, and Brunetti took the opportunity to follow him. He stopped to ask Bocchese, 'Will you see to having the rooms sealed?'

'The hotel won't like it,' the chief technician answered without bothering to look up from his work.

'That's too bad,' Brunetti said flatly.

Outside the room, Alvise saluted; Pucetti turned to face him but said nothing. 'I'd like you two to stay here until they're finished and then see that the seals are put on the doors. After the technicians leave, no one is to go into either room until the magistrate who's put in charge of this says so.' Pucetti nodded and Alvise saluted: neither spoke.

Rizzardi chose to take the stairs; Brunetti caught up with him. 'Would you like a drink?' the doctor asked. 'They'll still serve us in the bar, I suppose.'

'I have to talk to the man who found her.'

'Ah,' Rizzardi said with something that sounded like a sigh. 'I don't envy you that.'

'He's a friend.'

'Even worse.'

'Yes.'

'Know anything about her?' Rizzardi asked as they turned into the final flight of steps.

'Not really. I met her only today. She came with my friend – the one I have to talk to – to arrange a memorial service for another friend of hers who died recently.' Though Rizzardi was looking forward and could not see him, Brunetti shrugged at the strange symmetry of these two things.

'Friend of yours, as well?'

'Yes. He was walking on the street with his sister, and he fell down dead.'

Rizzardi stopped on the last step and turned to Brunetti. 'My God: things I've seen, I'd wish that for everyone.'

'Me, as well.'

'I hope you get some sleep,' Rizzardi said, then walked to the entrance and left the hotel without saying anything further.

Rezzante was still behind the desk. 'It's the room on the right at the end of the corridor, Commissario,' he said. Holding up the key card, he added, 'We've put him in 203 and left toiletries and fresh pyjamas for him.'

Brunetti took the plastic card, thanked him, and went towards the lounge to talk to Rudy. He told Tomasini he could go home.

Rudy was sitting in an armchair in front of a gas fire, the sort with fake logs and a controlled open-gas flame that were now the only fires allowed in the city. Brunetti, who remembered the stove in his parents' home, had always found these fires disappointing. It was impossible to cook on them, to heat water, or to dispose of papers and packaging.

Rudy turned at the sound of Brunetti's footsteps and spread his palms on the arms of his chair to push himself to his feet. 'Don't get up, Rudy,' Brunetti said, then went over to his chair, patted his shoulder a few times, and sat on the sofa opposite him. He set the plastic card on the table between them and said, 'They've put you in another room: 203.'

Rudy looked at him but paid no attention to the card. Brunetti wondered if he had heard what he had said to him.

'I'm sorry, Rudy, sorry for your loss.'

Rudy tried to smile, but all he succeeded in doing was to make the wrinkles around his mouth and eyes contract. 'She was my best friend, too, Guido.' Though the shock of having found her was gone, mention of her made the tears start to slide from his eyes. He wiped at them with the back of his hands, then took the handkerchief from his breast pocket and blew his nose. He crumpled the handkerchief in his right hand and closed his eyes for a moment. When he opened them, he said, 'Well? What do you need to know, Guido?'

'I'd like you to tell me anything she said to you about what she was going to do today. We all came to the hotel together, and I remember her saying she was meeting someone in the afternoon and would be having dinner with British friends.'

Rudy nodded and said, 'There was a message waiting for her when we checked in. Lady Alison was not feeling well and asked Berta if they could cancel the dinner.' He smiled and said, 'I love the British and their "not feeling well". It could be cholera or it could be a better offer, but they are always not feeling well and beg you to excuse them.'

'And the other appointment?'

'She didn't say anything about it.'

'Do you know who it was?'

'No. She never said, but I knew it was important to her.'

'How do you know that?'

'I sensed it from the way she spoke about it, but she was very cryptic.'

'Tell me,' Brunetti said.

Rudy rested his head against the back of his chair and closed his eyes.

'Tell me, Rudy,' Brunetti repeated.

'She sounded excited but not particularly eager.'

'Tell me what she said, Rudy.'

The tone opened Rudy's eyes; Brunetti's expression opened his mouth. 'She said she wanted to talk to someone who was supposed to love Gonzalo and see if she could find out whether the love was real.'

That was certainly cryptic enough. 'Who?'

'I have no idea. I don't even know if it was a man or a woman. She spoke about a "person".'

'Are you telling me exactly what she said?' Brunetti asked, doing his best to sound calm.

'That's what I remember,' the other man answered, close to exhaustion.

'Did she ever say anything about Campo Santa Margherita?'

'No.'

'Did she know the city well?' Brunetti asked.

'Why do you ask that?'

'I wondered if she knew it well enough to walk there or whether she'd take a taxi.'

Rudy smiled involuntarily at the question. 'Ah, you've got the wrong idea of Berta. All right, her husband is endlessly rich, but she's a Chilean whose father was a member of Allende's Cabinet.'

Brunetti failed to see what relationship her father's politics had with taxis. 'I don't understand.'

'The family was socialist, fervently so, and so was she. Her father disappeared soon after Allende died, and Berta had to go into hiding until she found a way to get out of the country.'

'I still don't understand,' Brunetti said.

'She'd walk to Milano if she couldn't find some form of public transport to take her there,' Rudy said with soft insistence. 'Her husband could easily charter a plane to bring her here,' he began, his face suddenly filled with a boyish wistfulness. 'We came on easyJet.' His voice broke as he said the name, and he gave a nervous giggle.

'I see,' Brunetti said and did not ask why her principles didn't have them staying in the youth hostel. 'Did she say anything else that you remember?'

Rudy sat forward in his chair and crossed his hands primly on his lap. His eyes closed. Brunetti wondered if the day's events had caught up with him and he had fallen asleep. He let some time pass, and then some more. Tiredness, until then kept at bay by action, found the opportunity to approach him. He sat back in the sofa and crossed his legs.

Rudy opened his eyes and looked across at Brunetti. 'Only that she had something to do for Gonzalo,' he said and reached forward to take the key to his new room.

Brunetti could think of nothing else to ask him and so got to his feet and asked Rudy if he'd like him to take him to his room.

Rudy surprised him by saying that he would and held out a hand to Brunetti, who helped him to his feet. They took the elevator to the second floor, and Brunetti walked with the other man down the corridor arm in arm, looking for the room. In front of it, Rudy handed him the key. As if he were a bellhop, Brunetti pushed open the door and went around the room, switching on lights.

A pair of pyjamas in a plastic wrapper lay on the bed, and in the bathroom there was everything a person would need as well as two bottles of mineral water, one natural and one sparkling.

Rudy lingered on the threshold and seemed confused about where he was. He watched Brunetti move about the room. When Brunetti stepped back out of the bathroom after his quick examination, he found Rudy standing near the bed, looking down at the packaged pyjamas.

'I'll go to bed now,' he said. 'Thank you.'

Together they walked to the door, which Rudy had forgotten to close. Brunetti stepped into the corridor and turned to the other man. Rudy put his hand on the side of Brunetti's face and said, 'Gonzalo was right. You're a kind man. Goodnight, Guido.'

Before Brunetti could speak, Rudy quietly closed the door.

CHAPTER 21

Brunetti stopped at the desk to tell Rezzante that his two men would be spending the night outside the sealed rooms and asked that chairs be taken up to them and that they be offered coffee during the night as well as anything they wanted to eat. He took out his wallet and extracted his credit card.

When he offered it to Rezzante, the man whipped his hands behind his back, as though Brunetti were offering him a burning branch. 'No, please, Commissario. You are all our guests. I'll send someone up with the chairs, and we'll take care of your men during the night.'

Brunetti hesitated a moment but decided to accept. He put his card back, saying, 'Thank you and thank the hotel. I believe the technician has called the hospital and asked them to send an ambulance.'

'They'll be discreet, won't they?' Rezzante asked.

'I'll call them when I'm outside and tell them,' Brunetti said. 'I'll also call tomorrow morning to let you know when the rooms can be opened again.'

'Thank you, sir.' Rezzante looked as though he were going to say something else but stopped.

'What is it?' Brunetti asked, stepping closer to the desk.

'It's a terrible thing for us when a person dies here.' Before Brunetti could say anything, Rezzante went on. 'I don't mean here, this time, but always. A hotel – any hotel – isn't the same for days, even longer. It's strange because that's what the person is, a stranger to us, and yet we all feel their death. Maybe it's the absence of any real involvement with the person that lets us feel the mystery of death.' He stopped, shrugged, and added, 'I don't know.'

'We'll try to cause as little confusion as possible,' Brunetti promised.

'I hope you can . . .' Rezzante began but substituted a wave of his hand for the ending of the sentence.

'Thank you,' Brunetti said. He realized that the barber they had in common was irrelevant: he felt sympathy with Rezzante because he could speak of the 'mystery of death'. 'And thanks again for your generosity to my men.'

'It's nothing, Commissario,' Rezzante said, and then, '*Buona notte*,' as if Brunetti were a frequent guest he was sending off for a good night's sleep.

Just outside the door, Brunetti stopped and called the emergency room at the hospital and identified himself, then asked the man who answered to tell the ambulance team that would be sent to bring a woman's body back to the hospital to be as discreet as possible when they were inside the hotel. The man he spoke to assured him that things would be handled correctly.

Brunetti started home, thinking of the things he should have done, and hadn't. He'd made no search of Berta's room for her *telefonino*, nor to see if she had been robbed. There'd be no knowing that until he had spoken to her husband and asked what she had brought with her. He had Berta's landline number but needed to delay the call until he was home and in surroundings that would work against the cost of having to call and announce, not only death, but death by wilful violence.

It was well after two when he let himself into the apartment. The light in the corridor was on. He hung up his coat and went down to the living room. A tray sat on the low table in front of the sofa, on it a bottle of their best whiskey and a glass as well as a metal thermos bottle and a cup and saucer. He sat on the sofa and uncapped the thermos: verbena tea. He poured himself a cup, then poured a generous shot of whiskey into it.

He did not allow himself to taste it yet but pulled out his notebook to find Signora Dodson's number, then dialled the English number. After three of those distinctive double-buzz rings, the phone was answered by a man's voice, inquiring, 'Berta, is that you?' If he had expected the gruff reproach of the English lord or the quaver of a worried old man, Brunetti was to be doubly disappointed. The voice was rich and low, the consonants chiselled, the tone one of enthusiasm at the thought that they might be able to continue the interesting conversation they had not finished the last time they spoke.

'Signor Dodson?' Brunetti asked.

'Yes. May I ask who's calling?'

'This is Commissario Guido Brunetti, from the Venice police.'

Silence filled the space between them. Beneath it, Brunetti could sense the other man considering possibilities, excluding some and not liking the ones that remained. He was suddenly aware that he could hear the man's breathing, deep, heavy, laboured.

'What is it?' he asked.

'I have bad news for you, Signor Dodson: the worst news.'

Again, a long silence. The breathing stopped, then started again, faster, more laboured. Did the Englishman want to remain in free fall, knowing what must come but wanting to delay for as long as possible the news that would change things for ever? Brunetti imagined him, watching the ground speed closer, closer, the only choice to close his eyes or to keep them open and ask.

'Berta?'

'Yes, sir.'

'Tell me.'

'Your wife is dead, Signor Dodson. I'm sorry, sir, but there's no other way to say it.'

'How?'

'This is worse, sir, if that's possible. She was killed.' He couldn't bring himself to tell the man that she had been murdered; it was too vicious a word to use.

The breathing thickened, deep and slow now, rasping at the beginning of each breath. Brunetti waited.

'How?'

'She was killed in her hotel room,' Brunetti said, then, having no other choice, he explained, 'Someone killed her.'

'Ah,' the man said, sounding as if he had just been punched in the back of his head. Brunetti cradled the receiver between his shoulder and his chin and picked up the cup; he held it beneath his nose and inhaled the combined scents, then set it on the saucer to let it cool a bit more.

'How?' her husband asked. Brunetti knew that those left behind needed to know this, even before they asked who it was who had done it.

'She was strangled, sir,' Brunetti said, pushing himself against the back of the sofa and closing his eyes.

'I'm sorry. Tell me again who you are, please.'

'Commissario Guido Brunetti. She was found by her friend, Rudy Adler, and he was allowed to call me. The hotel gave me your number.'

'"Was allowed"?' Dodson asked and then, after a significant silence, said, 'Could you tell me what that means?'

'As I said, sir, he found her body. He went to his room and found her there.' When Dodson remained silent, Brunetti added, 'He's a friend of mine, Rudy. So he called me. "Allowed" was perhaps the wrong word: he asked them if he could call me, and they told him that he could.'

'I see,' Dodson said softly. He remained silent so long that Brunetti leaned forward and took a sip of the tea, and then another.

'Do you have any idea of what happened?' Dodson asked.

'No, sir. Not yet. We've examined the room,' Brunetti said, failing to mention the examination of his wife's body.

'And my wife?' he asked, as though she were still alive.

Brunetti listened to the relentless breathing for what seemed a long time. 'She's been taken to the hospital, sir,' he said, unable to be the one to introduce the word 'body'. Nor did he want to talk about what would be done to her later this morning.

'I see,' Dodson said, and then, 'I can't come.'

'I beg your pardon, sir? Would you say that again, please?'

'I can't come. I'm in bed and can't leave it. Even for this.' Brunetti waited for him to explain. After a long pause, the man said, 'Even for Berta.'

'I didn't know that, sir.'

'No. We don't tell people. It isn't done, you know,' he said, reminding Brunetti that he was English.

Brunetti had no idea what to say in response.

240

'I'm sorry, sir. But I assure you that we will do whatever we can to . . .' he began but let his voice trail away, fully aware of how little they could do that would be of any help to this man. '. . . to make it less horrible for you, sir.'

Brunetti heard a grunt, and then Dodson said, 'Thank you for that, Signor . . . sorry, but I've forgotten your name.'

'Brunetti, sir.' He thought of telling him that he was the son-in-law of Conte Orazio Falier: his wife might have mentioned il Conte to him. But it didn't matter, not in the least.

'Ah, yes. Brunetti. Thank you for your honesty. It's all I have time for now.'

'If there's anything I can do, Signore, that might help you in any way, please tell me. I promise to do what I can.'

'That's very kind of you, Mr Brunetti,' he said, and made a noise that suggested he was about to continue, but then stopped.

Brunetti waited, silent.

'My illness has made me dependent on Berta. Well, on her and the people around me.'

'I see, Mr Dodson,' Brunetti muttered, not seeing anything.

'After her friend Gonzalo died, she went to Madrid for a day, and then she asked me if she could go to Venice to arrange a final party for him.' He sighed deeply but continued. 'He was the other great love of her life, Gonzalo. She told me that when I asked her to marry me.'

241

Brunetti reached for the cup and emptied it, holding the phone away so that the other man wouldn't hear the noise.

'So I told her to go and take care of it. And she did. And now this.'

The sigh became a cough, and when it stopped Dodson said, 'I'm sorry. I was telling you that I can't come.' With no change in tone, he asked, 'What's your first name, Mr Brunetti?'

'Guido.'

'May I leave it to you, Guido, to do this?'

'Yes, sir.'

'Good. I can't do this any more now. Talk.'

'I understand, sir.'

'Call me when you can, please.'

'Yes, sir.'

'Goodnight, then,' he said and was gone.

Brunetti broke the connection and leaned forward to pour himself another cup of tea. He did not add whiskey this time.

CHAPTER 22

Brunetti reached the Questura before nine the next morning, shaky and cranky from having slept too little, and that badly. He went directly to Bocchese's office and found the chief technician at his desk, a few papers in his hands. When the technician saw Brunetti, he said, 'Here's the report. I had them do it when they got back last night because I knew you'd give me no peace until you had it.'

Brunetti smiled in thanks. 'Handbag and *telefonino*?' he asked.

'Handbag, yes; *telefonino*, no,' Bocchese answered. Then, before Brunetti could ask, he continued, 'Which suggests that whatever kind of phone she had was more interesting than a wallet with . . .' he paused to look at the paper . . . 'one hundred and fifteen pounds, three hundred and twenty Euros, and three credit cards.'

'I spoke to her husband last night,' Brunetti said, 'but I forgot to ask if she wore or brought any good jewellery with her.'

'Men usually don't know that sort of thing,' Bocchese said. 'She was wearing her wedding ring and one large solitaire diamond.' He looked at Brunetti and added, 'Worth more than the *telefonino*, I'd guess.'

'No doubt,' Brunetti agreed. 'Did it look like anyone had gone through her things?'

'Her suitcase was unopened and still neatly packed. Her coat was in the closet.' Brunetti was about to speak when Bocchese said, 'But.'

'But?'

'But there are scratches on her side of the connecting door. We took samples from her hands last night, and there were fibres under her fingernails. We took them there, in the room, and put bags on her hands so the nature of the material can be confirmed.'

Brunetti came over and sat in the chair beside Bocchese's desk. The technician said, 'We're finished there, so there's no need to keep the rooms sealed now.'

Brunetti nodded, telling himself that, even though Bocchese needed a lot of deference, he was a reliable colleague.

As Bocchese started to say something, Brunetti said, '*Oddio*,' slapping his hand to his mouth.

'What's wrong?' Bocchese asked with real concern.

'I forgot about Alvise and Pucetti. I put them on duty in front of the doors to the rooms, figured they could keep one another awake all night.' Brunetti stood and said, 'I'll go and see they're sent home.'

As he was leaving the office he heard Bocchese

say, 'How easy, to forget about Alvise,' but chose to ignore the remark.

He went up to the officers' squad room, found Vianello, and explained what had happened: the Inspector laughed at first but then said he'd call the hotel and have the men sent home.

'Come up when you can,' Brunetti said and went to speak to Signorina Elettra. When he entered her office, Signorina Elettra said, by way of greeting, 'He's heard, and he wants to see you.'

Brunetti nodded his thanks and knocked at Vice-Questore Patta's door.

'*Avanti,*' the deep voice called out, and Brunetti entered.

He had expected to find himself confronted with Patta Furioso: the Vice-Questore's response to attention-getting crime was usually anger, as if the criminals had offended him personally. Part of his wrath was always directed at those in the Questura who had failed to apprehend criminals before or while they were committing their crimes.

And so it proved to be. 'What was this woman doing in Venice?' Patta demanded as soon as Brunetti had closed the door. 'Why did she let a stranger into her room?'

'Why a stranger, Vice-Questore?' Brunetti inquired as he crossed the room.

'She certainly didn't come here to let a friend kill her, did she?' Before Brunetti could answer, Patta pointed to a chair and said, 'Sit down, Brunetti. Tell me about it.'

Brunetti did as he was told. 'I went to the hotel last night, just before one. Tomasini took the call, and Pucetti and Alvise were there when I arrived; so were Bocchese and his crew.'

'Why did it take you so long to get there?' Patta asked.

'I was there twelve minutes after I got the call, sir,' he answered, inventing the number.

'And?'

'The woman was staying there with a friend, a German who lives in London. They'd come to the city for a few days.' Thus Brunetti avoided mentioning that Rudy was also a friend of his and that the victim had come as the result of the death of another person she knew. Patta would have fallen upon these details as a beast upon prey and torn into them in an attempt to find nourishment.

'Someone got into her room, or she invited someone into the room, and that person choked her to death, probably with a scarf, either hers or his own.'

'Why are you so sure it was a man?' Patta asked, as if he'd caught Brunetti in a lie.

'It might have been a woman, Vice-Questore. Of course. But the statistics are against it.' He wanted to ask Patta if he had ever worked on a case where a woman had strangled another woman but decided to let statistics do the arguing for him.

'All right,' Patta agreed, but grudgingly, 'a man.' And then, 'Did anyone see her? Or him?'

'The men at the desk in the hotel told me there

was a dinner for forty last night, so there would have been a lot of people moving around, aside from the guests booked into the hotel.' Before Patta could ask, Brunetti explained, 'I didn't have time to study the disposition of the rooms or the restaurant, but it might have been possible for someone to walk up the stairs or get into the elevator.'

'I suppose so,' Patta agreed, then asked, 'Signs of theft?'

'There was no *telefonino*,' Brunetti said. 'She was still wearing a large diamond, and her wallet hadn't been touched.'

'Why would anyone steal a *telefonino*?' Patta asked. 'Everyone has one already.'

Experience, patience, good sense, and the love of survival kept Brunetti from suggesting that perhaps the killer had wanted to have a pair. Instead, he said, 'There might have been a record of calls, or photos, or searches for websites. Any of those is possible, Signore.'

Patta interrupted him, sounding disgruntled. 'I've already had a vice-president of the chain of hotels that owns that one on the phone this morning, asking when this is going to be settled. It's terrible publicity for them.' Brunetti was convinced that the sincerity of Patta's words was in direct correlation to the size of the multinational company that owned the hotel where the murder had been committed.

'I'll keep that in mind, Dottore,' Brunetti said, getting to his feet. 'I've got some things I'd like to ask Signorina Elettra to look into, so if you have no objection, I'll go and speak to her.' Then, with faint, but audible hesitation, he added, 'If that's acceptable to you, Signore,' and left without hearing Patta's response.

He approached Signorina Elettra's desk, saying, 'The Vice-Questore's given me permission to ask you to do a few things for me.' He permitted himself a smile and added, 'He also tells me you can do anything.'

'How very complimentary of him,' she said with unaccustomed warmth.

Surprised, Brunetti failed to prevent himself from saying, 'I think you're the only person here he respects.'

She looked up and smiled modestly. 'I think it's more accurate to say I'm the only person here he fears.'

Oh so young and so untender, Brunetti thought. He had long been enamoured of the idea that Signorina Elettra had discovered where Patta had buried some of the Questura's bodies, but now he began to suspect that Patta might have slipped a few into their graves with the help of his secretary. Much to his astonishment, Brunetti felt betrayed, as though she had no right to be loyal to the Vice-Questore or to preserve his secrets. And why had this not occurred to him before now?

Caught by surprise, he could say only, 'I certainly hope you're right,' before he turned to the things he had to ask her to do. 'I'll try to get the dead woman's *telefonino* number for you this morning. When you have it, please get a record of her calls as well as any sites she might have looked at.'

'Going back how far, Signore?' she asked, pencil in hand.

Gonzalo had died on the last day of her vacation, he remembered, and named a date three weeks earlier. 'If she called anyone here, I'd like to know who it was and how long the calls lasted. In fact, could you go back even further than that for calls made to any Italian numbers?' He thought about how small was his understanding of the cyber-reality in which he lived and said, 'I don't know if you can find out where a *telefonino* actually was when someone called it or used it.' It was a statement, but both of them knew it was a question.

'That can be done, Signore,' she answered mildly, then, 'Anything else, Signore?'

'No, not for the moment,' Brunetti said. 'I'll have a word with Dottoressa Griffoni, and then I'll be back in my office.'

Signorina Elettra nodded, then returned her attention to the papers on her desk.

Upstairs, he found Griffoni at her own small desk in her very small office.

'Yes, Guido?' she looked up and asked as he stopped in front of her door.

'I'd like you to make a phone call for me, Claudia.'

'About the woman who was murdered?'

'Yes.' Brunetti wondered if this would have been easier if they'd just had a coffee together.

'To whom?'

'The husband.' Before she could question this, Brunetti said, 'It's easier to speak to a woman.' She stared but said nothing.

'I spoke to him this morning, about two o'clock our time. And told him what had happened.' She remained silent. 'He was very English,' Brunetti limited himself to saying. 'He told me, though, that he can't come. I think the reason is sickness, though he didn't say that outright.'

'If he's English, he wouldn't,' Griffoni said.

Griffoni moved her knees to the side to allow Brunetti enough room to come into the office and take a seat on the other chair. 'All right,' she said. 'What do you want me to tell him?'

'Ask him, really,' Brunetti said. 'Only two things: the number of his wife's *telefonino* and whether she was carrying anything valuable with her.'

'Can't Signorina Elettra get the number?' she asked.

'I don't know if she used her own name or her husband's, and it might take Signorina Elettra some time to get into the English phone system to look for it.'

'I see.' She extended a hand to Brunetti, who set his notebook on her desk, opened to the page with Dodson's phone number.

Griffoni picked up her phone and waved away Brunetti's when he offered it to her. She put in the numbers and pushed her chair halfway into the doorway to cross her legs.

Brunetti heard the double-buzz and then a male voice saying something he could not understand. 'Good morning, sir,' Griffoni said, speaking English with an accent mild enough not to interfere with understanding. 'This is Commissario Claudia Griffoni. From the Venice police. My colleague Dottor Brunetti has given me your number.'

She listened for a short time and said, 'No, nothing, sir. It's still early, and we're trying to find information that will help us in our work.'

Again, Brunetti heard the low sound of the man's voice.

'Only two things, sir: the number of your wife's *telefonino*, and whether she brought anything of value with her.' She paused as he answered and then said, 'No, that's all, sir.'

This time the man spoke for a longer time. Griffoni leaned towards her desk and slid Brunetti's notebook towards her. She wrote some numbers, set down the pen and looked off towards the windowless wall behind Brunetti's head.

As the man continued to speak, Griffoni closed her eyes and, occasionally, nodded. Finally she said, 'No, sir, I'm not. It's Commissario Brunetti who will be in charge.' He spoke, this time for a shorter period, and then apparently stopped.

'Yes, I'll tell him, sir. And please accept my . . . sympathies for your loss.'

There were some low sounds, and then he

seemed to be gone. Griffoni whispered, 'Goodbye,' and set her phone on the desk.

She opened her eyes and looked at Brunetti. 'He gave me her number,' she said, sliding his notebook back towards him. 'And he said she had no jewellery. Not that she didn't bring it: she never wore any except for the two rings.'

Brunetti could ask this of a woman. 'How did he sound?'

'Like a dying man,' was all Griffoni said. Brunetti asked for no explanation.

CHAPTER 23

The autopsy was done the day after her death, and there were no surprises. Alberta Dodson had been strangled: Rizzardi found haemorrhaging in the strap muscles and on the tissues around the larynx. She had died of suffocation: Brunetti was relieved to read that it had probably been swift.

Some sort of cloth – perhaps a scarf – had been used. Her killer, who had stood behind her, was no taller than she because the bruising on the sides of her throat sloped down towards the back. The scratches on her neck could have been caused by her own nails, but proof would be found only after the lab results were returned.

The rest of the report catalogued good health and the likelihood that she would have lived many more years. Brunetti read such information with a haunting sense of loss, thinking of what the dead might have done with those years.

The waiting began. There was no way to speed up a process that for years had remained unchanged in the face of all technological progress in the examination and assessment of evidence. They waited until the labs got to their samples and did what they had to do in order to find what they were told to look for. Were samples misplaced, did labels fall off and get put back on the wrong bottle? Who knew? Last month, a train had slipped off the rails because the place where two sections of track joined together had for months been supported by a piece of wood. A man was declared innocent of a crime but remained in prison for another three years because no one thought to inform him or his lawyer. So things went.

The day after the autopsy, the manager of the hotel called Brunetti to tell him that their chief of security had downloaded all of the surveillance videos taken on the day of the murder and that he would send them by computer if he would only supply the correct address.

Brunetti, embarrassed that he had not thought to ask about surveillance cameras, thanked the manager and asked if they had had time to look at the videos. The manager explained that there were hours of recordings from four different cameras, and they didn't have the personnel to check them.

Brunetti gave him the address and thanked him again, then immediately called down to Vianello, asking him to assign two reliable men to watch the films. He told the Inspector that Bocchese's men could provide photos of Signora Dodson's body so they'd have an idea of what she was wearing.

'Tell the men looking at the videos that I'm

interested in,' Brunetti started, speaking as a friend, 'anyone she spoke to except the man she checked . . .' He paused and then, speaking as a policeman, continued, 'anyone she spoke to.'

'I'll see who's on duty,' Vianello said. 'Not Alvise or Riverre, I assume,' he added neutrally.

'No, better not,' Brunetti answered, thanked him, and broke the connection.

When Brunetti returned from having a coffee, he found a folder of documents on his desk. He opened it and, without bothering to look at the cover letter, glanced quickly through the first few pages, all of which, he discovered, were written in Spanish. The addresses at the top of each showed that he was looking at email correspondence between Gonzalo and Berta Dodson. He turned quickly back to the cover letter, from Signorina Elettra, which read, 'The phone number was in her own name, and I found these between the two deceased persons you mentioned. Xavi is already translating them. I told him about the writers and what they might have been discussing, so he's put brackets around some of the passages that might be relevant, with translation. The complete translation should be ready tomorrow.' When he turned again to the documents, he saw the pencilled brackets, each followed by an Italian translation. He had ignored them when he'd first glanced at them. Perhaps the documents would allow him to recreate the story or at least give him some idea of what the story had been.

He checked the date of the first mail and saw that, five weeks ago, Berta had written, '*Precisamente porque soy tu mejor amiga puedo decirte la verdad.*' It was almost exactly like the Italian: 'It's precisely because I'm your best friend that I can tell you the truth.'

The same day, Gonzalo shot back, '*Tú no eres una amiga.*' So after all these years, she was no longer his friend.

A few days later, Berta replied, '*Somos los únicos que sabemos que no puedes hacer algo así.*' Here Brunetti was forced to turn to the Italian translation: 'We alone know that you cannot do this.' He wondered whom she had included in that 'we' and what it was that Gonzalo must not do. Was she advising him or forbidding him? He could stare at the phrase as much as he pleased: that made it no more understandable.

Gonzalo replied the same day in Spanish so clear that Brunetti didn't even bother to look at the translation of the first sentence: 'Friends don't give commands.' Then Gonzalo got on his high horse and declared that '*Un amigo nunca haría daño a un amigo*', which the translator told him meant, 'A friend never does anything that will hurt a friend.'

It took a week for Berta to respond to this: the email consisted of only one line, '*Incluso si para pararte los pies he de destruir mi propia reputación.*' After it the no less threatening Italian: 'Even if to stop you I must destroy my reputation.'

The correspondence ended there. It was not difficult to see that they were discussing the adoption. Only something they both considered as important and irrevocable as this was likely to have so incensed them. But what might she have done that would destroy her reputation? Her reputation as what? The daughter of a man killed by Pinochet? The wife of an English nobleman? Unless the voice that had come through the phone line to Brunetti belonged to an imposter. And why her reputation and not her husband's?

Brunetti sat and chased his tail around his desk until someone knocked on the door and Signorina Elettra came in.

She had a folder in her hand. 'Dare I say "*Buenos días*"?' Brunetti asked.

'Not if you pronounce it like that,' she replied with an entirely friendly smile. Then, ignoring their exchange, she came over to his desk and set the papers in front of him. 'These are the complete translations of the mails Xavi thought were related to their disagreement.'

He took the papers and set them beside the others. 'Did you have time to read them?'

'No, Signore. I thought you might be in a hurry,' she answered and left the room.

The idea surprised Brunetti. In a hurry? For what purpose? To solve more quickly the puzzle of Alberta Dodson's death and win a prize? To provide the press with its daily ration of fact and insinuation?

257

It was the appearance of haste that was important in these matters: urgency was felt by very few. The discretion of the hotel had been absolute; her body had been removed before daylight. When the reporters and photographers of the two local newspapers arrived, there was nothing to photograph but the façade of the hotel, the same façade that appeared on the hotel's website.

Brunetti wrote a short statement and sent it to the press by email, saying only that the investigation of the murder of Signora Alberta Dodson had begun and the authorities were questioning anyone who had been in the hotel at the time of the crime. This included Rudy as well as leaving him unmentioned, and it resembled the truth so closely that Brunetti had no compunction about writing it.

Both papers reported that the victim, Chilean by birth, was the wife of an English nobleman and was in the city as a tourist. They also lamented that the streets of Venice were no longer safe after a certain hour, ignoring the fact that Alberta Dodson had been killed inside the hotel.

Not spurred by any sense of urgency, Brunetti returned to the Italian translation of her correspondence with Gonzalo. She had indeed claimed to be his best friend and to know the truth, though that truth was neither named nor described. Gonzalo had replied that it was not the voice of a friend he heard but a desire to hurt him.

The 'we' who knew that he must not do whatever they were discussing remained equally unspecified in the translation. And her remark that he 'must not do this' retained its grammatical force in both languages but still remained as unclear after translation as before.

Gonzalo's response, that friends do not command, seemed entirely justifiable to Brunetti, as did the statement that this was a cause of pain to him: Brunetti had understood the Spanish well enough to know this.

With diminishing concentration, he read through the translation again but still he found no hint as to why her reputation might be damaged. Surely no one would be foolish enough to suspect her of being Gonzalo's lover. Gonzalo was one of the few men Brunetti knew who had never pretended not to be gay. Such openness was common today, but il Conte had told him that Gonzalo had made no secret of it even as a teenager in school, more than half a century ago. Thus he had been spared the years of pretending, of going through the fake marriage, raising – perhaps even siring – the children.

Brunetti spent a long time reading through all of her other mails, all written in English, and then reading through them again. Signora Dodson revealed herself to be kind, generous, patient with her friends, and not judgemental, although occasionally she could not resist the lure of the British sense of irony in commenting on their behaviour.

Relaxing into her native language with Gonzalo, she revealed the same qualities, at least when they were not discussing his plans to adopt. In this case, the flexibility and irony vanished, and she grew rigid in opposition to his idea, not in relation to any specific person but in general, viewing it as 'dishonest', and 'liable to end in disillusion for the person you adopt'.

Brunetti was tantalized by this but not at all certain about what she meant. The best he could come up with was some sort of financial scandal about which Berta knew, although with Gonzalo it would probably be a mess and not a scandal. Thus the adopted son's hopes would be raised at the thought of becoming the heir to a wealthy man, only to inherit debts and ruin, and an apartment owned by the bank. But then he recalled what Padovani had said about what riches were to be found in Gonzalo's home.

Brunetti sat up straight in his chair and folded his hands on top of the print-outs of the emails. He stared across the room and out his window, where he saw a patch of pleasant sky and the arriving green of the vine that grew on the wall on the other side of the canal. He turned his thoughts to his professional ethics and the law, to the impropriety of ever using his position to solicit in any way the divulging of privileged information. The confessional-like confidentiality between a lawyer and his client continued after the death of the client, privacy to be preserved even beyond the grave.

In a nod to his current state of cyber-capability, Brunetti refused the lure of the phone book in his drawer and, instead, turned to his computer to find the website of the *studio legale* of Costantini e Costantini, Gonzalo's lawyers and, more importantly, a legal studio where the junior partner was Brunetti's former classmate in the Faculty of Law at the University of Ca' Foscari.

He gave his rank and name to the woman who answered the phone and asked if he might have a word with Avvocato Giovanni Costantini. Her silence lasted three beats, and then she said she'd ask the Avvocato if he had time. Brunetti pushed his chair back and crossed his legs, then heard a click, and then the voice of Nanni Costantini. 'Ah, Guido. I haven't heard your voice in a long time.'

Brunetti laughed and answered, 'Say it clearly, Nanni: not since the last time I needed a favour.'

'Yes, it could also be described that way,' Nanni conceded in lawyerly fashion. 'What is it you'd like to know? I can't talk long. I've got a client sobbing in an office next door.'

This would be a minor impediment to Nanni, Brunetti knew, and so asked, 'Did a recently deceased client of your father's manage to leave everything to a younger man?'

'Ah,' Nanni whispered, and Brunetti could almost hear the wheels beginning to turn in his head as he considered the various possibilities of disclosure and refusal. 'First thing: he was my client: my father passed him on to me.'

'Are you at liberty to tell me why?' Brunetti asked.

'Now that he's dead, poor man, I believe I am. I suppose I'd tell you anyway, though. It's very simple: my father had been his friend before he became his lawyer, and he didn't want to ruin that by refusing to do what Gonzalo wanted, so I became his lawyer.'

'I'll repeat the question then,' Brunetti said. 'Did your client leave everything to that handsome man from Piemonte?'

'Does that mean you haven't seen him since Gonzalo died?' Nanni asked, sounding amused.

'I saw him only once,' Brunetti said. 'At that dinner.'

'Since Gonzalo's death, he's become very serious in his speech and demeanour with me,' Nanni said, 'as would be only right and proper for a person who has inherited such an estate.' Then, in a more reflective voice, he added, 'If he were an ancient Roman, he'd probably already have put a funeral mask in the atrium of the house.'

Encouraged by Nanni's willingness to pass on information about his client, Brunetti asked, 'Did you try to persuade Gonzalo not to do it?'

Nanni gave a weary sigh. 'I gave up, Guido. To try to argue with him about this was to pass endless billable hours listening to his refusal to listen. I've always believed I should do something like that only when I'm planning a particularly expensive vacation and need the extra money.' After allowing Brunetti to digest that, he added, 'Besides, it's not my job to try to reason with clients.'

'You've grown no less high-minded since the last time I spoke to you, Nanni,' Brunetti observed. 'Did you ever suggest – merely suggest – that he might give some thought to his decision?'

Nanni sighed melodramatically and went on, 'About a month ago, he showed up here and told me what he wanted to do; he asked me to turn it into legalese and write a will. He named Attilio Circetti di Torrebardo, his son, as his universal heir.' Nanni paused to allow Brunetti to comment, but he said nothing, and the lawyer continued. 'Two days later he came in to sign the will. Two of my secretaries witnessed his signatures, and he gave me a copy of the adoption decree and asked me to keep it with his other papers.' After a moment he added, 'I did not ask the name of the lawyer who obtained it for him.'

Suddenly, Nanni broke off, and a voice could be heard at a distance from his end of the line. 'Give me five minutes, and I'll be there,' he said sharply and returned his attention to Brunetti, saying, 'And then, he fell down and died, and il Signor Marchese will inherit the lot.'

'Which is?' Brunetti asked.

'You know I'm not supposed to tell you this, don't you?' Nanni asked.

'Of course I do, Nanni. Didn't we learn our reverence for the law at the same university?' Brunetti asked. 'And I also know you weren't supposed to tell me what you just did, either.'

'All right. The apartment and everything inside

it and a bank account somewhere that you didn't hear me tell you about.'

'Much in it?'

'That's none of my business,' Nanni said curtly.

'Sorry, Nanni,' Brunetti said, meaning it, although he knew enough about bank accounts 'somewhere' to know that they were unlikely to be mentioned in the will but only in some private understanding between lawyer and client.

'Anything else?' Brunetti asked.

'A few hundred thousand Euros in stocks and bonds,' Nanni said with the cavalier dismissal that only the wealthy can give to mention of such sums. 'And a chunk of land somewhere in Chile that Gonzalo inherited from someone he said was the relative of a friend.'

'Was it you who informed il Marchese of this?'

'Yes. It was my responsibility.'

'And how did he take the news?'

'He was, of course, grief-stricken,' Nanni said with an intonation that suggested he had not finished, as, indeed, proved to be the case. 'But grief-stricken in the manner of people in bad films or amateur theatrics, who think it's shown by pouring ashes on your head or tearing at your cheeks. Or wailing.' He paused, and then added, 'As I said, a Roman.'

'I see,' Brunetti said. And did. 'Was anyone else mentioned in the will?'

'His *maggiordomo*, or butler, or whatever you want to call him. Bangladeshi, Jerome, though don't ask me how he got a name like that. And his house-keeper, Maria Grazia. They've both been with him for as long as I can remember. Jérôme sobbed when I told him what Gonzalo left him; she couldn't even talk, she was so moved.' Brunetti noticed that, with these people, Nanni behaved like a lawyer and revealed nothing about their bequests.

'How was it you spoke to them?' Brunetti asked, knowing that the will could not have been probated so quickly.

'Gonzalo had always spoken so warmly of them, I thought I should go and see them.' A chill passed through Nanni's voice when he went on, 'Some people have called me or met me on the street and asked about Gonzalo. Mostly they wanted to know who would get the apartment and the rest of the loot, but they're ashamed to ask outright. It made me feel sorry for Gonzalo, though I never had before: he always seemed to be having so much fun.'

Brunetti listened, recalling funerals he had attended where the conversation centred on specu-lation about the will and who would get what, although this was, of course, done in a very elegant way.

The thought sobered him, and he said, 'How sad: you live your life among people you think are friends, giving them parties, taking them to lunch, having big dinners at your home, never forgetting a birthday. And in the end, all they care about is who inherits your stuff.'

'I have to get back,' Nanni said abruptly. 'Is there anything else?'

'No. And thanks, Nanni.'

'Does it help, what I told you?'

'Not really, I'm afraid,' Brunetti admitted. Then he added, 'If anything, it's merely confirmed my worst suspicions.'

'All part of a lawyer's job,' Nanni said and broke the connection.

CHAPTER 24

Two days after the murder, Rudy was given permission to return to London. After three days, Rizzardi released Alberta Dodson's body, and it was returned to Yorkshire, a cousin of her husband, Roderick Dodson, having sent his plane to bring it back. One of the two officers assigned to view the hours of surveillance films from the hotel came down with flu, joined by his colleague the day after. No one could be found to replace them, so Vianello and Pucetti volunteered to spend a few hours a day looking at the videos. On the first day, they both noticed the advanced ages of the persons who were at the hotel that evening; by the second day, Pucetti said he felt like a custodian in a retirement home rather than a policeman. On the third day, Pucetti called across the room to Vianello and told him to come and look.

When Pucetti moved the video back a few minutes, they both saw a grey-haired woman walk into the bar of the hotel and look around. After having watched so many white-haired people during the last days, neither of them was sure until

Pucetti stopped the video for long enough for them both to consult the photos of her taken in death. The camera gave a long shot down the length of the bar to the woman standing at the far end; she wore a calf-length black dress like the one the dead woman had worn. As if someone had spoken to her, she turned her head to the left, towards one of the three booths.

Her face relaxed and she walked to the booth. She slipped into it, still facing the camera, said something to the person opposite her, then shifted farther into the booth and more than half disappeared.

Occasionally, people came into the bar and walked through the range of the video camera. Four large men entered, then two more. The first were tall and robust and might have been the sons of the other two, who were markedly stooped and bald. The six men scrummed at the bar, their backs to the booth where Signora Dodson was sitting. The two largest put their arms around one another's shoulders and became a broad-backed, two-headed creature as they drank something out of short glasses. They remained in place; two hands appeared from the left and set two more glasses on the bar, then two more, and then two more. As they drank, one of the men almost lost his footing, as if pushed from the side; later, all six of them walked away, passing both the booth and the camera.

After the wall of men had disappeared, two couples

entered. The two men slipped into the booth where the woman had been sitting, and the two women sat opposite them.

'The men blocked them when they left,' Vianello said.

Pucetti checked the screen and wrote down the time displayed: 23:17, then pushed Play and continued looking at the screen in the hope that Signora Dodson would return. Vianello went back to his desk and resumed looking at the video of the front entrance of the hotel.

Two hours later, just as he was getting to the point where he thought he'd begin to scream at the sight of so many walkers, wigs, and false teeth, Vianello had a split-second's sight of a woman with grey hair approaching the bottom of the staircase to the upper floors, only to be instantly blocked from sight by three men who were descending. By the time they were out of the picture, she was gone. The Inspector stopped the video and rewound it to watch again, but once again she was blocked by the bodies of the men, and he could not be certain it was Alberta Dodson. The time at the bottom of the tape was 23:19.

Knowing that Rudy had called the desk around midnight, he continued until that point, hoping to see her again or to see another person with her. When the clock at the bottom of the last tape said 00:11, Vianello clicked stop, explained his uncertainty about what he'd seen, or not seen, in the previous tape, and suggested the younger man take the two videos up to Commissario Brunetti.

Brunetti, spared hours of watching the elderly guests, was stunned by the sight of the living woman. He recognized her instantly, the smile, the cap of short grey hair. Seeing her moving her hand towards her heart, as if to identify that she was the woman the person in the booth was waiting for, completely unnerved him, and he had to look away from the screen.

'Did you know her well, sir?' Pucetti asked.

'I met her the day she died,' was all the explanation Brunetti would permit himself to give.

Brunetti looked back at the screen and saw her slip into the booth and be reduced by half, then disappear fully, when substituted by the two-headed man.

After Pucetti changed videos, Brunetti watched a woman who might have been Alberta Dodson for an instant before she was blocked from sight by the three men coming down the stairs. He watched her again, and again, and even though he wanted to say it was she, he could not. 'That's all there is, sir,' Pucetti said when Brunetti looked up from the screen.

Brunetti looked at the time on the bottom of the screen. 'Eleven nineteen,' he read aloud. 'Less than half an hour later, she was dead.' Then, to Pucetti, 'Have you spoken to the waiter or the bartender?'

'No, sir. We saw these just now, and I brought them up immediately.'

'I want to talk to them,' Brunetti said. There had been more than forty guests at dinner, as well as the normal number of hotel guests, but it was possible the men at the bar would remember the woman. But perhaps not: Paola had once told him that women, after a certain age – especially if their hair was white – were virtually invisible. Well, he'd see.

Had there been a god of discretion, the concierge could have modelled for the statue. Neither short nor tall, neither thin nor stout, he had a straight nose set correctly between grey-green eyes and a smile that implied humour without displaying it. He spoke Italian with a slight accent that suggested he had no native language, only a wide range of lightly accented languages. His professionalism was displayed by the fact that he recognized Brunetti immediately as a police official and moved away from his place behind the reception desk to greet him and walk him a few steps away from where clients were standing.

'How may I help you, Signore?' he asked Brunetti, leaving the rank unnamed but recognized.

The crossed keys on his lapel gleamed, and Brunetti could easily picture him wiping them down each night with a moist suede cloth. 'My name is Brunetti. Commissario. I've come about Signora Dodson.'

It was the business of the concierge, Brunetti knew, to be a party to the needs of his guests, and so he lowered his head and muttered, 'Terrible, terrible,' before looking up at Brunetti and saying, 'Your men were very prompt in finishing their work in the room, sir.'

'I hope they,' Brunetti began, intending to say 'left no traces', but, given the circumstances, that sounded ominous to him, so he finished by saying, 'were careful.'

'Indeed, sir. There was no sign they had been there. Very professional.' The man's mouth moved in something that resembled a smile.

'I'd like to speak to the waiter and bartender who were on duty that night,' Brunetti said.

'Of course, sir. If you'd wait for a moment, I'll check the staffing rosters and give you their names.' He returned behind the counter and called up some information on his computer, allowed a few moments to pass and reached under the counter to pull a sheet of paper from the printer.

When he came back to Brunetti, he said, 'The waiter is on duty now, for another hour, and the bartender will be here at six. He'll be on duty until two.' Seeing Brunetti's surprise, he explained, 'It takes him some time to clean up the bar, and the night manager doesn't clear the till before one-thirty.'

'Long night,' Brunetti said.

'Even longer for Sandro: he lives in Quarto d'Altino.' It surprised Brunetti to hear the man sound sympathetic about his colleague's commute and realized it would surprise him to hear the concierge be sympathetic about anything.

'I'll take you to the waiter,' the concierge said, resisting the temptation to give the deferential half-bow he no doubt gave to all guests. He moved off towards the part of the hotel that faced the Grand Canal. It was a long, narrow room with wooden tables bearing up under enormous bouquets. Hotels like this seemed to have a special fondness for gladioli: Brunetti disliked them, thought them overdressed and too tall.

A white-jacketed waiter about Brunetti's age stood at the bar, waiting for the bartender to set two tall drinks on a small tray. As soon as he set them down, the waiter turned and took them to a young couple sitting at a small table with a view of what must be the most beautiful City Hall in Europe. So intent were they on one another that they didn't notice the waiter's arrival and had to lean back from where they sat with hands joined across the table to make enough room for him to set down the drinks.

When he turned away, the waiter was smiling and didn't bother to remove the smile as he approached the bar. 'We all were like that once,' he said to the concierge as he reached him. 'Thank God happiness is contagious,' he concluded and looked at Brunetti, who smiled at the idea.

'Gino,' the concierge began, 'this is Commissario Brunetti. He'd like to ask you a few questions.' That said, he bowed to Brunetti and nodded to

273

the waiter and headed back towards the front desk.

He'd seen the waiter before, probably passed him on the street for years. He was tall, his remaining hair cut short in a half-tonsure around the back of his head. He had the alert eyes common to waiters, always checking whether someone might want his attention. 'Do you mind if we stay here, sir?' he asked and turned to cast his eyes across the few tables that were occupied.

'Not at all,' Brunetti said. 'You were on duty the night the woman was killed here, is that right?' he asked.

'Yes, I was, Commissario,' he said. 'She sat in one of the booths.'

'It's a strange choice for a woman alone,' Brunetti said. 'They often sit at a table, don't they?'

'That's right, sir. But she wasn't alone.'

'Ah,' Brunetti said. 'I didn't know that. Was her companion a man or a woman?'

'A man, sir,' the waiter answered and turned to glance at the tables where people were sitting. When no one signalled to him, he returned his attention to Brunetti. 'It was a man. Quite a bit younger than she was, I'd say.' He listened to himself say that, shrugged, and added, 'That night, there weren't many young people in the place, so maybe he looked young because everyone else looked seventy.'

'Could you describe him?'

The waiter smiled again. 'I can describe his left cheek, sir. He was looking at the menu, had his

274

head turned down, propped on his left hand, menu flat on the table.' Then, at the sight of Brunetti's disappointment, he added, 'He had brown hair.'

'Do you remember anything else?'

'Not really, sir. It was pretty obvious he didn't want to be noticed, so I didn't bother to look at him when I took the drinks to the table.'

'Did you have an impression of how well they knew one another?'

'No, sir. I didn't hear them talk to one another, and it was the lady who ordered the drinks. I remember that.'

'But did they behave in a friendly manner?' Brunetti asked.

'I can't say, not really, sir. The place was full that night because of the dinner. I was on the run all night, especially after dinner.' His eyes played over the tables again, but still no one raised a hand or tried to catch his attention.

'I understand,' Brunetti said. He decided not to mention having seen the videos: perhaps the staff didn't know they were being filmed. If so, it was better to leave it that way. 'Did they leave together, do you know?'

'Oh, I've no idea, Commissario. There was a table of Englishmen over by the window. They're terrible drinkers, the English. I must have gone to their table six times that night. Maybe more.' Then, remembering Brunetti's question, he said, 'When I came back to the booth, they were gone and new people were sitting there; two young couples.'

'How did those people pay, the man and the woman?' Brunetti asked, hoping it had been a credit card, and the man had paid.

'They left the money on the table. And a tip. The young people pushed it towards me when I came to take their order.'

'Did you see either of them again?'

'No, sir.'

Now came the time for Brunetti to ask the question the waiter might not want to answer. But he was curious and so he began, 'When you learned that this woman had been killed . . .' He paused and saw the waiter sweep his eyes across the people in the room, his expression now like that of a lost child on the beach, searching for someone to help him find his mother.

Brunetti continued. 'Why didn't you contact us?'

A few seconds passed. The waiter lowered his head and studied the tips of his shoes. He looked up and asked, 'There's no law that says I have to, is there?'

'There's no law that says you're obliged to do so, no.'

'No one goes to the police,' the waiter said resignedly, with no evident desire to offend Brunetti. 'It's only trouble.'

'You really believe that?'

'*Sì*, Signore,' the waiter answered. Then, seeing a hand raise to summon him, and making no attempt to disguise his relief, he asked, 'Is that all, Signore?'

'Yes, it is,' Brunetti answered. 'Thank you for what you've told me.'

The waiter nodded and was gone. Brunetti decided to go home.

Later that evening, after dinner, he walked back to the hotel to speak to the bartender, a quick-gestured man who apparently had been informed that the police wanted to question him. He smiled at Brunetti and offered him a drink. Even though Brunetti refused, the bartender asked how he could help.

Yes, he had been on duty the night of the birthday dinner, but he had paid no attention to the people in the booths, only prepared their drinks. When Brunetti questioned him about this, the bartender told him that all he had to do was turn around and look towards the booths to see what he meant. When Brunetti did, he saw that the booths ran in a diagonal away from the bar in order to create a space in which people could stand. Thus the bartender could see into only the first booth. 'If you'd like to see from here, sir . . .' Brunetti smiled and shook his head to show that wasn't necessary.

Brunetti could see from where he stood that it would be impossible to see into the booths, so thanked the man and left. Both of them gone by 23:17. Two minutes later she – perhaps she – started up the stairs of the hotel and went to her death.

On the way home, he stopped in a bar and had a grappa that burned his throat as it went down. He didn't care.

CHAPTER 25

The following morning, as soon as he got to the Questura, Brunetti banished all thought of discretion or correct police procedure and gave in to curiosity. Without bothering to consider the reason for or the possible consequences of his behaviour, he called Nanni Costantini's office, again identified himself, and asked if he might have a minute of the Avvocato's time. This time the secretary transferred the call without asking Brunetti to wait.

Nanni provided the *telefonino* number of il Marchese di Torrebardo – careful to call him that – and said that he was very curious to know why Brunetti wanted to speak with him.

'All in good time, Nanni,' Brunetti replied. 'I don't think I know myself.'

His friend laughed and ended the call.

Using his office phone and not his *telefonino*, Brunetti called the number Nanni had given him and waited while it rang eight times. A man's voice answered, saying, 'Torrebardo.'

'Ah,' Brunetti said. 'This is Commissario Guido Brunetti. I'm calling from the Questura.' When the expected response failed to come, Brunetti went on, 'I've been assigned the investigation into the death of Alberta Dodson,' still not addressing the man by name or title.

The continued lack of response had a special resonance for Brunetti. 'I'm trying to contact anyone who might have known her,' he said with calm amiability, as though his statements were no more than part of an ongoing friendly dialogue.

'What makes you think I knew her?' the voice finally asked.

'The fact that you're the son of her best friend,' Brunetti explained. Then he decided to risk it, thinking that Torrebardo might well have spoken to her after Gonzalo's death: 'And the fact that you're one of the people who spoke to her recently.' He tossed it off, as though he were reading the man's name from a printed list of the calls registered on Signora Dodson's phone.

There was a short silence before the man said, 'I'm sure many people have spoken to her recently.' It was the voice of a cultured person, light and clear, each syllable distinct from the next. Polite but not affable, as though the latter would be reserved for friends, certainly not wasted on police officers. Or officials.

Years of experience and scores – perhaps hundreds – of conversations with people even distantly involved with a crime raised a tumultuous babble in Brunetti's memory. Why did they

279

always begin the same way, with the attempt to deflect the possibility that they were involved – even in the most minimal way – with what had happened? Innocent, guilty, it mattered not at all: most people reacted the same way, like a patient whose doctor asks if they eat a lot of sweets.

'Of course, of course, but we've decided to call everyone on the list to see if they can remember anything that might be apposite to what happened to Signora Dodson,' Brunetti said blandly.

'Apposite?' Torrebardo asked instantly, as though driven by instinct to reprove a servant he caught wearing one of his shirts.

'It means having something to do with something else,' Brunetti answered neutrally, hoping to bait him with his inability to be embarrassed by the other man's sarcasm.

'Ah,' Torrebardo whispered, and to Brunetti it sounded very much like the noise an outboard motor made when it was suddenly switched into reverse. 'Of course. I must not have heard you correctly.'

'It's nothing, sir. Bad line,' Brunetti said affably and decided to strike while his opponent was down. 'I wonder if you'd have time to come and see me, perhaps some time today?'

Brunetti listened to the silence on the line, resisting the impulse to say something to make it disappear. Instead, he sat quietly, receiver turned away so that the other man might not hear his breathing.

'What time would be convenient, Commissario?' He could not have sounded more cooperative.

'After lunch, perhaps,' Brunetti said lightly. 'I've a few people to see this morning. Perhaps at three?'

'Certainly, Commissario. And your name again?'

'Brunetti.'

'Until three, then.'

After he hung up, Brunetti thought of something his mother's father had often said: 'You catch more flies with honey than you do with vinegar.' He'd known a thing or two, his grandfather had, Brunetti thought. Even without knowing Latin, he'd known about *captatio benevolentiae*. He was a fisherman, but he was also the man people in Castello went to see when they received any official communication. Not only could he read them; he could sometimes make sense of them.

Torrebardo understood the importance of the trick, although it had taken him some time to switch registers and use his honeyed voice when speaking to Brunetti. Too much time, Brunetti thought. The arrogance had flared up at the first mention of Signora Dodson but had begun to change at the suggestion that the police knew he had spoken to her. Torrebardo had not confirmed this, but Brunetti had gone ahead as though he had.

As he stared out the window and mused upon il Marchese, whom he now had to consider Gonzalo's son, his thoughts turned to Rullo's son and his own failure to do anything about Patta's problem with his neighbours. Was the boy nothing more than selfish, wilful, and badly behaved, or was something wrong with him that was not going to change as he grew older? For the child's sake and for that of his parents, Brunetti wished it to be the first. Patta's desire for peace at home paled in comparison to the other possibility.

He went down to Signorina Elettra's office and found her at the window, looking at the wisteria on the other side of the canal. It had not been trimmed in living memory, and now it hung down the wall, almost making contact with the water of the canal.

When she saw who it was, she asked, 'Aren't plants supposed to grow upwards?'

'I think so. Phototropism, I think it's called,' Brunetti said. 'They search out the light.'

'Then why is that one growing downward?' she asked, pointing an accusing finger at the plant.

'No idea. Maybe it's simply perverse.' Then, to prod her without having to ask, he added, 'Like the son of the people who live below the Vice-Questore.'

'Excuse me?' she asked, visibly confused.

'The little boy who hit Dottor Patta's wife,' he supplied.

'Ah, of course,' she said, surprised and making no attempt to disguise it. 'I forgot,' she said and blushed. 'I forgot to tell you.' Then, to save face, perhaps, 'I did inform Dottor Patta.'

'What?'

'About Rullo. The boy's father.'

'Tell me.'

'It's a common enough story, Commissario. He's a violent man: his wife has gone to speak to the Carabinieri about him twice during the last two years.' That, Brunetti knew, meant that it had become so bad that she had finally gone to the authorities, though not to the local police. If she was Venetian, she probably didn't want to go to a place where people might know her or her family.

'She'd never filed a formal complaint, but last week he put her in the hospital with a broken cheekbone.' She closed her eyes after saying this.

When she opened them to go on, Brunetti nodded, puzzled that there had been no report, at least none he'd noticed.

'While she was in the hospital, she called Aurelio Fontana,' Signorina Elettra continued, naming a lawyer in Padova whose fame as 'Dottor Payout' had spread through the entire North-East.

'Oh my,' Brunetti said. He knew that to hire a lawyer was to cross the Rubicon of divorce. To hire Fontana was to cross the Mississippi. 'Don't tell me she's going to spend her husband's money to hire Fontana.'

'No. She's the daughter of Barato,' Signorina Elettra explained, naming the owner of one of the largest chains of supermarkets in the Veneto.

Brunetti turned his hands palms up and began to rub his fingers against them.

'What's the matter, sir?' she asked.

'I feel money in the air,' Brunetti answered. 'Falling from the heavens, leaking from the ceiling, seeping out of the walls.' Still holding his hands out and still wiggling his fingers, he turned full circle. 'And all falling into the pockets of Aurelio Fontana.'

Signorina Elettra smiled at this gesture of *lèse-majesté*. So far, she told him, Fontana had secured a writ that banned Rullo from his home, ownership of which was in his wife's name. Rullo had also lost his position as director of one of the Barato supermarkets. Apparently Rullo had underestimated his wife's – as well as his wife's father's – wrath.

Signorina Elettra had called a friend who worked in Fontana's offices and learned that a quiet divorce was already being planned, as discreet as the wedding of a pregnant woman had once been, and Signor Rullo was going to be issued with another writ, this one forbidding him to contact his wife or to come within 250 metres of her, his son, or their home. In return, no charges for assault would be made against him, and the divorce would go ahead unopposed on his part. The amount of his monthly payment to his wife was being discussed.

'And the boy?' Brunetti asked.

'It's anyone's guess,' she answered. 'He might quieten down because his father's not there, or he might get worse because his father's not there.' She paused, then added, 'There's nothing in his school records that suggests he's a problem. In fact, two of the teachers have remarked on what a sweet boy he is.'

Brunetti didn't bother to comment on her access to this information. Entering the files of the Ministry of Education could probably be done with a nail file and a paper clip or their cyber equivalents.

'Thank you for telling me, Signorina,' he said, adding, 'And the files on Signora Dodson and Signor Rodríguez de Tejeda?'

He saw her lips tighten. 'I've written again to try to encourage the people in Chile to send me their information about her, but they say that, because of the political unrest at the time . . .' Brunetti nodded. So that's what it's called now.

Signorina Elettra continued. 'It's the third time they've given that explanation, Commissario.' She disguised her exasperation badly. 'I'll try the Spaniards now. She went there directly from Chile. She worked as a translator for years, but then she more or less dropped out of their system after she married the Englishman.'

Her voice changed at the mere mention of her marriage. 'The story is quite remarkable: she met Signor Dodson about twenty years ago, in Cairo. He was an official in the British Embassy there, and she was a tourist staying at a hotel where he was having dinner. And six weeks later they were married in the Coptic church in Cairo.' She looked up and smiled, as at the end of a happy film. 'In

Cairo. She simply stayed there, then stayed on with him another four months until he retired and they went back to England.'

'Sounds like something you'd read in a novel,' Brunetti said.

'Only bad ones tell stories like that, I fear.'

Brunetti thought it best to let that remark pass uncommented.

'Let me print out the English information,' Signorina Elettra said, 'and I'll put it on your desk. There's a lot of society stuff: photos of her with famous people, and quite a few photos of her with your friend Gonzalo. Handsome man, wasn't he?' she said.

'He'd have been happy to hear you say that, Signorina,' Brunetti said, smiling at the memory of how proud Gonzalo had always been of his appearance.

'Let me know if the Spaniards ever answer,' he said and decided it was time to go home for lunch.

Before three, he was back in his office, reading through the folder on Alberta Dodson that Signorina Elettra had left on his desk.

He read the more complete account with some interest, for she had had a life far more varied and active than his own. Truth to tell, more active than that of most people. She'd left Chile a year after the *coup* that had brought the quietly monstrous Pinochet to power: the report made no attempt to connect these two events. She'd gone to Spain and was very soon a citizen, working as a translator from both French and English into Spanish. The fairy tale began in the late Nineties, when she met an Englishman in Cairo and fell in love. After that, she'd lived, it seemed, happily – not ever after, but until she was murdered in a hotel room in Venice.

She had, as did many wealthy English ladies, done charity work, though hers seemed more genuine than most. She founded, and apparently supported, three hospices in Chile for abused women and children. Until three years before, she went often to Santiago to work at the hospices for weeks at a time. She also went to costume balls, apparently rode to hounds until no one could any more, and was often photographed in the company of persons who had titles, as did her husband.

Her husband had two children by his former wife, who had died at least a decade before he met Alberta. He and Alberta had no children, although she was often photographed with his sons in poses that suggested easy familiarity and affection.

Although married to an English nobleman, Alberta had never become a British citizen, saying once in an interview, when asked why she chose to retain her Spanish citizenship, 'This passport and the person who helped me acquire it saved my life. I could never abandon either one.'

Brunetti was reading these words when there was a knock at his door, and Alvise entered, saluted, and said, 'Il Marchese di Torrebardo to see you, Dottore.' Alvise moved parallel to the open door and held his salute as il Marchese came into the room. Resisting the temptation to follow the Marchese across the room to pull out his chair for him, Alvise substituted this with a click of his heels, after which he did a quick turn to the right and left the room, closing the door silently behind him.

Neither man commented on Alvise's behaviour, Brunetti because he thought it embarrassing, the other man, perhaps, because he thought it only correct.

The younger man started to walk across the room. Brunetti got to his feet and came around the desk. He noted that Torrebardo seemed smaller than he had the other evening. His head came to just above Brunetti's shoulders, and the rest of his body was in proportion to his height. He extended his hand, and Brunetti took it, only to be surprised by the force of Torrebardo's grasp.

'Thank you for coming to see me,' Brunetti said and released the hand without entering into a contest of strength. He retreated around his desk and resumed his seat.

He waved Torrebardo to the seat opposite him and studied his face: dark eyes and hair, fine nose, skin smooth and clear with good health. His was the sort of masculine face often seen in television ads for breakfast cereal, a symmetrical face that inspired trust.

'It's my duty, isn't it?' Torrebardo asked in the same precise voice he had used on the phone.

'If more citizens thought like that, sir, my job would be a great deal easier,' Brunetti said in his most friendly manner, then added, as though the idea came to him that instant, 'Speaking of duty, Signor Marchese, it's mine, as the officer assigned this case, to keep a record of whatever information I obtain, however irrelevant it might be.' He saw, and ignored, the sharpening of Torrebardo's attention. 'So I inform you that I'm obliged to record any conversation I might have about the death of Signora Dubson,' he added, intentionally mispronouncing her name.

Torrebardo nodded but said nothing, so Brunetti reached to the side of his desk and clicked on the microphones placed under the top.

'How is it that you knew her, if I might ask?' Then, as if himself uncomfortable with the idea of speaking for a recording, Brunetti said, pronouncing clearly, 'Alberta Du . . . Dodson.'

Torrebardo pulled at the left leg of his trousers to smooth out a wrinkle. 'She was my father's best friend and had been for ever. He often spoke of her.'

'Do you know where they met?'

'In Chile. That's what he told me. My father worked there for some years, until Pinochet.'

'He was farming there, wasn't he?' Brunetti asked, avoiding the word 'farmer' and its suggestion of toil.

'Yes. He had a cattle ranch. But he chose to sell up and leave,' il Marchese said. 'I suppose he sensed what was coming.'

'Yes. Terrible, terrible,' Brunetti said in his most solemn, and equally noncommittal, voice.

When he said nothing further, Torrebardo continued. 'He seldom talked about those times. He said terrible things happened, and he never knew whether he was safe or not.' Listening to the other man talk about Gonzalo, Brunetti asked himself if he would be able to refer to his friend as this man's 'father' or whether he would continue to avoid saying it.

'Is that why he left?'

Torrebardo was visibly relaxing. He'd put one arm over the back of his chair and had ceased to draw his mouth closed and chew at his bottom lip.

'He told me once he had to leave to save someone else, but it wasn't anything he ever explained to me,' he said, then added, 'Getting out was certainly the right decision at the time.' There was that word, 'save', again. Hadn't Berta said that Gonzalo had saved her life? On the boat, coming into the city. Then Rudy had interrupted, and she had changed the subject without explaining.

'So they met there . . .' Brunetti said, hoping to prod an explanation.

'As I told you, he never talked much about those times,' the younger man answered. 'After all, it was a long time ago.'

Brunetti nodded as though he understood the need to abandon the past and concentrate on the present.

'Did you ever meet her?'

Torrebardo might have been expecting the question, so prompt was his answer. 'We met in London, about two years ago. My father and I were there for a weekend, and we met her for tea.' He's going to tell me where they had tea, Brunetti thought, and as if the idea had brushed the words off the edge of Torrebardo's tongue, he added, 'At Claridge's.'

'Ah,' Brunetti let fall, as if he dared not repeat the name. 'I've heard of it.'

'Quite nice,' il Marchese conceded.

'Since you'd already met her, did she by any chance contact you to tell you she was coming to Venice?' Brunetti asked.

'No,' the younger man answered instantly and then, as if startled by what he had just said, flashed a glance at Brunetti. 'That is,' Torrebardo continued, as though there had been only a comma after his last word, 'she didn't call me to tell me that she was coming. She called me when she was here.'

'When was that?' Brunetti asked amiably.

'The afternoon she got here. It sounded as though she was calling me from the taxi.' This, Brunetti reflected, was what Paola called 'verisimilitude', a technique used by writers of fiction: the small detail, seemingly meaningless, tossed into the story to make it more resemble the truth.

'Ah, from the airport, you mean?' Brunetti asked.

'Yes, it must have been.'

'What did she say?'

'That she'd arrived in the city and wanted to tell me she was here, although she had no time to see me. She didn't want me to find out from someone else that she had been here and not called.'

'That was gracious of her,' Brunetti said in a soft voice.

'Yes,' Torrebardo said with an even softer smile. 'She was very kind.'

'Did she say anything else?'

'She told me she was planning a memorial service and would call me when she was sure of when it would be, and where, so that I could come.'

He paused to give Brunetti the chance to ask, and he did. 'What did you tell her?'

Torrebardo made no effort to hide his surprise. 'That I'd come, of course,' he said, turning the surprise into astonishment that anyone could ask such a question. Then, seeing Brunetti's expression, he added, 'He was my father.'

Brunetti lowered his head and nodded a few times, then asked, 'Then you didn't get to see her?'

'No. In fact, I'm sorry now. My father adored her.' When Brunetti said nothing, the younger man went on, 'It's tragic, that she'd come here to do him honour and something so horrible should happen to her.'

Brunetti looked at the surface of his desk and

let the moment pass. 'The night she was killed, could you tell me where you were?' he asked.

'It was Thursday, wasn't it?' Torrebardo asked.

'She arrived on Thursday, yes,' Brunetti said. 'And she was killed that same night.'

Torrebardo looked down at his knees, as if unsure how to remember where he had been. 'I was home,' he said. 'I'd had an invitation to dinner, but I cancelled it because I had a migraine and didn't want to go out or have to talk to people.'

'I see,' Brunetti said, pulling a pad towards him. 'Could you tell me who the host or hostess was?'

'Conte Fabrizio Urbino,' Torrebardo said, almost as if he were happy to have such a name to throw at Brunetti. 'We were at school together, and he was here for a few days. I called him at his hotel and told him I had to cancel.'

'And where does Conte Urbino live?' Brunetti asked.

'In Milano, but I don't know the address.'

Torrebardo pulled out his phone and clicked a few keys, then read out the Conte's phone number to Brunetti, who wrote it down and thanked him.

'Thank you for your cooperation,' Brunetti said, pushing himself to his feet.

Torrebardo failed to hide his surprise. He stood and stepped forward to shake Brunetti's hand, started to say something – perhaps to thank him – but changed his mind and said nothing. He made his way to the door, and let himself out of Brunetti's office.

CHAPTER 26

So that was Gonzalo's son, the young man his friend had watched with 'shark's eyes', the young man who had swept it all up: the apartment, the bank accounts in 'somewhere', the paintings, the prints, everything Gonzalo had owned at the moment he fell forward to his death while on his way to look at paintings.

Conte Falier, his oldest friend, had tried in vain to talk to Gonzalo about what he was planning; his lawyer had ceased attempting to dissuade him; Brunetti wanted not to be involved; while Berta, his best friend, had persisted over the course of months, trying to make him see his own life with his other eyes, the human ones. And now she was dead, as was Gonzalo.

Brunetti opened the drawer of his desk and pulled out the folder Signorina Elettra had given him containing the print-outs of the emails between Gonzalo and Berta. And there it was again, reference to something that 'we' both knew that would prevent Gonzalo from doing what he wanted to do, presumably the adoption. 'We alone know you cannot do this.' Brunetti told himself to stop inventing plots to discover who the other side of the 'we' might be and simply assume the easiest: it was Gonzalo, and Berta, who was writing to him, completed the 'we'. What could they two have known that would prevent him from adopting il Marchese?

If they were both dead, then the secret would lie silent with them. Unless . . . unless . . . someone else had learned what it was . . . Brunetti dismissed this possibility as the stuff of bad movies: letters discovered after death; long-lost children stepping forward; the map to the hidden will placed inside the family bible and discovered only at the funeral, when a passage was to be read from that bible. Berta was willing to risk disgrace in order to stop the adoption. Had she risked death, instead?

He returned to reading and found again Berta's warning that the person Gonzalo adopted – never named in this correspondence – might be disillusioned after Gonzalo's death. What greater disillusion than to discover there was little to inherit? Had lust driven Gonzalo to this sort of deceit? Brunetti, suddenly recalling his conversation with Nanni, realized that there was, in fact, no question about the extent of Gonzalo's wealth nor about the person for whom it was intended.

Brunetti leaned forward and picked up the phone. He looked at the paper on his desk and dialled the number he'd been given for Conte Fabrizio Urbino, who confirmed what Torrebardo had told him. Urbino displayed no curiosity whatsoever that the police should be calling him to check on Torrebardo's story, and Brunetti was left to wonder whether it was because people like that did not care what the police did or thought or because he did not want to be involved in any way with what Torrebardo might have to do with the police.

There was a knock at his door. '*Avanti*,' Brunetti called and was pleased to see Signorina Elettra open the door, some papers in her right hand.

'Signore,' she said as she approached his desk, 'I've just had an email from the Spanish police.' Her voice was not the same; he found himself thinking she sounded stunned, like someone who has suddenly come upon an accident, smoke still rising from the wrecked cars.

'Tell me,' Brunetti said.

She held up the papers, as if she wanted to demonstrate the source and validity of what she was going to say. 'They were married.'

'I beg your pardon?' Brunetti said, not understanding.

'Your friend Gonzalo and Signora Dodson; they were married. That's how she got out of Chile.'

She placed the papers on his desk, but Brunetti barely saw them, nor paid much attention to her as thoughts assailed him. Signora Dodson had said more than once that Gonzalo had saved her life. Rudy joked that they behaved like an old married couple.

'When?' Brunetti asked. 'Where?'

'In the Spanish Embassy in Santiago, the year after Pinochet took power,' she answered.

'But she's married to her Englishman,' Brunetti protested.

Her response was calm. 'So it would seem. But the Spanish can find no record of her divorce.'

'What's that worth?' Brunetti asked, tone flirting with condescension.

Signorina Elettra's voice changed as she said, 'If you're looking for someone to accuse of being bad at record keeping, Signore, Spain is not the place to cast your eye. In fact, they responded almost immediately when we told them that a Spanish national had been murdered here.'

Signorina Elettra paused to give him the chance to ask about this, but when Brunetti failed to speak, she went on. 'I sent them a copy of our documentation.' Before he could ask, she added, 'All of it. And I asked them to give me any information they had about her.'

'You've dealt with them before, haven't you?' Brunetti asked.

'Yes, but never with this office,' she said, hesitated, then added, 'It's not like it is here, Dottore. The person who gives the information doesn't have to be the cousin of your brother-in-law or someone you went to elementary school with.'

Brunetti nodded to encourage her to continue. 'They had records of her marriage to a Spanish national in Chile and the concurrent application for citizenship, then of her emigration to Spain.

They had the date when citizenship was granted and when and where she lived and voted in Spanish elections after that, and then her address in England.' Signorina Elettra paused and then repeated, quite unnecessarily, 'They can find no record of her divorce.'

To Brunetti, it was as if the horizon had suddenly shifted to a new place and he was being asked to examine the new arrangement. 'That means he's not adopted, doesn't it?' he asked.

'If I remember the law correctly, Signore, no, he isn't,' she said. It wasn't necessary that she spell it out to him – the law was both clear and wise: the adoption of an adult by a married person was valid only if both husband and wife agreed to it.

'Thank you,' Brunetti said and slid the papers towards him. He didn't hear her leave, so fierce was his desire to read the documents. He read the first three pages twice but still failed to understand what he was reading, though the vocabulary of bureaucratic Spanish was markedly similar to the Italian. He knew the dates, recognized the names, but he could not concentrate on the facts because of the shadow they cast on what was to come later.

He stood and went to the window and studied the sky, seeking, perhaps, illumination there. He found none, nor in the canal beneath his window.

Finally he broke the code of the documents and pieced together the chronology, then added his own facts. Berta had been of an age to believe in the efficacy of political protest; Pinochet's officials learned her name and came looking for her; Gonzalo did the gentlemanly thing and saved the damsel in distress, defeating the dragons in Chile by marrying and carrying the princess off to Spain. They had remained friends and perhaps decided to forget the marriage. After all, who would remember the marriage between – Brunetti had to look at the papers – Alberta Gutiérrez de Vedia and Gonzalo Rodríguez de Tejeda in the midst of martial law, political tumult, and thousands of unexplained disappearances? Time passes, governments change, people forget.

Who would ever have imagined that the self-confidently gay art dealer would have a wife, especially one who was apparently married to an English nobleman and who had ridden to hounds?

To the Spanish police, however, Berta Dodson was still Alberta Gutiérrez de Vedia, wife, and then – very briefly – widow, of Gonzalo Rodríguez de Tejeda. Thus she, not Gonzalo's fraudulently adopted son, would be his heir. Brunetti found himself wondering who her heirs would be but no sooner thought it than backed away from the idea. It didn't matter, and there was nothing that could make it matter.

Memory mugged him, and he found himself thinking about *The Trojan Women* again and about the Greeks and what animated them. How different were their motives, how absent the thought of material gain. They defended their honour, both men and women; they defended it with violence or cunning or some combination of both, but not for gain. Clytemnestra did not kill Agamemnon to inherit the house, and Medea was not interested in Jason's wealth. He remembered a speech in one of the plays; he couldn't remember which one. He recalled only the disgust felt by a character who thought another had been animated by the desire for profit. No baser motive could be imagined.

And here we were, two thousand years later, and greed was the common denominator of human action.

He went back to his desk, muttering, 'Follow the money. Follow the money.' Surely, he was a man of his times.

The trail led to il Marchese di Torrebardo, the person who would have profited from her death. If only she had been Gonzalo's best friend and nothing more, she might have been spared. The list of might be's was discouragingly long.

Brunetti imagined the scene in which he attempted to persuade a magistrate that the flash he'd seen in the eyes of il Marchese di Torrebardo was evidence of his involvement in Berta's death, and turned away from the idea in embarrassment.

For no better reason than to have something to do, he decided to go and talk to the waiter again and see if he could, having had time to think about it, remember anything about the man in the booth.

The day was enticing and pulled at his senses, tempting him to walk along the *riva*, but Brunetti chose to take the vaporetto and got off at San

Tomà, the stop nearest the hotel. He was quickly there and walked into the half-filled bar, where he saw the waiter standing with his back against the bar.

He nodded and half smiled as Brunetti approached the bar. '*Bon dì, Commissario,*' he said.

Sandro, the bartender, approached their end of the bar and asked Brunetti, 'May I offer you something, Signore?'

'I'm on duty,' Brunetti answered. When he saw the man's surprise, he smiled and said, 'Well, maybe a glass of white wine. It's after five, and I don't have to go back to the Questura.'

'Pinot Grigio?' the bartender asked.

'Yes. Thanks.'

In response to a waved hand from one of three women sitting at a table near the window, the waiter went over to take their order.

'Is there something you forgot to ask?' the bartender asked as Brunetti sipped at his wine.

He'd come to talk to the waiter, but Brunetti decided he might as well include the bartender in his curiosity. 'I'd like to ask both of you if you've remembered anything about the person who was with Signora Dodson in the booth.'

The bartender picked up a cloth from the counter below him and wiped at the surface of the bar a few times. Then he rinsed the cloth in running water, wrung it out, and draped it over the tap. 'May I ask you something, sir?'

'Of course.'

'You think the man in the booth with her was the man who killed her?'

Brunetti considered answering for some time before he said, 'It's possible.' He took another sip of wine and wished he had something to eat with it. Peanuts, perhaps.

As if he'd read Brunetti's mind, the bartender opened a drawer and pulled out a bowl of salted almonds. He slid them towards Brunetti and nodded. 'They're nice with white wine.' His face softened, Brunetti noticed, as often happens when a person offers someone food.

Brunetti picked up a few almonds and placed two in his mouth, wondering why we always ate almonds one or two at a time and didn't fling them into our mouths with the reckless abandon with which we treated peanuts. They were very nice.

The waiter came back and said, 'Three champagnes.' Turning to Brunetti, he asked, using the plural, 'Am I allowed to ask if you've found out anything?'

Brunetti took another small sip, set the glass on the counter, and said, 'Yes, you're allowed to ask, and no, we haven't found anything.'

'Sandro and I were talking about it,' the waiter said, tilting his head in the direction of the bartender, who was at the other end of the bar, unwrapping the cork on a bottle of champagne.

'Either of you think of anything?' Brunetti asked casually.

'Well,' said the waiter, and then allowed himself time to pause by casting his glance across at the tables. When there was no sign from anyone there, he went on hesitantly, 'I don't know if they told you about the video cameras.'

'Yes, they did, and we looked at them,' Brunetti said. 'Nothing.'

'You looking for anyone in particular?' the waiter asked.

This, Brunetti reflected, is how privileged information ended up on the front page of *Il Gazzettino*. To answer this man's question would be to reveal information to which only the police were privy.

'Yes. We have someone in mind.'

The waiter started to say something, stopped, looked back at the tables, at Brunetti, and asked, 'The guy in the booth?'

Brunetti smiled and gave a slight nod, as if to indicate his approval of the man's cleverness without actually answering his question.

The bartender came back with three flutes held in the triangle of his hands. He set them on the waiter's tray; the waiter moved them apart from one another and told his colleague, 'They gave him some videos, but there was nothing there.'

He shrugged, picked up the tray, and moved off towards the table where the three women were sitting. The bartender wiped the counter down again, and Brunetti ate a few more almonds.

When the waiter returned, he again leaned back against the bar and gave a sigh of relief. 'You don't know what it does to your back to be on your feet for so many hours.' He put his hands on his hips and leaned forward, then twisted from side to side. When he was upright again, Brunetti gave a sympathetic nod.

The other two men exchanged a look that Brunetti did not understand. After a moment, the bartender asked, 'They give you all of them?'

'There was one from the front desk, looking at the door, and then one from the door to the front desk,' Brunetti said. 'There was another in here,' he began and twisted around and glanced up to look for the camera. 'There, that one up there,' he said, pointing to a single glass eye that peered out, almost invisible, from the moulding above the mirror on the back wall of the bar. 'And there was one of the staircase going upstairs from the lobby.'

'That's all?' the bartender asked, sounding faintly puzzled.

'Yes,' Brunetti answered.

'Ah.' The bartender sighed and looked at the waiter. From the side of his eye, Brunetti caught a slight motion of the waiter's head but kept his own attention trained on the bartender, who finally said, 'There's another one.'

'They probably didn't want to tell him,' the waiter said to no one in particular.

Brunetti decided not to ask and to see what they would tell him, knowing that they now had no choice.

'I suppose I ought to be the one to tell him,' the

waiter said. The bartender took his cloth and wiped the bar again. Brunetti picked up his glass to let him clean under it.

'It happened about five months ago, just at the beginning of winter,' the waiter said. 'There were still a lot of guests – there always are now – so we were pretty busy.'

The bartender, not bothering to rinse his cloth, draped it over the edge of the sink and stepped back from the bar. He folded his arms.

'I was on duty one night,' the waiter continued, 'and it suddenly came to me that two men had been in the bar on a couple of weekends – I hadn't paid them any notice because that's when there were even more people and we had a lot of work. One of them was sort of blonde, and the other one had very curly red hair. I'd guess they're both in their twenties. Anyway, they were here Friday and Saturday nights. I recognized the blonde one because he worked in a clothing shop across the street from my house. I knew him but didn't know him, if you see what I mean.'

He paused to give Brunetti the chance to comment. Brunetti nodded but said nothing. Venice was filled with people he knew but didn't know.

'The one I recognized caught my attention. Why didn't he go to the bar in our neighbourhood where he knew people? And how was he paying for the drinks here – I know what they cost – when he worked in a clothing shop?' There was a more than mild tone of irritation under the waiter's voice, surely out of proportion to a salesman's presence in the bar of an expensive hotel.

Suddenly the waiter excused himself and walked over to a table where two men were seated and came quickly back to give their order to the bartender. After he took their drinks to them and gave a look around the other tables, he returned to the bar and resumed. 'So I started to pay attention to him and to the other guy, who always paid in cash, too.' When he saw confusion cross Brunetti's face, he explained. 'Guests always put the bill on their room.'

'Anyway,' he went on, 'I noticed that they both came in alone but always seemed to end up talking to someone else, then moving to his table.' So, Brunetti said to himself, it was always men they spoke to.

'Then one night I noticed that the guy I recognized would disappear for a while, and then the man whose table he had gone to would follow him after about a minute, and neither one of them would come back for about ten minutes.' He stopped and gave Brunetti a long look, managing to appear very embarrassed by what he had just said.

As if to wipe away any suspicion Brunetti might have about his bothering to tell this long story, he said, 'At first I thought they were going outside for a cigarette, but they didn't go to the front of the hotel and the exit but back towards the men's room.'

Brunetti pulled his lips together and raised his eyebrows. The bartender moved forward and asked if he'd like another glass of wine, but Brunetti refused.

'So what did you do?' he asked the waiter.

'I watched them for the next few weekends, and I realized the other guy had the same pattern, more or less, though not every night he was here.'

His eyes flashed across to the tables, but when no one signalled, he continued. 'I didn't like it. It's not my hotel and it's none of my business what people choose to do, but for the love of God, not in the men's room in a public place. What happens if there's a family here or someone brings his kid in for a Coke during the summer, and the kid goes to the bathroom, and he sees two men coming out of the same cubicle or he sees something else, I don't know what.' He looked out over the tables again, but no one tried to catch his eye.

'What did you do?' Brunetti repeated.

'I told the boss, and they put a camera in the men's room. Well, not really in the room, but on the far wall, inside, and it's trained on the door, so you see whoever comes in.'

Brunetti did his best to hide his excitement and asked, 'What did you do about the two men?'

The waiter and the barman exchanged a long look, and this time the barman spoke. 'The day after it was installed, the first one came over to pay his bill when he was leaving, and I asked him if he knew that there was a video camera in the men's room.'

He pressed his lips together and tilted his head to one side, as though he wanted to give evidence of his confusion. He glanced at his colleague, who nodded, so he continued, 'We thought it was right to tell him.'

'How did he react?'

'He dropped his change. Didn't even bother to try to pick it up. He left, and I haven't seen him again.'

'And the other one?'

The waiter interrupted. 'He never came back after that night, either.'

Keeping his voice as calm as he could, Brunetti asked, 'Is the camera still there?'

Again, the two men looked at one another. The waiter said, 'I suppose so. There's no reason not to have it there.'

Brunetti finished his wine. He reached for his wallet, but the waiter put his hand on his arm. 'Please, Signore. You're our guest.'

'Am I allowed to leave a tip?' Brunetti asked with a broad smile to show he was joking.

'The very idea,' the bartender said in the voice of a maiden aunt at the sight of a too-short skirt.

'Thanks, then,' Brunetti said, leaning over the counter to shake the hand of the bartender. The waiter's hand was waiting when he turned, and Brunetti shook that, as well, then said, 'If I can ever fix a parking ticket for you, gentlemen, my name's Brunetti, and it would be my pleasure to do it.'

Both men laughed, and Brunetti went back to speak to the concierge.

CHAPTER 27

With no explanation of how he had learned about it, Brunetti asked the concierge to send the file from the video camera that filmed the door of the men's room to his private email address so that he could have a look himself. When he got home, he poured himself a glass of white wine, sat in front of Paola's computer, and opened the file attached to the email. He moved the timer at the bottom of the screen to six o'clock of the night of the murder and settled down to watch.

He had had no idea of how tedious it would be to keep his eyes on a door that repeatedly opened to allow a man to pass through it, either entering or leaving. After less than half an hour, he found himself agitated at the constant flash of the faces and heads of men entering and leaving the men's room, as if he were looking at an American comic film from the Twenties played at double speed. Viewing turned to something approaching pain. Each man was visible for, at the most, three seconds and was replaced instantly. No matter how much the flashing images troubled Brunetti, he could not take his eyes from the screen. If he wanted to glance away or close his eyes, even for an instant, he had to stop the tape and stare at the far distance for a moment, then resume. Twice, he had to stop the video and move it back to see the last man to come through the door, only to discover that he could not remember if he had seen the face or not. At one point, he stopped the video and went to the window to study the tree in the courtyard below their apartment, then went back to the computer.

He heard the front door open and close and Chiara call out, 'Who's home?'

'I am,' Brunetti called out, feeling a bit like Papa Bear.

She came in, carrying her backpack, and walked over to kiss him on the top of his head. She looked at the screen and asked in her sweetest voice, 'Have they demoted you to watching surveillance films?'

'You watch too much television,' Brunetti said in his roughest voice.

She kissed him again and went back towards the kitchen.

He was vaguely aware that she later passed down the hall to her room. He stopped the video and got up to turn on the lights and saw that it was after seven. He went to the kitchen and drank a glass of water, wished he had the patience to make himself a coffee or that they lived on the first floor and he could go down to Rizzardini to get one.

He sat again and was about to continue when

311

he heard the front door open and close and light footsteps come down the hall. Paola was at the door, smiling, curious. 'You? At the computer?' She laughed, then asked, 'What are you doing?'

'Looking for a killer,' he said.

'Same old work day, eh?' she asked as she came across the room. Like Chiara, she kissed him on the head and looked at the screen. 'But there's nothing there,' she said, puzzled. 'Just a door.'

'I had to stop,' he confessed.

'Why?' Paola asked, coming around to stand beside him.

'You'll see,' he said and clicked on the arrow.

After three minutes of watching the continual in and out of men through the door, Paola said, 'It's a good thing you keep your pistol locked up in the wardrobe somewhere.'

'Because I'd shoot myself?' Brunetti guessed.

'Exactly,' she said and then asked, 'What is this?'

'It's a video of the door to the men's room at a hotel.'

She leaned to the side and dragged a chair over beside him and sat. 'Tell me why you're watching this.'

Brunetti repeated what the bartender and waiter had explained about the video.

'And you're waiting for Gonzalo's young man to come through the door?' she asked. 'Or hoping?'

It took him a moment to think about that. 'No, I'm not hoping.'

'Why?'

'Because I don't want Gonzalo to be responsible for her death.'

'Ah,' she said and went silent for a long time, until she added, 'I see.'

Brunetti leaned forward and started the video again. They sat, silent, side by side, for ten minutes until Paola said, 'I find this frightening.'

'What?'

'Look at their faces,' she said, voice surprisingly sober. 'These are men on their own for a few minutes, with no one to talk to, no one to boast to, no one to tell their stories to. And just look at their faces. Have you ever seen such misery in your life?'

With newly-focused eyes, Brunetti observed what he now saw as a cavalcade of sadness and woe. He studied the faces of the men entering and those leaving: they could have been on their way to their own funerals, so grim were their expressions, so dejected their posture. Why had he not noticed that before? He watched two more case studies in despair, and stopped the video. 'Why don't you sit on the sofa and read, and I'll watch this until the end?' he asked Paola.

'Why don't I make dinner, instead?' Paola asked and patted his shoulder.

'Bless you,' Brunetti answered, though not to any of the men who were passing through the door.

A few minutes later, Chiara brought him a glass of wine and then came back after what seemed a long time to tell him dinner was ready. Brunetti emerged from the room red-eyed and exhausted, battered down by the sight of so many hard-faced men. Dinner helped, but he was in front of the computer as soon as he finished eating, refusing Paola's offer of a grappa.

He started anew, fighting off food-induced drowsiness. And then, when the clock at the bottom of the screen read 23:22, the door opened and Attilio Circetti, Marchese di Torrebardo, walked into the men's room. He made no attempt to lower his head or put his hand over his face: he was a man in a man's world and held himself up straight and proud. Three minutes later, he walked out: Brunetti noticed the light-coloured coat he was wearing and the dark blue scarf around his neck. Brunetti clicked off the video and decided he would have the grappa.

CHAPTER 28

The next morning, Brunetti remained in bed until after nine, drinking two cups of coffee and reading that morning's *Gazzettino*, those things supplied by his wife, who applauded him in his lethargy and negligence.

After Paola left for the university, he called the magistrate who was in charge of the investigation of Berta's murder and asked if he could meet her at the Questura in an hour, when he would tell her what he'd discovered since last they spoke. Then he called Torrebardo, asking him to come back that afternoon at three to answer a few more questions.

The young man's peevish agreement pleased Brunetti; a person who is worried does not easily succeed at indignant refusal: the Marchese didn't even attempt it. Or perhaps the desire to find out what Brunetti knew proved irresistible. Il Marchese did at least make it clear that he would have to cancel an appointment in order to be at the Questura at three.

On his way to the Questura, Brunetti had another coffee, this one with a brioche, and arrived at the same time as the magistrate. They went up to his office, and he explained the importance of the Marchese's appearance on the video in light of his insistence, registered on tape during their interview, that he had spent the evening of the murder at home because of a headache, even cancelling a dinner engagement to do so.

After assuring her there was no doubt it was Torrebardo who appeared in the video, Brunetti easily persuaded her to agree to order a DNA test of Torrebardo's clothing to see if there were traces of the DNA of the murdered woman he insisted he had not seen in Venice.

There remained time for lunch; Brunetti called Paola and told her he was too restless to eat, only to have her say, laughing, 'I'm writing the date down, Guido. I'll put a notice in the papers.' Then, still laughing, she said, 'Try to calm down in time for dinner. We're having *peperonata con polenta*,' and hung up.

He pulled out the folder of Berta Dodson's emails and started to read them through again, interpreting them in light of her still being married to Gonzalo. The texts made sense now: once the missing piece of the jigsaw puzzle was slipped into place, the entire scene came into perfect focus and made it easy for him to abandon the possibility of some murky financial scandal that would be passed on to any heir Gonzalo named.

What animated Gonzalo's deceit was – at least to Brunetti – of an entirely different order, and far worse. He had bought the favours of this young man with a promise of financial reward knowing that his – say it – wife would reveal their marriage after his death. And so, blinded by love – or perhaps it was lust – Gonzalo had gone ahead with the adoption, aware that his son would eventually be stripped of his inheritance: no apartment, no paintings, no anything. What he had not calculated was that his best friend would be stripped of her life because he had so badly misjudged his heir.

Brunetti closed his eyes and the papers disappeared, taking with them the last words of his dead friend and that man's best friend. He thought about Gonzalo and what he had done, and why. He stared at the top sheet of paper, then swept them all into his drawer and locked it. He left the Questura and started walking down towards Castello with no destination in mind.

He paused after an hour and went into a bar, where he had a very bad *tramezzino*, most of which he left uneaten on his plate on the counter, along with his unfinished wine. When he got to San Pietro di Castello, he sat on one of the benches on the tiny patch of grass in front of the church and watched the advance of the pigeons, optimistic in the belief that he was yet another large creature with some bread in its pocket. They gave up after five minutes or so and tried the same tactic, with significantly greater success, on a grey-haired woman wearing a coat over her apron who stood on the pavement near the canal.

Brunetti found it surprisingly relaxing to watch her pull pieces of bread from the pockets of her coat and then from those of her apron, tear them in pieces, and toss them to the pigeons. The birds all seemed to be old friends: there was no crowding, no pecking each other. They put their heads down and ate their lunch quietly, something Brunetti still had no desire to do.

He glanced at his watch and saw that it was after two, got to his feet, and headed back towards the Questura. He saluted the man at the door, who said nothing this time about anyone's having come to see him, and so went back to his office. He was hungry now but told himself to ignore it.

About an hour later, Pucetti knocked on his open door. He stepped back, and Torrebardo walked in front of him as though the officer were invisible.

Brunetti looked up at the young aristocrat and whispered under his breath, '*Mirabile visu*,' for Torrebardo was wearing the same light coat he had been wearing in the video. 'Ah,' he said with unfeigned pleasure. 'Thank you for coming.'

Petulance is not an attractive thing to see in an adult. In fact, it's not a pleasant thing to see in anyone above the age of four. Brunetti steeled himself to the look on Torrebardo's face and walked towards the door to meet him. When Torrebardo removed his coat, Brunetti took it from him, careful to lift it by the tag on the inside of the collar. He folded it backwards and laid it over the second chair in front of his desk. 'Have a seat, please,' he told Torrebardo and went back to the door. In the corridor, Pucetti stood talking to one of the translators.

Brunetti called and waved Pucetti back with a quick gesture. When the young officer was in front of him, Brunetti leaned close and said, voice urgent, 'Call Dottoressa Baldassare and tell her I need those papers now.'

Pucetti remained silent for a few seconds, and when Brunetti said no more, saluted and turned away to go and make the call.

Brunetti returned to his office; when he was seated, he reached to the side of his desk and made it obvious that he was switching on the micro-phones again, then put his elbows on the desk and folded his hands under his chin. 'The last time we spoke, Marchese Torrebardo, you told me you'd had a telephone call from Signora Dodson.' He paused.

Torrebardo nodded, and Brunetti said, without bothering to state the obvious, 'Could you state your answer, please?'

'Yes,' the young man said.

Calmly, Brunetti continued. 'Could you tell me in more detail about the conversation and how it was you happened to speak to Signora Dodson?'

When he began to answer, it was clear to Brunetti that il Marchese had told himself to remain calm and agreeable and to give every appearance of friendliness and willingness to cooperate. 'I think I've told you everything, Commissario,' he said in a voice from which had been erased all annoyance or irritation. They might have been two close friends in easy conversation.

Brunetti was well aware that he'd been told all there was to say about that conversation, but he hoped Torrebardo would see it as an opportunity to perform once more as an innocent man being patient with the authorities.

When it became obvious that Brunetti was not going to ask again, Torrebardo gave a long sigh and said, 'As I said the last time, I first met her two years ago, in London, when my father introduced me to her as his best friend. I'd often heard him speak well of her. We had tea together and had a very pleasant conversation, and then I didn't hear from her again until the other day, when she phoned me to say she was already in Venice and busy trying to arrange a memorial service for my father. She told me she'd call me again when she had the date and place for the occasion.' He'd let his voice fall into the descending cadence one puts at the end of a conversation and looked across at Brunetti to show he was finished.

'She did not tell you the name of her hotel?'

'Why would she?' flashed out before Torrebardo could stop himself. Hearing it, he quickly added, speaking in a patient, reasonable voice, 'There was no time for us to meet, so there was no need for her to tell me.'

'I see,' Brunetti said and named the hotel. 'Are you familiar with it, by any chance?'

'No one I know has ever stayed there, so there's no reason I'd go, not really.'

'Not even to meet someone for a drink?' Brunetti prodded.

'Commissario, I have no idea why you're so insistent in linking me to this hotel where I've never been and where I did not know Signora Dodson was staying,' Torrebardo said, finally loosening his hold on his anger.

Brunetti turned his hand up and gave a weak smile. 'I'm simply trying to exclude the possibility of your involvement in this, Signore.'

'Well, you can do that without this cross-examination, Commissario. I give you my word as a nobleman that I've never been in the hotel, that I did not see Alberta Dodson while she was in Venice this time, and that I had nothing to do with her death.'

'"*La nobiltà ha dipinta negli occhi l'onestà*", ' Brunetti whispered.

'Exactly,' Torrebardo said, failing to recognize the reference and deaf to Brunetti's irony.

'Well, then,' Brunetti said, pushing his chair back from his desk. Seeing this, Torrebardo had put his hands on the arms of his chair and started to stand, but when he saw that Brunetti remained seated, he lowered himself back.

'Is there something else?' Torrebardo asked.

'Yes, there is,' Brunetti said. Unexpectedly, his thoughts turned to an email in the folder, from Berta to Gonzalo, written months before his death, in which she had reproved her friend for the step he intended to take, saying that it saddened her immeasurably to see him, at his age, so consumed by lust as to betray even the object of that lust.

In the next paragraph, she had said that she was beyond the lust that still held Gonzalo captive and lusted only to understand and caress Roderick's thoughts and spirit as he confronted the devastation that was slowly consuming his life.

Brunetti had stopped reading then, the force of taboo rendering him incapable of prying any deeper into her thoughts and spirit. He returned his attention to il Marchese di Torrebardo.

'I'd like to discuss the lies you've told me about where you were on Thursday evening and talk about the reason you killed Signora Dodson.' Watching the shock plaster itself across Torrebardo's face, only to disappear immediately, driven off by force of will, Brunetti added, 'The wife of Gonzalo Rodríguez de Tejeda.'

'You can't prove . . .' Torrebardo said, giving in to his rage for just long enough to pronounce three words and then immediately closing his lips and pulling them into his mouth, as though that would somehow erase what he had just said.

Brunetti took his phone and dialled the number of Magistrato Baldassare. 'Petra,' he said when she answered. 'Do you have them?'

'They've been sent to Signorina Zorzi as an attachment, so you can act on them now. There's also a hard copy – signed and with the proper office seals – on its way by courier.'

'Grazie, Petra,' he permitted himself to say, not wanting Torrebardo to have any idea of what he was talking about.

'Signor Torrebardo,' he said, finished with using the title or showing any deference to a man he was about to arrest for murder, 'I *can* prove. I have proof that you were in the hotel the night of the murder.'

This time, Torrebardo's mouth fell open in surprise, and Brunetti saw how his teeth matched the other perfections of his face. It was about time for him to protest that he didn't understand what Brunetti was talking about, but he disappointed Brunetti by asking, 'Am I allowed to call a lawyer?'

'*Sì*,' Brunetti answered.

Suddenly deferential, Torrebardo asked, 'May I use my own phone?'

'Of course,' Brunetti agreed.

Torrebardo took out his phone and found the number he wanted. Brunetti listened to it ring: it was picked up on the third ring.

'Nanni, it's Attilio,' Torrebardo began, fighting to control his voice. The other man said something, and Torrebardo said, 'I don't know. I think I'm being arrested.' He listened quietly for an instant and said, 'No, it's for something I didn't do. That woman who was killed in the hotel. They think I did it.' Brunetti could hear Nanni's voice but kept his head down and pulled his desk calendar close to study it.

'I know you don't do criminal law. But can you give me the name of someone who does?' This time the pause was longer until he said, 'It doesn't matter what he costs. That doesn't matter, either. I can borrow it.' He listened for a longer time, crossed and re-crossed his legs, and then said, voice veering towards anger, 'Nanni, I'm not asking for your advice. I'm asking you to recommend a criminal lawyer. Give me the name of the best, and I'll take care of it.' Torrebardo used his other hand to dip into the pocket of his coat.

Brunetti got up and walked to the window, not wanting to be asked to give him pencil and paper. On the far side of the canal the end of the vine was submerged in the water, he noticed.

He ignored the fumbling sounds behind him and pretended not to hear the phone fall on the floor, nor Torrebardo's obscenity. After a moment, Torrebardo snapped, 'All right. Give it to me.' There was silence, and then there was more silence. 'd'Acquarone?' There was a brief pause, no doubt as Torrebardo wrote down the name. Then the young man snapped out, 'I don't care if he's in Verona. If he's the best, I want him.'

Brunetti heard something hit the desk, and when he looked back at Torrebardo he saw him sitting with his head lowered, hand covering his phone, which he'd apparently slapped down on Brunetti's desk.

'Excuse me,' the younger man said, not looking up. His voice had grown somehow smaller.

'Yes?'

'Is there a bathroom up here?'

'Yes,' Brunetti answered. 'Wait a moment and I'll have someone sent up who can take you there.'

Torrebardo raised his head as Brunetti walked to his desk, and Brunetti saw the terror in his eyes as he thought about his future. Brunetti dialled the number of the front desk and said, 'Send an officer to my office. Quickly.'

He walked back to the window and stood, thinking about weakness. In the truly weak, it was the object of pity, while in the arrogant it most frequently educed contempt, as was the case now.

After about three minutes, Bassi appeared at the door, and Brunetti asked him to accompany the gentleman to the toilet – he intentionally used that word – wait for him, and bring him back. Torrebardo pushed himself to his feet and followed the officer, walking with what appeared to be some discomfort.

Brunetti turned back to face the room, and his eye fell on Torrebardo's coat. The video was clear, and if there were traces of Berta Dodson's DNA on that coat, there would be very little for Avvocato d'Acquarone to do. Brunetti had the warrant, and now he had the coat.

His thoughts turned to Gonzalo, the father of all of this. Brunetti had always thought he loved the Spaniard; after all, Brunetti had married into a family of people who loved him. But now he found that he felt nothing for Gonzalo beyond pity. He had known Gonzalo was selfish and a fool about young men, but he had always seen those as weaknesses and never bothered to question Gonzalo's character because of them. 'Oh, that's just Gonzalo.'

But now his weaknesses had destroyed the two people he cared about the most. Brunetti could no longer attribute to Gonzalo the capacity to love, at least not in a way that he could understand that word. And because of that, his own love for the man had been dismissed or banished, or had simply died.

How strange, Brunetti reflected: we choose to love people despite their flaws and weaknesses. We train ourselves to overlook or ignore them; sometimes these failures of character even fill us with a special kind of tenderness that has nothing whatsoever in it of a sense of superiority.

Like bombs, these flaws tick quietly through our lives, and theirs, until we learn to ignore them, and then forget them. Until some unlikely impossibility causes them to explode, when finally we recognize how dangerous these people are and have been all along.

If Gonzalo had not told Berta of the adoption, if she had not come to Venice, if and if and if, there would have been no explosion, and Brunetti would remember his late friend Gonzalo with love and laugh fondly at what a goose he could be about young men.

Even now, remembering Gonzalo's frequent kindness, his habitual generosity, his love for his and Paola's children, Brunetti felt his heart begin to warm towards him. He thought of something his mother had often said. Brunetti used to think she was talking about his father when she said it, but as he grew older, he began to suspect she was speaking in general. 'It would be nice if we could choose the people we love, but love chooses them.'

He heard a noise, and when he looked, he saw Bassi at the door, bringing back the man Brunetti was about to charge with murder.